Praise for Leslie O'Kane
and her Molly Masters mysteries

"Endearing characters, touching family and friend relationships, and a feisty heroine."
—DIANE MOTT DAVIDSON

"O'Kane delivers a satisfying whodunit."
—*San Francisco Chronicle*

"Molly Masters is a sleuth with an irrepressible sense of humor and a deft artist's pen."
—CAROLYN G. HART

"Molly is a realistic heroine you'll feel you've known for years."
—*Romantic Times*

DEATH OF A PTA GODDESS

Leslie O'Kane

FAWCETT BOOKS • NEW YORK

A Fawcett Book
Published by The Ballantine Publishing Group
Copyright © 2002 by Leslie O'Kane

www.ballantinebooks.com

ISBN 0-449-00721-9

Manufactured in the United States of America

First Edition: October 2002

OPM   10   9   8   7   6   5   4   3   2   1

For Carol,
who is a much better driver than Karen
(and is not allowed to date until she's twenty)

Chapter 1

Brake Fast

"What!?!" my daughter, Karen, cried as I tried to relax my two-handed, white-knuckled grip on the dashboard. "You said 'Stop,' so I stopped!"

"Yes, but the brake doesn't need to be stomped on as though you're crushing a cockroach. Neither does the accelerator."

I gave a glance behind me at my best friend, Lauren, and her daughter, Rachel. Lauren's face was almost as pale as the whites of her eyes, although Rachel was smiling and appeared to be enjoying our bone-jarring ride. Lauren and I had combined forces, thinking a joint driving lesson for both of our daughters at once would be killing two birds with one stone. We had miscalculated; this was killing two mothers with one car.

Softening my voice, I added, "They're pedals, not on-off buttons."

"How was I supposed to know that?"

Silently I retorted: By listening to my instructions and observing how we've been hurled forward or backward like crash dummies! My reply, however, was a reasonably even-voiced "Now you do," while I reminded myself that, although there were nicer ways to spend a chilly Saturday morning than circling a deserted parking lot at Carlton Central School, there were worse ways, as well. Not that I could think of any at the moment.

"Jeez, Mom!" Karen cried. "If you think I'm such a hopeless case, why can't I just get Dad to teach me?"

The true answer was: Because I lost the coin-flip, but I replied, "I *don't* think you're a 'hopeless case,' and you *will* get plenty of lessons from your father." Starting tomorrow and lasting for many, many months. Even if that required my buying a two-headed coin. I took a calming breath, which didn't seem to do the trick. "Let's go over the basics again, starting with the pedals."

"I'm never going to be able to drive! I'll be the only graduate in the history of Carlton Central School without a driver's license!"

"That's not true. My sister didn't get her license until she was in college."

"So it's hereditary?" Karen shrieked. "I come from a line of slow learners behind the wheel? This is going to kill my popularity at school! Nobody's ever going to want to hang with someone too stupid to drive!"

I was not about to enter into a catastrophizing contest with my daughter. At sixteen, Karen had mastered that particular skill, and I would lose. "Okay, then." I clapped my hands once in a smack-something-other-than-your-daughter move. "Back to the basics. Long, thin pedal on the right—gas pedal. Requires a *light*, steady pressure to make the car go. Squarish, high pedal on the left—brake pedal. Activates our *power* brakes and stops the car. Use your right foot only and, remember, both pedals are *never* pressed at the same time."

"I didn't! I was . . . transitioning."

That excuse was a new one on me, and I had no response. I rubbed my eyes, trying to quell the nervous tic that was developing. I turned to Lauren and Rachel behind me. "You're sure that the driver's ed class has no openings?"

"Not till June," Lauren replied.

I returned my attention to Karen. "And we can't wait three months because . . . ?"

Karen clicked her tongue again at my profound ignorance. "All our friends are driving already. Tell her, Rachel."

"All our friends are driving already," Rachel dutifully repeated.

"You know, Mom, if you didn't want to give me driving lessons, you should have given birth to me earlier in the year, like all our friends' moms did. They all got into driver's ed this semester."

Matching my daughter's tone of voice, I snapped, "Sorry if that strikes you as shortsighted of me. For some reason, while I was busy giving birth to you, it never occurred to me what impact your having a March birthday would have on your social life."

Time for another calming breath. Actually, this called for those breathing exercises they'd taught us in birthing class to shift focus away from the pain. I did a quick "hee-hee-whoo," then said, "You're going to make a slow turn now, drive to the other side of the parking lot, and stop."

She shot me a dirty look and crossed her arms.

"Karen, do you want to learn how to drive or not?"

"Yeah, but not if you're going to look at me the whole time!"

"Oh, my God. Fine." I rotated a little in my seat, but my heart rate was increasing despite my best efforts to stay calm. "I'm looking forward, see? I'm looking at that little bird sitting on the asphalt just a few short feet ahead of us." It was a brown sparrow, bathing in an icy puddle in the parking lot. I tried to send him a telepathic message: *Fly! For God's sake, use your wings! Save yourself!*

The next several seconds were a literal blur, with Karen

somehow managing a hairpin turn just before we ran off the parking lot and into the surrounding trees. I got the distinct impression that only two wheels made actual contact with the pavement. All the while, I was shouting, "Slow down! Turn! Look out! Brake! Brake!" and a couple of major curse words right at the end when I really thought I was about to get a face full of air bag.

Next thing I knew, we were facing the high school building and all trying to catch our breath. This time, Karen and Rachel were shaken, too. I looked at my daughter's features in profile and could only think how desperately I never wanted that perfect, beautiful face of hers to be sent through a windshield.

Lauren broke the silence. "Maybe we should get out of the car for a while, Rachel."

"No, you're safer inside it."

"Mom's right," Karen said, her voice sounding on the verge of tears. "I might hit you."

"Don't get discouraged, sweetie. This—"

"Mom, *you* get out."

I glared at her, bristling at the implication that she considered me more expendable than Rachel or Lauren, but she went on: "You can teach Rachel how to drive, and Lauren can teach me."

"That's a great idea, honey," I said, just about to turn around to try to sell Lauren on the notion. Her daughter was a much better student so far.

"That's a thought," Lauren said, but while she spoke, she reached around my seat back and pinched my arm.

"Ow! I mean, I can't really agree to that, on second thought. For one thing, it looks like Lauren's getting a little carsick."

"Let me just try one more time to drive all the way around the lot, then we'll go home. Okay?"

"Okay," the three of us said in unison.

Rachel said, "Don't push so hard with your foot this time."

"Oh. All right," Karen replied as if this were brilliant advice that she'd just been given for the first time.

I braced myself, and we set off on another nauseating trip, giving our seat belts a workout as Karen tried to find a happy medium on the gas pedal. Up ahead of us, a car pulled into the lot.

"There's a car coming! What do I do?"

"Don't panic!" I cried, panicking on all of our behalfs. "Just take your foot off the gas pedal and—"

She stomped on the brake again. We came to a screeching stop. I cleared my throat and said as pleasantly as I could, "That stop was a little better. My neck hardly got hurt." Also, remarkably, my nose was not bleeding.

The other car stopped, and the driver got out.

"Oh, it's P-Patty," I stammered, having accidentally almost called her by her nickname: Perfect Patty. I don't know who had given her that name originally, but it certainly fit. She was hands down the most impressive person I'd ever met. Despite the early hour, she looked fresh and wide awake, and as though she'd stepped from the pages of an L.L. Bean catalogue in her khakis and knit sweater. Seeing her, our PTA president, reminded me that the secretary/treasurer had called last night and left a message that there was "a crisis brewing." I'd simply cried, "*Another* one?" at my machine and decided to call her back later this morning.

Patty approached from the passenger side, and I rolled down my window, happy to see her friendly face. She was a trim, attractive woman in her early fifties, with bright blue eyes and dark blond hair that she wore in a flattering, short style. "Hi, Patty."

"Good morning, Molly," she said with a brilliant smile. "I thought that might be you." She shifted her gaze and said, "Karen, you're learning to drive, I see. Good for you! I'm Patty Birch. We've never met, but I've heard so many terrific things about you that I feel like we have."

Karen smiled. "Nice to meet you. My mom says a lot of nice things about you, too."

I couldn't help but give Karen a double take at her unexpectedly gracious response. These days the only thing I could predict about her was that she was unpredictable.

Patty then looked past my shoulder and said, "Hi, Lauren. And . . . you must be Rachel, right?"

"Yes. Hello, Mrs. Birch."

Although she had kept her married name of "Birch," she was divorced and always corrected people to "Ms. Birch," but she said, "It's Patty to all of us young adults." She gave me a wink. "We still qualify as young, right?" She looked at Lauren, then at me, maintaining her smile.

These days, I truly didn't feel all that young, especially not while this driving lesson was rapidly aging me. I skirted the question and asked, "What are you doing out here at six o'clock on a Saturday morning?"

"Getting some work done. Kelly is at her father's house this weekend, so I'm not on breakfast duty. Besides, it's nearly seven-thirty."

"It is?" I glanced at my watch. She was right. We'd lost all kinds of time dawdling before we got out here and had spent quite some time on Rachel's lesson. "Time flies when you're having . . . fun." Or a series of minor heart attacks.

"The building's locked," Lauren said.

"Oh, I have my own set of keys. I can get so much done when the school's deserted like this." She turned her smile toward my daughter. "Karen, what do you think about driving so far?"

"It stinks. I've decided to wait till I'm thirty." She unfastened her seat belt. Without looking at me, she muttered, "Let's just go home, okay?"

"Oh, hey," Patty said. "Don't get discouraged. Would you mind giving me a crack at riding shotgun? I've taught half a dozen teenagers how to drive."

"You have six teenagers?" Karen asked incredulously.

"Only one of them was my own. I just have a knack for teaching people your age."

I hesitated, thinking this was above and beyond the call of our relationship, but Karen resolved my dilemma by saying, "Get out, Mom."

"We'll just go on a little spin around the campus, all right?" Patty said to Karen as Patty and I traded places.

"The entire campus? Dream on! I can't even get ten feet without making everyone sick to their stomach."

"Do you play the piano by any chance?" Patty asked.

"Yeah," Karen said slowly. "For eight years now."

"Wonderful! You're used to working the piano pedals, then. I'll have you driving before you know it."

Karen giggled and said, "That'd be great!"

Stepping on a piano pedal would have been a better analogy than crushing cockroaches. I'm sure I'd have come up with it myself, if a piano came equipped with an engine and a steering wheel. I bent down to speak to Lauren through my still-open window. "Rachel, Lauren, do you want to wait here or do—"

"No way!" Rachel cried. "I'm gonna hang with Karen and Patty. Mom, you go keep Molly company."

"Answers that question," Lauren muttered as she got out beside me.

Patty said, "We'll be back in ten or fifteen minutes. Why don't you two just wait in my car so you can stay warm till we get back. All right?"

"Sounds good," I replied. It was downright chilly out here. We were having what was graciously referred to as a "warm" March for upstate New York, which only meant that areas such as this one, covered in black asphalt, had warmed enough to be free of ice and snow. But the sparrow I'd seen bathing in the puddle had to have been part penguin.

Lauren and I got into the front seat of Patty's Ford sedan and kept an eye on my Honda CRV. As grateful and relieved as I was to let somebody else help my daughter learn to drive, I felt a bit, well, jealous, too. Both teens were clearly enraptured by Patty's presence. Karen was nodding her head, as was Rachel, who'd scooted forward in her seat as they both sat with their attention riveted to whatever Patty was telling them. Short of smearing grape jelly on my face and dumping an ant colony over my head, there was no way I could capture those girls' attention so fully.

"Ever since I quit as secretary at the high school, I've lost track of the town's teens," Lauren said. "Didn't Perfect Patty's son graduate from Carlton recently?"

"Yes. He was valedictorian last year."

"That's right. I remember now. Where did he decide to go to college?"

"Harvard."

"Wow. I didn't realize that."

"She made a point of not telling anyone, unless you asked more than once, like I did. She also kept it out of the press release about his being valedictorian. Which she wrote herself." A bit of rancor had slipped into my voice, and I cleared my throat. "She said with the university's name recognition being what it is, just saying your child goes there makes it sound like you're bragging."

There was a pause. "Well, she's got a good point, I guess."

"She always does."

I could feel Lauren's eyes on me, and my cheeks

warmed. In an oral argument with myself, I said, "She's a great PTA president, and I don't mind that she could give Martha Stewart cooking and arts-and-crafts lessons, and that everyone in this entire town loves her. But—"

"I wouldn't go that far. It's not like all of Carlton is enamored with her. Parents and teachers at the school are just excited about the possibility of winning a national PTA award. That's all. And, if we do, it's to all of our credit, not just hers."

"Sure, but to be honest with you, for once I really feel for Stephanie. She'd been PTA president for, what? Ten years? Then, two years ago, Patty moves into town and takes over as PTA president. Bam! The Carlton PTA instantly becomes a finalist for a prestigious award from national headquarters. And there's Stephanie, left behind to eat Patty's dust."

"Poor Stephanie. Couldn't happen to a nicer woman." Lauren's voice dripped with sarcasm.

"True, but still." I sighed. Karen waved and grinned as she drove past me, suddenly looking utterly at ease behind the wheel. "The thing is, had our positions been reversed just now, it never would have occurred to me to offer to help teach her child to drive. Does Patty have to be so much better a mother than I am? I mean, that's the one that really rankles, you know?"

Lauren averted her eyes and looked thoughtful, then finally said, "Remember that famous poem that starts: 'Go placidly . . . ,' which someone put background music to, and it became a pop-hit when we were kids?"

"Yeah. I remember some of it . . . 'Go placidly amongst the . . . turnips and collard greens . . .' "

" 'Noise and haste,' " Lauren corrected.

"Oh, right. That's much better. But I was close."

"It mentions the wisdom of not comparing yourself with others."

"Right. I remember that part. Something about how there's always going to be people who are 'lesser and greater than you.' I should go reread it. Now that you reminded me the poem wasn't about strolling through a vegetable garden."

"All I'm saying is, regardless of how . . . astonishing Patty might be, you're a terrific mom."

"Oh, hey thanks. Fortunately, my kids tell me that all the time, so my self-esteem never sags."

Lauren chuckled a little. "Same here."

"And they say parenting teenagers is *hard*."

"But not for us." She held up her palm, and I gave her a high five.

We sat back in our seats and stared through the windshield. My car, driven by Karen, had long since disappeared beyond this closest of school buildings on the large Carlton Central School campus. It hit me then just how many students this place held and how desperately I hoped that my two could come through without a single tragic event, and how unrealistic that hope was. In Lauren's and my graduating class—roughly the same size as Rachel's and Karen's—three of our friends had died in two separate accidents during our senior year.

Swallowing a lump in my throat at the memory, I told Lauren, "I'm not going to make it another four-plus years, till Nathan graduates from Carlton. When one of our kids made a bad choice, it used to just be a learning experience. Now, suddenly, bad choices are life-threatening . . . there's AIDS, riding around in cars with inexperienced drivers, alcohol and drugs. I want Karen and Nathan to socialize. I just wish they'd wait till they're in college, so I can hold on to the inane notion that what I don't know about can't hurt me."

"I know what you mean," Lauren replied. "If only blissful ignorance were an option."

"Here they come again. They're slowing down."

Karen managed to bring the car to a smooth stop. Patty, all smiles, emerged from my car just as Lauren and I emerged from hers.

She said quietly, "Molly, I hope I wasn't stepping on your toes just now. It's just easier to teach driving to someone other than your own child, and you were looking pretty exasperated."

Trust Perfect Patty to read my mind. Now I felt bad for having whined about my squashed toes. "Any help you or anyone else can give my daughter to teach her to be a good, safe driver is always appreciated."

"Thanks. Tell you what, two years from now when both of our younger children are going through this, let's trade services. You can teach Kelly how to drive, and I'll teach Nathan."

I intended to reply: It's a deal, but was dumbstruck at the reminder that, two short years from now, I'd be going through this yet again with a second child.

Karen rolled down the window and called, "Hey, Mom? I've got stuff to do. So can we leave soon?"

"Okay. Just a minute." I returned my attention to Patty. "Thanks again, Patty."

"Anytime." She called out to Karen and Rachel, "I agree with you both about Adam and Rick. You're making wise decisions."

I gave a quick glance at Lauren, who gave me a shrug and shook her head. The boys' names meant nothing to her, either. "Adam and Rick?" I repeated.

"Never mind, Mom. You wouldn't understand."

"Actually," Patty immediately interjected, "your mom is one of the most understanding people I've ever met. So is *your* mom, Rachel. And don't hesitate to call me if you need any help with your trigonometry, Karen." She returned her attention to me. "I minored in mathematics," Patty explained, rolling her eyes teasingly.

We watched and waved as Patty got into her own car and drove over to the entrance of the high school. Making no move to get into our car yet, Lauren and I exchanged glances. After checking to make sure the girls had shut the windows again, I said quietly, "From the snippets of Karen's phone conversations I've overheard, Adam and Rick might be the ones code-named 'He Who Must Not Be Named' and 'Too Cute.' "

"Must be. I wonder which one is which." Lauren put her hands on her hips and said under her breath, "Maybe we should ask Patty."

"Knowing Patty and her strong sense of ethics, she might consider that a breach of confidence. Have you ever heard her say anything negative about her ex-husband or his new wife?"

"No. Have you?" Lauren asked.

"Nope. She moved here because she felt her kids needed to live near both parents. Even though *he* was transferred here after their divorce, and *she* had custody. And he'd dumped *her* for a twenty-year-old ski bunny. If Jim ever did something like that to me, there's no way I'd be able to relocate to his new town and never bad-mouth him."

"Me, neither. Not even close."

We stood there in silence.

"Okay, Lauren, I'm just going to say this, and then, I swear, I'll go placidly strolling through a vegetable garden and mull over how petty I am to be so envious. The woman's too good to be true. Nobody can be *that* terrific. She's everything I wish I could be. And the worst part is, she's so darned likable, she's impossible to hate."

"My thoughts exactly, Molly. And you know what? I hate that about her. Sometimes I wish her ex-husband would get transferred again, and they'd move to a town far away."

The girls rolled down the front and rear windows and cried in unison, "Mo-o-om!"

"Duty calls."

I made Karen switch into the backseat so that Lauren could sit up front with me. Just as they fastened their seat belts, a BMW came zooming into the lot. I caught sight of the "Steffi" vanity plates and tried to hurry up and get into my seat, with the hopes of ducking out of view.

Too late. Stephanie had spotted me. She hit the brakes, then turned the wheel to race over to me, pulling her car to a screeching stop with her window just two feet from mine. She glared at me and gestured impatiently for me to roll down my window.

"Morning, Steph—"

"Have you seen Patty Birch, by any chance?"

"—anie." Gesturing at the high school building behind me, I said, "Yes, she just went into the—"

"I'm going to kill that woman!" Stephanie snarled.

She drove off before I could reply.

Chapter 2

My Kingdom for a Porsche

During our drive home, Lauren and I discussed Stephanie's outburst and concluded that she must be angry with Patty over the brewing PTA crisis that Susan Embrick had called me about last night. That subject matter had now taken on a whole new level of seriousness for me. It was too early on a Saturday morning for me to return Susan's call, however.

Once home from dropping Lauren and Rachel off at their house, which was one cul-de-sac down from mine and next to my parents' home, my thoughts eventually returned to Karen and her driving. I exorcised my worries in my usual fashion—by drawing cartoons. My cartooning was ostensibly for work, but it also relaxed me. So even if my one-person company went belly-up—and it had been doing the back float for quite some time now—I would continue cartooning for my own sake. My business, Friendly Faxes, required me to create humorous faxable greetings, plus I freelanced to major greeting card companies.

Sketches of mother-daughter tugs-of-war with car keys and steering wheels somehow led me to draw a king, looking baffled as he stares at a man in ragged clothes emerging from a sports car. The ragged man says to the king, "Oops. My mistake. Could have sworn you said 'my kingdom for a *Porsche*.' By the way, the salesman says the leather seats and undercoating cost extra, so he wants you to throw in France, as well."

The phone rang. Just as Karen raced past Jim—who was still poring over the sports section at the kitchen table—I said, "Sounds like Stephanie's ring. It's got that hint of haughtiness."

Karen stopped short. "I don't want to answer if it's going to be Stephanie."

Neither did I. Especially because I knew that she would be calling to rake *me* over the coals regarding whatever Patty had done to anger her so badly. "We'll let the machine get it."

We waited, and after our pleasant, musical recording of Karen's and Nathan's voices, Stephanie said, "Oh, for heaven's sake, Molly, pick up. I know you're home. I'm on my cell phone in the car, just a mile or two from your place. You can either talk to me now, or I'll head over there now and camp out on your doorstep until you—"

I picked up the phone and immediately asked, "Why are you angry with Patty Birch?"

"That's why I'm calling, my dear."

I rolled my eyes. I was not Stephanie's "dear," nor was she mine.

"Thanks to Patty, our privacy has been egregiously violated," she said.

"Huh? Whose privacy are you referring to?"

"That of the entire Carlton PTA."

"But how can—"

"We've scheduled an emergency PTA board meeting at Patty's house to discuss that very topic this evening."

"A 'board' meeting? Is that spelled b-o-a-r-d, or are we talking about a meeting for particularly dull and disenchanted PTA'ers?"

No answer, save for a noise that sounded like Stephanie clicking her tongue at me. Maybe it was just static.

"Am I even on the board?"

"Oh, Molly, don't be obtuse. The board consists of everyone who holds an important position or has headed a committee this year. You are the vice president. Draw your own conclusions."

"Okay. That lets me off the hook, then. I don't have an *important* position. You said when I became VP that that was just a figurehead who had no actual—"

"Just be there, Molly. Regardless of how important your post may or may not be, *this* is. It starts at seven." She hung up.

"Trouble in PTA land?" Jim asked as I let out a growl that made our cocker spaniel rush over to look up at me expectantly, her stubby tail wagging.

"Yes." I knelt and stroked the soft, red fur on Betty Cocker's back. She immediately rolled over for a tummy rub. "Apparently there's a dispute between Patty and Stephanie, involving some sort of privacy issue. Susan Embrick called me last night, saying there was a PTA crisis brewing, but we average one a month. She should have said that this was an *important* crisis. Meaning, one likely to cause us all to get harangued by Stephanie."

"Is she in the PTA, too?" he asked, meaning Susan Embrick. Everyone within a hundred-mile radius of this town knew Stephanie was PTA Queen Bee. Jim had heard me mention Susan's name dozens of times, but was still reading the paper, his attention divided.

"She's our secretary-slash-treasurer. I'm calling her back now."

I punched in her number and waited. It rang once, then a deep but young male voice intoned, "Yo, babe."

Yo, babe? I lowered the phone to stare at it for a moment, then asked, "Is this the Embrick residence?"

He chuckled. "Yeah. This is Adam. What's up?"

Adam? Surely not of "Adam and Rick," I thought.

Then again, Susan did have a son who was a junior in high school. I glanced toward Karen and saw that she'd migrated back into the room to read the paper. She seemed to be playacting at being uninterested in my phone conversation. "Could I speak to your mother, please?" I asked.

"She doesn't seem to be here. She must be out someplace."

Quelling irritation at his bad phone manners, I asked evenly, "Could you take a message? Could you tell her that Molly Masters returned her call, and could she please call me back?"

There was a pause. "Uh, sure. Does, um, Karen happen to be around?"

That cemented things; Adam was not that common a name. There could not be two boys with that name at Carlton High School who both knew my daughter. Was this Nameless or Too Cute? And what was this "wise decision" that Karen had made toward him? Karen's cheeks had reddened a little, and she was staring at a full-page advertisement for lawn mowers as if transfixed. "Just a minute. I'll check."

Karen met my eyes. I pressed down on the holes over the receiver so hard that the imprint might prove to be emblazoned on the heel of my hand for days. "This is Adam Embrick. He wants to talk to you."

She held out her hand, and I passed her the cordless phone, but the action felt as though I'd very unwillingly handed her a mantle that symbolized her entrance into adult relationships. She'd gone to boy-girl group functions and outings, but we'd said she had to be sixteen before we'd let her go on actual dates. She'd had her sixteenth birthday last week. What the hell had we been thinking? She was way too young. Or maybe I was. Or too old. In any case, *I* wasn't ready!

She said, "Hello?" listened, and then grinned. As she was leaving the room and trotting up the stairs to her room, I distinctly heard her say, "I'm sorry, too."

Oh, crap! Was that apology undoing the "wise decision" that Patty had complimented her for?

Meantime, Jim was oblivious and still reading the sports section. "Jim! Get your nose out of the newspaper! Our little girl is passing before our eyes!"

"What?" he asked, deserting the paper and sitting bolt upright. "What happened?"

"I think Karen is being asked on a date with some upperclassman named Adam Embrick who says 'yo, babe' instead of 'hello.' "

Jim looked baffled and blinked a couple of times before speaking. "How did that happen? You were on the phone with some PTA person. How did that wind up with Karen's dating someone?"

"He's the secretary-slash-treasurer's son."

"But she's too young to . . ." Jim's eyes widened as, no doubt, the significance of her last birthday dawned on him. He got up and started pacing, pulling on his mustache, a habit whenever he was upset. "Our daughter can't go out with some guy who refers to people as babes. Did his family used to live in L.A. or something?"

"I don't think so."

Nathan, who has that special antenna that allows children to sense when a sibling is perhaps about to get yelled at, came bounding up the stairs from the basement. He'd been playing a computer game in my office. He took one look at our faces and asked, "What's going on?"

"Nothing," Jim replied harshly, but added under his breath, "just that my only daughter is about to go out with some dolt who thinks he's Joe Cool." He shifted his attention to me, his brow furrowed. "What do you know about this guy?"

"I think his mom said he's president of the junior class. Either that or the glee club. He's president of something, though. Or maybe that's a sibling of his in junior high. It's so hard to keep everyone's kids straight when the PTA has to deal with all thirteen grade levels at Carlton Central."

We spent the next few minutes in shared, speechless anxiety, unwilling to discuss things further in front of Nathan, who was, in turn, unwilling to leave us alone and miss out on anything. The beacon that had kept me going during occasional dips and dulls of my twenty-year relationship with Jim was the realization that marriage meant my never having to date again. Yet another miscalculation on my part. I'd neglected to factor into the equation the vicarious element of motherhood: the fact that worrying about my daughter felt even worse than actually experiencing her travails myself.

Karen came skipping down the stairs and hung up the phone. "Adam and I have a date tonight. Before you ask, he's president of the junior class, and I've known him from pottery class last year and choir this year. He'd been going out with someone, but broke up with her a couple months ago because she wanted to spend every minute with him, and he's in all these honors classes and has to study a lot. And, Mom, he . . ." She'd started laughing so hard that she had to stop and get her breath, but finally managed to say, "He said to tell you he was sorry for saying 'yo, babe' when he picked up the phone. He thought you were a guy friend of his, and he was goofing around."

Jim's and my eyes met. Apparently the boy had much more going for himself than I'd assumed, but in some ways that only posed a bigger threat. "So what was Patty Birch saying to you about him and Rick?"

"Rick's this jerk who hits on everybody because he

thinks of all girls as conquests. He's been asking both Rachie and me out. Adam warned her about him because she was tempted to say yes. Anyways, I'm going over to Rachie's now. Okay? Then we're coming back here so she can help me figure out what to wear."

"Fine," I said, too stunned to think of another response.

"How about overalls and that . . . that one-piece, long-sleeved bodysuit you wear for dance class?" Jim suggested, but she was already closing the door behind her. He sighed and looked back at me. "Does she own any really ugly outfits with lots of buttons?"

The day passed of its own volition and far too quickly. I was in no hurry either for my meeting or to see Karen off on her first date. I'd told her I wasn't going to fuss, but asked her to commit to memory my one piece of general advice about dating: If you ever feel you have to do something just because otherwise he might not like you, he *doesn't*, so dump him and wait until someone else comes along who *does*. Then I'd made several phone calls on the pretext of discovering the source of the PTA turmoil, and then asked "by the way . . ." if they'd ever met Susan's high-schooler son. I could get no information on either issue, and Susan herself never returned my call.

The doorbell rang at a quarter to seven. Jim and I both answered. There stood a painfully—to me, at any rate—handsome young man with curly blond hair and brown eyes, wearing baggy khakis and a leather bomber jacket. He was, indeed, Too Cute. *Much* too cute.

"Hi. I'm Adam Embrick, here for Karen."

Jim said nothing.

"Come in. Karen will be right down."

He stepped inside. Karen came down the stairs. Jim had taken a step back to allow Adam to enter, but was standing directly between him and Karen, and now stood glaring at the short hemline of her purple-and-black dress.

Adam said, "Nice to meet you, sir," and held out his hand.

"Nice to meet you," Jim said with no smile as he shook his hand. "Her curfew is midnight. Where exactly are you taking her?"

I glanced back at Karen, who rolled her eyes and got her coat out of the closet.

"I have dinner reservations at the Captain's Table at seven, then we'll go to a movie." Jim continued to glare at him, and he added, "Something rated PG. By Disney."

"Have a nice time," I said as Karen squeezed past her father.

"Thanks, Mom."

"Be home by midnight," Jim said again. They disappeared around the corner to the garage, but he continued to watch out the door.

"Well, I've got to go. Although Stephanie's having threatened to kill Patty this morning pales in comparison to knowing that Karen's off on her first date."

Jim shut the door and slumped into the nearest chair. "I'm staying right here till she's back."

"He seems like a nice kid. Don't worry so much."

He looked up at me. "Easy for you to say. *You* were never a teenage boy."

Not wanting to explore that notion any further, I grabbed my coat and left for Patty's.

Patty's house was a ranch-style, three-bedroom house, the smallest home in her neighborhood. Tacked to her front door was a hand-painted paper marionette wearing a leprechaun outfit. That reminded me. It was time to throw out the jack-o'-lantern on our back porch. I studied the little paper dude as I rang the doorbell. In typical Perfect-Patty style, the leprechaun's face had been hand-painted, and the paper had been molded so that he was somewhat three-dimensional. His clothes, from argyles to bow tie, were made from fabric. The red tresses poking out from below his little green hat appeared to be real. Patty's daughter, Kelly, had red hair. Maybe she'd had a haircut recently.

To my surprise the door was swept open not by Patty, but by Chad Martinez, a divorced father who had taken to volunteering for all sorts of PTA fund-raising campaigns and committees, ever since Patty had become president. He was a dark, tall, muscular man with a square jaw and deep-set eyes, and a mustache squared off at the ends to look a little too Hitler-like for my tastes. He gave me a sheepish smile and said, "Chad Martinez. I'm afraid I've forgotten your name."

"Molly Masters."

"Ah. Right. Come in, Milly."

"Molly." I removed my coat, which he immediately collected from me.

"I'll put your coat in the spare bedroom. Patty's in the kitchen." Apparently he had no problem remembering that her name was Patty, not Pitty.

"She made such delicious hors d'oeuvres . . . pastries stuffed with corned beef . . . that I ate most of them. She's just getting a second batch out of the oven now."

"Okay. Thanks."

He nodded and headed down the hallway, carrying my coat.

Although I recognized a few faces in the small gathering, I headed straight to Susan Embrick. She was a little older than I, in her mid-forties, with short, jet-black-dyed hair. She was standing a short distance from Mr. Alberti, a teacher at the high school, who was the only person so far that Stephanie would not have considered part of the "PTA board."

Susan blew on the surface of the liquid in her coffee cup, then I winced as she took what appeared to be a gulp of the very hot liquid. She smiled when she spotted me approaching.

"How are you, Susan?"

"Fine, Molly. How about you?" She ran a trembling hand through her hair. She always seemed to have a slight case of the shakes. She had four children, ranging in age from seven to seventeen. That would make anyone's hands tremble.

"I'm fine." Okay, we'd said something pleasant to each other; time to broach the subject matter so pressingly on my mind. "Our teenagers are on a date tonight."

"Yes, I know. Adam told me he has a nice evening planned. He's had quite the crush on your daughter for some time now."

"Oh? For how long? Karen doesn't volunteer much information to me, now that she's in high school."

"Really? Adam tells me absolutely everything." She crossed her eyes to let me know that she was joking. She took another gulp of coffee. "I threaten to withhold his allowance each week till he opens up with at least one tidbit of personal information."

"Did he tell you I called you back this morning?"

She grimaced and said irritably, "No. That would require his remembering that there are other people . . ." She let her voice fade. "This isn't the right time to point out my son's typical shortcomings. He's a wonderful young man, Molly, and I hear nothing but good things about your daughter, so they'll make a terrific couple."

Oh, God. My little girl, one half of a high school couple! Why couldn't she be a late-bloomer like her mother? My stomach churning, I reached for a less-upsetting topic. "What's this emergency meeting about?"

"That's why I called you last night, to see if you knew what was going on. Stephanie had phoned me a while earlier, saying that Patty had 'done something unconscionable' and videotaped us, but wouldn't tell me anything more."

"Hmm. She told me that the PTA's privacy had been violated. Which must mean that Patty videotaped our meetings, for some reason. But they're public, anyway, so I don't see why that would be all that upsetting."

"It's puzzling, all right." She glanced at her watch. "And now Stephanie is being passive-aggressively late to arrive."

"As opposed to my being *coincidentally* late to anything that Stephanie hosts."

Susan smirked. "Well, that's different. Stephanie deserves it."

"Deserves what?" Patty asked, appearing behind us with a steaming plate of puff pastries. Before Susan could answer, Patty smiled at me. "Molly, I'm glad you could make it on such short notice." She indicated her appetizers with a tilt of her head. "Try one of these pasties. Tell me what you think."

I'd thought "pasties" were those half-dollar-sized stickers that strippers wore to "cover" themselves; must be a dual definition because baked goods would never do the trick. Not even if the baked items were sticky buns. "Okay, but I've got to warn you, I'm not a big fan of corned beef."

"Fair enough. We'll trade warnings. Mine is to be careful. The cheese-and-beef innards are hot."

I bit into one of the flaky little treats and was rewarded with a wonderful blend of flavors, so much so that I didn't mind that, as forewarned, the insides seared my mouth a little. "Yum! Patty, this is delicious! Where did you get the recipe?"

"It's my own spur-of-the-moment concoction."

"Have you had any of these, Susan?" I asked.

"I'm a vegetarian."

Patty chuckled and said teasingly, "You are *not*."

"During Lent I am. I gave up meat."

"I guess your giving up booze doesn't count," Patty said.

Though Patty's voice had been completely casual, Susan stiffened and gave her a hateful glare. Surprised, I did a double take, not understanding the significance of the remark. Despite her moniker, Patty was, of course, not perfect, but I'd never heard her say anything hurtful before. Yet she'd obviously injured Susan's feelings just now.

"Here, let me help," Chad said to Patty from across the room. He took the tray from her. "Don't worry. As long as I keep both hands on the plate, I won't be able to eat them all myself."

"Thank you, Chad," Patty said. "Molly, could you come help me bring out one of the bowls of popcorn?"

"I'd be happy to," I said, following her into the kitchen, but casting a longing look at the pasties. Counting the yet-to-arrive Stephanie and, surely, Jane Daly, who never missed a PTA meeting and was an arts-and-crafts guru and self-appointed decorating-committee goddess, there would be seven of us non–Lenten vegetarians versus two dozen pasties. No way would they last until I had the chance to return.

I grabbed one of the two large bowls of popcorn from the kitchen counter. "The popcorn's got green sprinkles on it," I couldn't help but note with a smile.

"That's the salt. Hang on a moment. I think I'd better sprinkle a little more on before you take it out." Patty grabbed a shaker of bright green salt and started an elaborate procedure of tossing and sprinkling. "Green salt was the only way I could think to make popcorn seasonal."

"Seasonal seasoning," I mused. Looking into Patty's blue eyes, I asked, "Do you mind telling me why we're here tonight?"

Patty frowned. "It's going to be movie night, I'm afraid. Hence the popcorn. Stephanie Saunders objected greatly to the tape that the kids in Kevin Alberti's government class produced."

That explained why he was here tonight. "They finally got their camera? I'm glad to hear it." They'd lobbied the Carlton PTA for funds to pay for a video camera for months now.

"According to Stephanie, if you still *are* glad after you see the tape, that will make one of us. Well, two, counting me. I happen to support freedom of speech, regardless of whether or not it makes people uncomfortable. Stephanie complains that she wasn't portrayed in the best possible light."

I scoffed. "I've known Stephanie Saunders for years. Chances are that's nobody's fault but her own."

Patty raised her eyebrows and shrugged, and I reminded myself that Patty did not partake in gossip, which I, sorry to say, was very capable of lowering myself to. In fact sometimes I was a regular hot dog: doing so with relish. I winced at my own unspoken pun, chalking it up to an occupational hazard.

"I wasn't about to censor the kids, so I have no idea what they actually filmed. I haven't even seen their recording myself."

"That's surprising," Stephanie said, suddenly behind us, still in her coat. "Because the students themselves tell quite a different story regarding your level of involvement, Patty."

"Do they?" Patty said, her voice and facial expression inscrutable. She said, "Excuse me," and left the room.

"Popcorn, Stephanie?" I asked, holding the bowl in front of her.

My offer was met with a chilly glare. Stephanie said quietly, "Trust me, Molly. Once everyone sees this tape, Patty will lose the nickname *Perfect* Patty. Permanently."

Chapter 3

Rated PG-13 for Violence

Despite Stephanie's statement, I couldn't help but assume Patty was in the right. Over time, Patty could wear down one's ego a bit, but the fact that other people even *had* egos, not to mention feelings, had no relevance to Stephanie whatsoever.

When we returned to the living room, Susan was parting the Liberty print curtains to look out the front window. "Here comes Jane, so everyone's here."

"Wonderful." Patty attempted to carry a couple of chairs from the dining table, but Chad immediately rushed over and brought them in for her. I sat down in one, and Patty took the other. A wave of disappointment crossed Chad's features. He returned alone to the love seat.

The doorbell rang and Jane Daly let herself in, eyeing the decoration on the door at great length. She was a short woman with dirty blond hair. Her face seemed to be naturally set into a scowl. Tonight she was wearing a red stocking cap that accentuated her gnomelike appearance. She finally pulled her eyes away from the door to take in all of us in the living room. "Sorry I'm late. I haven't missed anything, have I?"

"No, not at all," Patty said.

Jane took off her hat and shut the door, casting another long look at the paper decoration in the process. "How did you make that leprechaun? Is that real hair?"

"Yes, Kelly did that herself. She had a haircut recently, and she taped her locks to the hat."

"That's just so very clever." Jane looked at a second cardboard doll, leaning against the side of the television. This one had plain, colored-in hair. "Good thing you didn't put actual hair on every single leprechaun. Your daughter would be bald."

Patty laughed. "That's why she's wearing a baseball cap these days."

"Really?" Jane asked, taking a seat next to Chad.

"Of course not. I'm joking. Since you asked, I made the template for the leprechaun from a—"

"Interesting as all of this leprechaun talk is," Stephanie interrupted from her stance in the center of the living room, "I'd like to get to the purpose of our being here tonight, if I might."

"Go right ahead, Stephanie," Patty said.

"I got your VCR ready to go, like you asked, Patty," Chad said, looking at her with puppy-dog eyes. The man couldn't be more obvious about his affection for her if he wore a heart-shaped pendant around his neck with both of their initials on it.

After removing a videotape from her purse, Stephanie gestured at Mr. Alberti, a large, bald man who seemed to be crammed next to the arm of the sofa to avoid getting too personal with Emily Crown beside him. She was Patty's closest friend. To hear her tell it, she was on a perpetual diet, but in my opinion she epitomized the phrase "pleasingly plump."

Stephanie cleared her throat. "I'm sure most of you know Kevin Alberti, a history and government teacher at Carlton. He was kind enough to give me this tape last

night, after I belatedly"—she narrowed her eyes at Patty—
"learned of its existence. As you'll soon see for yourself,
the students used the ruse of *claiming* that they needed
money for a video camera while secretly filming us in
action."

"Wait. You mean, they had access to a video camera
all along?" Jane asked.

Stephanie ignored Jane's question and handed the tape
to Chad. "Start this up." After voicing her command,
she strode to the back of the room and stood with arms
crossed near the door. Was she anticipating a need to
block the exit?

Chad, meanwhile, looked over at Patty, making it obvious that he would take orders from her alone. She gave
him a little nod. He loaded the tape in the slot, turned on
the television, and pressed the play button.

The opening shots were credits that listed each of the
four girls who had been lobbying us for money to purchase
a video camera this year, then showed them mugging for
the camera. This took an inordinate amount of time, and
they were suffering from a bad case of the giggles. We
could wind up as PTA *bored* members, after all.

Next came a shaky view of Stephanie heading toward
the camera on what I recognized as the sidewalk in front
of Carlton Central School. The date readout on the bottom corner of the screen showed that this was filmed last
September, six months ago. Just as Stephanie started to
open the door to the lobby of the elementary school, a
girl not shown by the camera asked, "Excuse me. Are
you Mrs. Saunders?"

Onscreen, Stephanie paused and turned toward the
voice, but the camera was significantly below her gaze.
The girl must have been carrying the camera inside her
purse or knapsack. "Yes, hello." She stared for a long moment, then asked, "Are you a friend of my daughter's?"

"Not really. I mean, I knew her well enough to say hi to her, you know? But she was already a senior when I was a freshman. You're the president of the PTA, right?"

She smiled broadly. "Yes, I"—her smile faded—"or rather, no, but I was until recently. Is there something I can do for you?"

"Yeah, um, I'm in Mr. Alberti's government class? And we need to get five hundred dollars from the PTA? So that we can buy a video camera? It's for, like, filming projects and things?"

It was clear from Stephanie's frozen expression that her patience was already wearing thin. "I see. Well, have your teacher put that on his wish list for the school, and we'll—"

"We want to keep him out of it. See, that's part of the learning process? For the government class?"

Stephanie started to turn away, waving her manicured fingers in the air in a gesture of dismissal. "In that case, you can talk to our treasurer, Susan Embrick. She can have you fill out the forms. Then you can come to the next meeting and plead your case."

"Is that all there is to it? We'll be able to get money for a new camera?"

Though Stephanie answered, "Yes," the girl kept asking questions. Stephanie gave increasingly snarky answers until finally she growled, "*Save it* for Ms. Embrick!" and shut the door in the camera girl's face.

The theme song from *Jaws* began to play, then a voice-over said, "And thus our story begins."

Though I could see why Stephanie would find this an unpleasant episode to have been captured on film, so far it was hardly grounds for an emergency meeting, let alone threats to Patty's well-being.

"Stay in your seats, boys and girls," Stephanie said as if anticipating this reaction. "It gets worse."

The next few minutes showed a series of vignettes featuring all four girls, at different times, trying to get the paperwork handled so that they could get on the agenda at the next meeting. They were bounced between Susan and Chad, getting misinformed by both. Susan, especially, came off as both addled and irritable, but overall, this was merely a valuable lesson to high schoolers about dealing with any kind of a bureaucracy, the Carlton PTA being no exception.

Next came scenes of our monthly PTA meetings, shown in chronological order. The time of day was on prominent display, and the editing demonstrated how endlessly Emily Crown could drone on. I glanced at her, and her hands were now over her lips. I tried to give her a reassuring smile, but her attention was focused on the screen. Although she could go toe-to-toe with me in terms of talking too much—and likely win the contest—she was likable and energetic.

My attention abruptly returned to the screen when the camera's microphone caught some unseen woman with a nasal voice saying, "How dare these amoral people show their faces at school, let alone call themselves PTA officers? Do they think they . . ." The voice faded as, apparently, the woman and whomever she was speaking to left the room. The camera, however, remained in place, aimed at the podium where Patty, Stephanie, Susan, and I were chatting, which we sometimes do after meetings.

"Who was that?" Susan asked, interrupting what was being said on tape. "What the hell did she mean, calling us 'amoral'?"

Mr. Alberti answered, "My students said it was some woman grumbling, but that the camera was unmanned at the time."

"Maybe she misspoke," I said. "Maybe she thought

the meeting went on for so long that she meant to say 'immemorial.' "

No one laughed. Chad muttered something about "replay" and hit the rewind button. We watched again, but the wording did not change, and the adjective was definitely "amoral."

My mind wandered as I tried in vain to think of why any of us on the board could be accused of lacking morals. But once again, an image on the screen quickly recaptured my attention. The camera had caught Patty in a haughty sneer as she turned to leave the podium. That one glimpse of Patty's facial expression startled me, because it was so unlike her typical public persona. The girls stopped Patty and complained. Once again all equanimity, Patty replied, "I'm sorry. This is the first time I've heard anything about your wanting to purchase a video camera."

One of the girls then spotted Stephanie and whined about what she'd told them to do. Stephanie gave her a blank look and said, "I don't recall anything about this matter. In any case, you should have talked to Ms. Birch long before now if you wanted to be on tonight's agenda. She's the president, after all. I can't believe nobody told you that."

Then Chad Martinez stepped right in front of the students to squeeze close to Patty. "How's the old 'alemana turn' going?" He did a couple of quick dance steps and chuckled.

"I'm just being friendly," Chad moaned, drowning out Patty's taped response. "An alemana turn is one of the dance steps from the class I teach. In the class that Patty's in."

"Shh!"

The camera focused on Chad and caught him trying to

peer down Patty's blouse while Patty jotted a memo to herself.

"Oh, God," Chad cried. "Patty . . . I was just . . . er . . . Al, please tell me you haven't shown this in your class already," Chad asked.

Mr. Alberti—whose real first name was Kevin but was nicknamed Al—said, "I did, but it's not anything you should feel—"

"Shh!"

This time I pinpointed our shusher, Emily Crown, Patty's best friend. Her attention was so riveted to the screen, my suspicion was she thought *she* was about to be caught on tape in an embarrassing moment.

I realized with a start, however, that the next image on the screen was my own.

The unseen girl reporter was saying, "Ms. Masters? We've been trying to—"

"Oh, my God," I muttered. "Are my nostrils that large in real life?"

"Shh!"

Shown from this angle, my nose looked hideous. I'd heard about the camera adding ten pounds, but not to one's nostrils. I tented my fingers over my nose and watched in horror.

". . . so we're, you know, doing this to learn what it's like, taking a problem to the government," the girl was saying. The date indicated this conversation took place last October.

"I've never actually tried to get money out of us, so I'm not going to be a good source of information," I was saying on the tape.

"We were told we should attend the next meeting and present our case."

"Really? Well, for your sakes, I hope you only have to

sit through *one* of them. They're dreadfully boring. It's like listening to a group of people impressed with the sound of their own voices. And I should know . . . I'm the worst offender of all. I'm a compulsive jokester."

To my mortification, they next showed a montage of my wisecracks at various PTA meetings this past year. A parent was calling for suggestions on ways to increase attendance at PTA meetings. My suggestion was "Say that we serve terrific snacks. That's the only reason *I* come." Next the principal was complaining that our school had done so well on standardized tests that he kept getting calls now from parents wanting to switch their kids into Carlton, which would overcrowd the classrooms. I said, "Tell them that our scores are high only because we encourage cheating." Next, someone proposing an Asian-Culture Day was talking about China and said, "They don't allow organized groups there," to which I replied, "Ah. Well, the Carlton PTA would be fine, then." The camera was focused on Patty's face during this last remark, and a look of pure fury passed over her features, though she'd assured me when I'd apologized at the time that she'd taken no offense.

Jane and Emily groaned repeatedly as the video showed the two of them, engaged in conversation at what was perhaps a table in the high school cafeteria. I was too consumed with my own shame to pay any attention. Though my quips, in context, had drawn big laughs, when edited this way, I looked like a pathetic buffoon. If I'd ever before felt this thoroughly humiliated, I certainly could not remember when.

A gasp went up from the audience.

"What happened? Can you rewind?" I asked.

Everyone ignored me. Damn! Had I blinked during the one moment when the Loch Ness Monster had surfaced?

Patty Birch was now being shown as the cameraperson approached. Patty's face was red, and she winced as a door slammed. She looked at the camera girl, smiled, and said, "Oh, good. A friendly face for a change. You're Skye, right?"

"Yeah, I'm, um, sorry to catch you at a bad time, but—"

"It's not a bad time. What can I do for you, Skye?"

"I just . . . came to ask you if there was any progress made on getting us that video camera we asked the PTA for."

"Not yet, I'm sorry to say."

"Yeah, um, I'll just come to the next PTA meeting and ask again. About the camera."

"I'll insist that that's the first item on our agenda next meeting, no matter what. You've been more than patient. And, if I could make a suggestion to you, once you do get the camera, you might want to do a documentary on us, on how frustrating this procedure has been and how inefficient the PTA process really is. You could surreptitiously interview us on tape." She looked straight at the camera. "That is, if you're not already." She smiled and winked. The picture faded to black.

Chad was too busy holding his head in his hands to continue with his audiovisual duties. Instead, Stephanie crossed the room, stopped the VCR, and turned off the TV. There was a stunned silence. "So. Does anyone have anything to say?"

The pause was long and heavy. "Could somebody please pass the popcorn?" I asked.

No one laughed.

"Anyone other than Molly?" Stephanie said.

"Sorry. Like I said, it's compulsive." I turned to Mr. Alberti. "I hope you gave your students an A."

"I did."

"They also deserve a civics lecture on respecting people's rights to privacy," Susan snarled.

"You can say that again. Can we buy the tape from them?" Chad asked. "And burn it?"

"Patty, how did you know they were taping you?" Jane asked.

"Because it was her idea in the first place," Stephanie interjected. "She's the one who suggested it as a possible project to Al."

"Patty! How could you!" Jane cried. "Why didn't you at least warn us?"

"We looked like a bunch of idiots," Emily said. "All except for Patty herself, of course." Even though she was supposedly Patty's best friend, she went on to say, "Since *we* were all at the disadvantage of having no idea that we were being filmed."

Still calm and the picture of reason, Patty maintained her seat on the couch and said, "I didn't know for certain that they were taping us. I suggested it, yes, but I didn't know that the students had taken me up on the idea. I thought it'd be such a wonderful opportunity for them to witness firsthand a government in action."

"There's an enormous difference between witnessing a group in action firsthand and secretly filming them," Susan said.

Patty scanned the room as if looking for sympathetic faces. "It's not as if the tape revealed anyone's private lives. They were simply taping public meetings in public places. There was no expectation of privacy."

"But we were recorded other times as well," Emily cried, "such as during our private conversations! All it would have taken was a word of warning from you . . . a mention at the first meeting that it was possible students would be taping us."

"Yeah," Jane said. "And what about the award from national that we're finalists for? If they catch wind of this video . . ."

Emily said, "This is so like you, Patty . . . forging straight ahead with your plans, no matter who or what stands in your way, leaving everyone else to pick up the pieces."

Clearly hurt, Patty scanned her friend's face. "After all this time, that's how you feel about me? So what you said about me on film *was* in context?"

Emily merely averted her eyes.

What *had* she said on that tape?

Mr. Alberti dragged a palm across his bald pate. "I apologize for my role in this. Yesterday in class was the first time I actually saw the video myself. The students had assured me that they'd left the embarrassing parts on the cutting-room floor. I should have given stricter guidelines, insisted that they not hide the cameras and never record someone without getting prior consent."

"And I, too, regret that I suggested this as a project in the first place," Patty said.

"It's a little late now, wouldn't you say?" Jane Daly cried, her focus still exclusively on Patty and not at all on Al's role.

Patty nodded and said nothing. "Clearly, the only ethical thing for me to do now is to resign. Molly Masters is going to have to take my place."

"Nobody wants this to go that far," I immediately said.

"I do," came a voice behind me.

"Me, too." It was Jane.

"All those in favor of Molly Masters taking over as—"

"Wait!" I cried, leaping to my feet. "Just wait. We're all reacting here in the heat of the moment. Let's let ourselves cool down and take another look at this matter when the full PTA is present at the regular meeting in two weeks."

"Sounding pretty presidential there, Molly," somebody remarked.

"Don't say that! I don't want to sound presidential. I don't want to be the president."

"Which is why you're not seeing that Patty should resign," Jane Daly said, getting to her feet. "Come on, everybody, let's get out of here."

They rose and headed out the door en masse. I knew the right thing to do was to stay behind and reassure Patty that she'd done nothing wrong. But I couldn't. Truth be told, I was angry myself. I came off looking like an idiot on that tape. The thought of having had an entire class in my daughter's school witness that aspect of my personality was excruciating. Every one of us on that video had to feel equally bad, with the possible exception of Patty. Could she have done this deliberately—engineered this so that she could show us what idiots we all were?

I left with the crowd, consciously trying to avoid anyone's eyes. Stephanie, however, was waiting for me by my car.

I held up a hand. "Not now, Stephanie. I need to be alone for a while and see if I can save face. Oversized nostrils and all."

She nodded. "Well, I told you so. They say that everybody loves a clown. Though some might quibble with the accuracy of that expression, it's indisputable that *nobody* loves a shrew. *You* have nothing to be ashamed of."

"Neither do you, Steph. You were curt with the girls, but we can all stand to be more patient at times."

She widened her eyes and said, "Yes, we can, can't we?" then grinned and went to her own car.

That "I told you so" of hers must have been building up for years now. I wondered if she'd be willing to serve as president again. Maybe for a second ten-year term.

I mulled things over during my drive home. Once again, I was embarrassed to admit to myself that I was feeling resentful toward Patty. Although I'd pulled into my garage and shut off my engine, I sat there for a couple of minutes, shivering from the cold, trying to put my thoughts in order.

Wait. There was a reason I was so cold—I'd left my coat at Patty's. That was an unconscious sign that I needed to say the things I was thinking to Patty's face, admit to her how bad the tape had made me feel, and suggest that we figure out a way to put the whole incident behind all of us. Maybe we could all learn and grow from the experience.

I pulled out and turned the car around, but cracked myself up at that last thought. Asking for personal growth from a half dozen people at once was as big a fantasy as the Easter bunny. Far easier to blame the person aiming the spotlight and exposing one's flaws than to perform cosmetic surgery on one's own personality. Truth be told, that tape could have been so much worse for me and, likely, every single person it depicted. Al's students were probably telling the truth about the embarrassing sections having been left on the cutting-room floor.

I parked in Patty's driveway, then trudged up the steps and rang the doorbell, which was oddly loud. Then I noticed something by my feet. It was the leprechaun, who'd seemingly been torn from his position on the door. The wind must have caught him and torn him free, I thought, retrieving it. I opened the glass outer door and tried to hang the leprechaun on his little hooks.

The door, which had been ajar, swung open from the gentle pressure of my attempt to rehang the decoration.

I stared in horror. Patty Birch was lying motionless in a pool of blood in the center of her living room floor, a knife handle protruding from her chest.

Chapter 4

Feeling Woozy

I screamed, my vision locked on her motionless body. This couldn't be happening. Surely Patty was just playing a macabre joke on me. I took a couple of steps toward her. Her eyes were open and unseeing.

Though I knew I should check for a pulse, I was so certain she was dead that I surrendered to my instincts and staggered back outside again, needing to get away from this house and the hideous sight.

"Help," I murmured, feeling dizzy. My knees were wobbly. I grabbed the railing on the front porch and steadied myself. I scanned the street, but it was quiet with no cars.

My vision locked upon the large two-story house directly across the street. Patty's ex-husband lived there, and the lights were on. I ran to the house and leaned on the doorbell.

A young blonde opened her door. I couldn't remember her name, but I'd seen her once or twice and recognized her as Patty's ex-husband's new wife. There weren't many twenty-somethings with teenage students, so she stood out at school functions. I saw a flicker of recognition in her features, but I said, "Mrs. Birch? I'm Molly Masters."

She must have seen how grave my expression was,

for she immediately demanded, "What is it? What's wrong?"

"Patty. She's been stabbed."

"Oh, my God! You mean . . . you . . . you saw . . . is she dead or just . . . bleeding?"

"She's dead. I need to use your phone." I grabbed the edge of the door and started to enter.

She put her hands to her face. "Poor Randy! He'll be so upset when he finds out! They were married for nearly twenty years."

"Oh, God," I said, and froze partway through the doorway, remembering now that Patty's fourteen-year-old daughter was likely home. "Kelly. Is she here?"

"She's in her room."

"She'll hear me. I can't—"

She held up a hand and shook her head. "Don't worry. She'll have her earphones on, listening to music. That's what she always does when we're here alone."

Her tone of voice was so matter-of-fact. What was wrong with this woman! Kelly was bound to be ten times as affected by her mother's death as Randy would be over losing his ex-wife.

"There's a phone in the kitchen," she continued. "I'll get it for you."

To steady myself, I leaned against the wall by the front door. Damn it! I should have stayed at Patty's. Called from there. I focused on the stairs directly in front of me, fearing that Kelly would come down those stairs and spot me shaking like a leaf.

The woman returned and handed me a bright blue cordless phone. "I'll call from outside," I said, shoving back out the door. I dialed 911 as I stepped onto the front porch. To my surprise, she came out with me. I slumped down on the wood floor of the porch, unable to support my weight any longer. A male dispatcher answered. I said,

"There's been a murder. A woman was stabbed to death. Patty Birch. Across the street from where I am now."

"Your name?"

"Molly Masters."

"Can you give me the address?" he asked.

"What's her address?" I asked the bleached blonde, holding the phone out so the dispatcher could hear.

"Thirteen forty-six Blackwood Drive," she answered.

I put the phone back to my ear. "Is there anyone else on those premises?" the man asked.

"I don't know. I don't think so. I just . . . came to her house. The door was open, and I found her like that. I'm looking at the house now, and I don't see anyone. My car's the only one in her driveway."

"What's your address?"

My entire body had such a case of the shakes that I was bashing my ear and lips with the phone. I wanted to ask if he meant my home address or the address I was calling from, but could only manage to mutter, "I feel sick." I thrust the phone into Blonde's hands.

"Hel-hello?" she said as I crawled as far as the railing to be sick over the side of the porch. "This is Amber Birch. The, um, the woman who called you is vomiting right now. Can I . . . answer any questions?"

She talked to the dispatcher, explaining her relationship to "the victim," while I tried to pull myself together. When I shakily got to my feet, I glanced up at the house and thought I saw the curtains part in an upstairs room.

"Is Kelly's father home?" I asked Amber.

She shook her head at me and said, "I hear the police sirens now," into the phone. She hung up.

"Kelly's going to see the police cars pulling in across the street."

"Shit!" Amber said, stomping her foot. "Randy is in Japan. I'll call him. He can't make it back here till tomorrow, even if he left immediately. I'm going to have to tell her myself." She went through the door, taking the phone with her. I felt too dizzy to do anything but sit down.

A moment later, Tommy Newton's patrol car came screeching to a stop in front of the Birches' house. He gestured at another pair of officers in a second car to go ahead across the street to Patty's house. By the time Tommy made it up the porch steps to me, an emergency van was pulling up in Patty's driveway.

"They're too late," I said to Tommy. "The paramedics, I mean." I hugged my knees to my chest while seated on the top step of Amber Birch's porch and shivered helplessly.

"Molly? You don't look so good."

I didn't feel so good, either, but mumbled under my breath, "Neither do you." Everything had such a surreal edge to it that his freckled features looked pale and gaunt in the bright light from the motion detectors above me.

"Where's your coat?"

"Patty's house," I murmured.

" 'Scuse me?"

"The victim's house. I left it there by mistake."

Tommy returned to his car, opened his trunk, and retrieved a blanket. He wrapped it around my shoulders. He peered into my eyes and said, "Let's get you out of the cold."

"I don't mind the cold," I replied, but only because I wasn't at all certain that I could get to my feet without fainting.

He put his arm around me as he led me to his car. He and I had known each other for more than thirty years, both of us having grown up in this town, along with Lauren, who was his wife in addition to being my best friend.

"There a reason you been sittin' out here by yourself?" he asked as he opened his car door for me.

"Because I'm a coward. Patty's daughter's in there, and I can't face her."

Tommy put me into his passenger seat, then got into the driver's seat. "Want to tell me what happened?" he asked gently.

His features and voice were so compassionate at that moment that I started crying. Tommy handed me a box of tissues and said nothing. When I managed to regain my self-control, I said, "Considering you're a police sergeant and all, this is the stupidest thing I've ever said, but I could kill whoever did this. Kelly's my son's age. They're in some of the same classes in junior high. What do you say to a fourteen-year-old girl whose mother's been murdered, right across the street from her?"

Tommy gave no answer.

"Everybody's always told me what a great sense of humor I have. But you know what? If positions were reversed right now, if I were . . . dead on the floor and Patty were the one to have found me, she'd have known what to say to my children. She'd have comforted them. I'd trade every ounce of my wit to be the sort of person with that kind of inner strength and poise."

Again, Tommy said nothing for a long time, then quietly said, "Let me take your statement, then I'll drive you home."

"Karen's on her first date." My eyes teared up again. "This is what she'll remember for the rest of her life. How she came home from her first date and learned that the nice lady who gave her a driving lesson that morning had been murdered."

I was sitting in the interrogation room at the police station. I'd already given my formal statement and called home to tell Jim what was going on, but felt strangely unwilling to leave. Tommy had gotten one of his men to retrieve my coat and had returned it to me—after deciding it wasn't evidence—so I couldn't even use the cold as an excuse to stay inside.

Because I'm ludicrously susceptible to caffeine but wanted the comfort of a cup in my hands, I was sipping water from a stained coffee cup that still bore a faint flavor of old coffee. Tommy watched me, his red hair in even worse than its typical hat-head state, with a cowlick standing at attention.

"I thought the curse was over, Tommy. I finally went two full years. Nobody was murdered. Does that sound to you like it should be reason to celebrate? Two stinkin' years without anyone I know getting murdered? Sheesh! What is it with me?"

Tommy shook his head and sighed. "I dunno."

"No, I'm really asking, Tommy. I'm just . . . a typical housewife. A suburbanite mom with a little cottage industry on the side that barely brings in enough revenue to require me to declare a profit. Why should *I* be more deadly than the bubonic plague?"

"You bring out the worst in people?"

I scowled. "Let's stick with your 'I don't know.' " I sighed. "Patty Birch, of all people. She was so . . . amazing. Who would do this to her?"

"You said that you and Lauren saw Stephanie early this morning. And that Stephanie had been furious with Patty."

I nodded. Both of us knew Stephanie too well to seriously believe that she'd committed this horrid crime. "That was because of the tape I told you about. Have you heard back from your crime-scene investigators? Was the tape still there, in Patty's VCR?"

"Yeah. Watched it when you were calling home. Didn't

make y'all look too swift, but that's about the sum of it. Can't see as it was worth bloodshed. Though maybe it was a last straw . . . a trigger. Anyone at the meeting strike you as bein' on the edge? Ready to snap?"

"Everyone did."

"Nothing stood out?"

"There was the unseen voice I didn't recognize who called us amoral. And one time when everyone kind of gasped."

"At what?"

"I don't know. Something Jane Daly or Emily Crown said. My attention had wandered."

He rose and gestured for me to follow him. "I'll replay it for you."

"That's hardly standard police procedure, is it?"

He shrugged. "You're a material witness. You know these people. Maybe you can tell better 'n me when someone's hittin' a nerve."

He led me to a second room where four officers were watching us on tape. They did a double take at me. To my chagrin, they were watching my aren't-I-funny . . . not section. Tommy explained that he wanted me to watch this without distractions, and the others left the room. He fast-forwarded till we reached the section I'd missed.

Emily and Jane were in the corner of the high school cafeteria. The camera appeared to be resting at the opposite side of the table. Jane was saying, ". . . because she doesn't *want* you to lose weight. I'm telling you, she's so competitive, she needs to have something over everyone else."

Emily sighed. "And now she's going to win yet another award. That's Perfect Patty for you, isn't it? She's so freaking perfect that it would never even occur to her that she's bringing us mere mortals to shame in comparison."

Jane rolled her eyes. "You can say that again. Try holding down a job for ten years that you and everyone else knows Patty could do better than you with one arm tied behind her back."

The screen image shook as if the camera had been jostled. Oblivious to whatever caused the camera motion, Emily cried, "That's exactly how she makes *me* feel! The truth of the matter is, Patty is as insensitive and egotistical as they come."

I caught my own breath at that, just thinking how Patty must have felt hearing that from her so-called "best friend" in front of a half dozen witnesses.

"If she ever once tried to—" Emily must have noticed then that the girl with the hidden camera was within earshot, for she stopped. She put on a smile and said, "Oh, hi, kids. Still trying to get your little camera?"

"Yes."

Jane smirked and crossed her arms. Again, the posture gave me the image of her as a gnome. If she commented, it was not recorded. Instead, the final scene with Patty began, and Tommy stopped the VCR.

"Any thoughts?" Tommy asked me.

"Well, it doesn't look to me like a motive for murder, but just shows how ... bitchy we can be sometimes when we think nobody is looking. Patty herself took the brunt, so if anything, *she* should have been infuriated. Though I'm sure Jane and Emily's getting caught talking about her behind her back was horrid for them, too." I winced, remembering how I'd been guilty of talking behind Patty's back just this morning. I sank my face in my hands. "How did this happen? Patty was such a terrific person, and her last day on this earth was spent learning that all her friends resented and betrayed her."

*   *   *

The next morning, my first thought upon waking was that I'd had a terrible dream but that everything was fine now—Patty was alive and well. But as I became fully conscious, I remembered the whole story and realized that Patty was dead. I pulled my pillow over my face, thinking there was no way I could face the day.

Jim was already showered and getting dressed the next time I opened my eyes. He saw that I was awake, knelt beside me, and stroked my hair. "You're coming to church, aren't you?" he asked.

"No." I didn't want to see any familiar faces, but also didn't feel like explaining this. "I'll go to a later service by myself."

Our dog, meanwhile, put her front paws on the edge of the bed beside Jim and shoved her cold, wet little nose into my face, whining for attention. I got up, put on my bathrobe and slippers, and went downstairs, just as Jim was trying to hustle everyone into the car. Karen gave me a reassuring smile before heading out to the garage. We'd both gotten home last night just before midnight. She'd said her date was "good," that dinner was "good," and the movie was "pretty good." She was horrified at my news, but at least she'd heard it directly from me.

Our fourteen-year-old, Nathan, stalled as he put on his coat. He was tall and thin with a band of brown freckles across his nose and cheeks. These days he kept his hair very short and combed with gel into what was called a "ski jump" in the front. He asked me what happened last night. I told him only that Kelly's mother was dead and that I didn't feel up to talking about it. Void of all energy, I sank into a living room chair and stared at the wall.

Not ten minutes later, the doorbell rang, which, great watchdog that she is, got Betty Cocker to start barking. "Hush, BC," I said. She looked up at me, continuing to bark. "On second thought, speak." We'd been working to train her out of the barking at the doorbell, but with a murderer on the loose, we could probably use as much protection around here as possible.

I cinched my robe tighter and approached the door, thinking if this proved to be a reporter, I would go into attack mode myself and save BC the effort. A second thought occurred to me: If this was Stephanie, I would *really* launch into attack mode.

The barking immediately stopped and turned to tail wags as I opened the door. Standing there was Lauren, who must have made the short walk between our homes. My eyes misted at the welcome sight of her attractive, round face. She had a small bag in her hand, which she ignored as she gave me a hug. "I should have gone with you last night."

"It wouldn't have changed anything," I said as she released me from her hug.

"You might not have doubled back. You might not have had to be the one to find her."

"It's the story of my life. I never arrive early enough to prevent the murder, just to find the body. I should run for county coroner."

She gave BC, whose interest had turned to sniffing the bag in her hand, a quick little pat. "Tommy said you were pretty shaken up last night."

I nodded. "I didn't feel like going to church this morning. So the place is quiet, if you can stay for a while." I put a hopeful tone in my voice, needing Lauren's companionship.

We automatically started for the kitchen, where, on our stools at the counter, we'd had so many heart-to-hearts over the years. "I brought you a muffin."

Our standard "comfort" food. "Thanks. Whatever would I do without you and your muffins?"

"I don't know, but since I bake when I'm upset, I'd weigh two hundred pounds if I didn't have you to eat them."

I chuckled a little, my humor returning. "You know, when the doorbell rang this morning, my first thought was that it'd be Stephanie, wanting to know who I thought—"

The doorbell rang, again instantly augmented by my dog's barks. Lauren and I exchanged glances.

"Couldn't be," I said. My parents were currently in Florida, so there was no way that this could be my mother. Reaching for an alternate explanation, I called over my shoulder, "Isn't this Girl Scout Cookie season?" as I went to the door.

It was indeed Stephanie. The sight of her on my doorstep made me want to join BC at barking. Stephanie was wearing a powder-blue tailored pants suit, her hair wrapped up in a scarf, turban style. I stared at her, speechless. She must really be in quite a mood if she felt inspired to dress like the Queen of Sheba on a Sunday morning. Her au pair must be watching her seven-year-old son, unfortunately; I enjoyed the little boy immensely. Stephanie shot a withering glare at Betty Cocker, who continued to bark.

Finding my voice, I said, "Hi, Stephanie. We were just talking about you."

She stepped inside and said, "We'll leave your conversation up to my imagination, all right? Hello, Lauren."

"Stephanie," Lauren said with a nod. She'd returned to the living room to give me moral support. Unfortunately, BC immediately quieted down.

"It's probably good that you're here, Lauren," Stephanie said. "We need to discuss what we're going to do."

"About . . . ?" I prompted.

"Solving Patty's murder, of course." She swept past us

and took a seat in the recliner, known in my house as "the big chair" from the days when my children were little enough to cuddle with me there.

I looked at Lauren, who gave me a slight one-shoulder shrug, then took a seat on the love seat and pulled a white paper napkin and a pink-colored muffin out of her bag, which she handed to me. I took a seat beside her as she held out a second muffin to Stephanie, who shook her head. BC was rapt in front of her, her little brown eyes pleading for the muffin that Stephanie had declined.

"As you both no doubt recall, at that ungodly hour yesterday morning when I ran into you in the school parking lot, I said something about wanting to kill Patty. Needless to say, that was just a figure of speech, and I'm completely innocent."

"Mm-hmm," I said, taking a bite of Lauren's home-made muffin. "This is delicious. You don't know what you're missing, Stephanie."

"Alas." She leaned back in her seat and studied my face. "We all know that you're going to look into this murder, Molly. You always do. So I thought I'd offer you some assistance."

"Why?"

She raised her eyebrows. "You don't think that I'm going to sit back and allow the gossipmongers to carry on at will, do you?"

"What are people saying about you?" Lauren asked. "That you did it?"

"I doubt anyone has *that* much misplaced nerve, no. Just that I . . . instigated it. Thanks to my making the meeting so inflammatory."

"They may have a point, there, Stephanie," I interjected. "I mean, obviously you didn't mean to get Patty murdered, but you could have handled the whole thing a bit more gently."

"More gently, you say? I was supposed to pussyfoot around when that . . . when Patty set me up to look like a complete bitch?"

That actually was an insult to my wonderful little female dog, but I decided not to call Stephanie on it. "You didn't look like a *complete* bitch. But my point is that people wouldn't have gotten so upset if you'd warned them about how they came off on the video, or if you'd allowed us to view the tape individually, in the privacy of our own homes, and then called a meeting to discuss it once we'd calmed down."

She examined her fingernails. "That was precisely how I told Patty I wished to proceed, but she insisted we do it as a group at her house. Anyway, what is important is that it seems as though this entire town has the misconception that I was jealous of Patty Birch. That's ludicrous. The best way to dispel such nonsense is if I play an active part in solving her murder."

"Stephanie, I just don't see—"

"Don't argue with me, Molly. My mind is made up. You've done this before, so tell me—what's the first step toward figuring out who the murderer is?"

"Jeez, Stephanie. I don't know." I glanced at Lauren, whose lips were pursed. "You just . . . try to talk to people in Patty's social circles . . . her menopause support group, for example. You figure out who had such a fractured relationship with her that they might have resorted to violence."

"That makes sense. Three heads are definitely going to be better than one." She gestured at Lauren. "I'm assuming you'll take advantage of your friendship with the police sergeant's wife, after all."

Lauren let out a guffaw. "Stephanie, Molly never takes advantage of our friendship. We've been friends our whole lives because we like each other. For good reason."

"You misunderstood the implication." She chuckled. "Molly, you know I didn't mean that you're friends with the chief investigator's wife because that's prudent. Now mind you, I'm assuming that you're innocent, despite how idiotic you were shown to be in the tape and the fact that you had the best opportunity."

I massaged my suddenly aching temples. "You know, I am not in the mood to put up with this. Please leave, Stephanie."

"Oh, I'm sorry. I obviously underestimated how touchy you would be the morning after your morbid discovery." She rose and headed for the door. "You know how to find me," she said over her shoulder as she shut the door behind her.

I growled in frustration and looked at Lauren, who gave me a smile. I said, "If only I could figure out how to *lose* her."

Chapter 5

A Different Drummer

The next couple of days seemed to pass in a colorless blur. After having given myself twenty-four hours to cool off, I had called Stephanie and initiated a peace-pipe exchange. She was just being herself, after all, and with a killer on the loose who was very possibly a fellow PTA member, none of us needed to make enemies. The passage of time, however, had done nothing to ease my guilt over my cowardly avoidance of Kelly Birch on the night of the murder. Nathan reported to me that she'd been absent from school both Monday and Tuesday. I planned to tell her after the funeral, which was scheduled for tomorrow afternoon, how very sorry I was about her mother.

But for now, I was seated in "the big chair" with my sketch pad, in search of a cartoon idea. Eventually I drew a couple of elderly women staring after a young man dressed in feathers and streamers who is cheerfully marching down the street while banging on a drum. One woman is gripping the other woman's sleeve and says to her, "Hold on, Agnes . . . this could be a trap. Are we supposed to march to the beat of a different *drum* . . . or to a different *drummer*?"

The phone rang. "And not a moment too soon," I said to myself as I dropped my feeble attempt at humor, stepped over my sleeping dog, and answered the phone.

"Molly?" The voice was tense and unfamiliar to me. "This is Jane Daly. You're down as a substitute chaperone for the eighth graders' ski trip this evening."

"I am?" I muttered, needing a moment to transition from stupid-cartoonist mode to addled-mother mode. "Oh, of course I am." This ski trip was an anticipatory celebration for the eighth graders who'd be graduating from junior high in a few months. With tomorrow and Friday scheduled as in-service days for the junior high, this was not a school night. "My son, Nathan, has been really looking forward to it. Somebody got sick?"

There was a pause. "Patty was supposed to be one of the chaperones."

I winced. "Oh. Of course. Stupid of me not to realize that."

"You couldn't have known she was going."

"Sure I could have. She started the whole tradition of the ski trip, after all."

"Yes. It was another of her terrific ideas."

Her voice sounded flat. Having witnessed her videotaped harangue of Patty, I immediately bristled and asked, "Are you being sarcastic?"

"No, it's not that. I'm just a little upset, because I just now found out that Kelly's going on the ski trip, in spite of everything."

"Kelly Birch?"

"Yes." She sighed. "Keep a special watch out for her, would you?"

"I will, but I'm . . . surprised to hear she's going. She hasn't been in school. I assumed she'd be needing time to cope with her loss."

"That's what *I* thought, too, but she's in school today, and I just got off the phone with her stepmom. Amber thought it'd be good for her. Amber's going to be working at the ski slope tonight. Wouldn't do to change one's routine, just because your stepchildren's mother died horribly right across the street from you, not four days ago."

"Yes, well . . ." I let my voice trail off, not really knowing what to say. On the one hand, I shared Jane's indignation at what appeared to be Amber's indifference to Kelly's grief. But Amber, as well as her stepdaughter, was a source of guilt for me.

After assuring Jane that I'd be at the school to help with the loading up of students and ski equipment, we said our good-byes and hung up.

I returned to my seat and pondered my feelings toward Amber Birch. Initially I had drawn nasty conclusions when I'd barged in on her to use her phone, yet it was impossible to say how I'd have reacted under those same circumstances. She was such a natural target for scorn from all of us forty-plus-year-olds who resented anyone's trophy wife. None of this could be easy on her. I could seek her out and give her a kind word. More important, establishing camaraderie between us would help allow me to discuss her relationship with Patty and learn if she was a suspect . . . said my one face to my second face.

After school, Karen reminded me that I'd promised her that, if I went on the trip, she could go as well. Since then I'd learned that the high school teachers did not have in-service days this week, so this *was* a school night for her. Even so, these days I was anxious to spend some time with my growing-up-too-fast daughter. So far, Jim and I had only managed to elicit her usual one-word responses to questions about her budding romance with Adam Embrick. That she was at all interested in going skiing with her mother and a hundred eighth graders was almost a welcome surprise. I told her that she could come skiing as long as she got her homework done first.

That evening, we each had a bowl of macaroni-and-cheese—the Goddess of Processed Food's little gift to us harried moms—and a Flintstone vitamin for dessert. Okay, so I'm not exactly centerfold material for *Good Housekeeping*. Or even *So-so Housekeeping*. Truth be told, *Unlikely-to-cause-permanent-damage Housekeeping* was more my speed. I left a message at Jim's office as to where we'd be. Then we took off to meet everyone at school.

It was a hectic scene in the junior high parking lot. In their excitement, the students had reverted to that peculiar tendency of young children to be able to spot a Cheerio in the dirt from a hundred paces, but not the twelve-feet-high, fifty-feet-long display of fine china directly in front of them. With many of them carrying skis, the trek along the sidewalk was hazardous to us non-Cheerios.

Jane Daly was the first person to greet me. Again, she was wearing her red gnome hat. "Molly. Several parents are driving up and hauling the kids' ski equipment."

"I can do that," I quickly interjected.

She shook her head. "Those slots have already been taken. We need chaperones on the buses. It's just you, me, and Chad on one bus, and we'll have our hands full."

I nodded. "Good thing it's just the first hundred eighth graders to turn in their permission slips and not all three hundred of them."

"Really." She patted my arm. "I've got some running around to do. You take the clipboard and start checking off kids as they get on the bus."

I got Karen and Nathan situated on the bus and began to check off names as a mob of eighth graders boarded. Their noisy voices were getting to me, so afterward I went outside to catch the few late-arrivals on my list. In the corner of my vision, I caught sight of Chad Martinez, who was pacing the sidewalk a short distance away, looking downhearted.

I smiled at him when he neared. He gave me a slight smile in return. "I'm really sorry about Patty's death, Chad."

"Me, too," he said, his voice choked.

"I know you two were close friends."

He made no reply, and the silence was heavy. As a less-somber conversation starter, I said, "Well. Two hours on the bus. With a group of young teenagers. Oh, boy."

Chad's deep-set eyes were now red-rimmed and appeared to be almost sunken into his skull. He said forlornly, "Patty used to lead us in song the whole way. She knew so many . . . great songs for groups. The only one I know is 'A Hundred Bottles of Beer on the Wall.' "

"That's quite a crowd pleaser. Wouldn't be appropriate now, though. Besides, I keep forgetting the lyrics."

He furrowed his brow. "It goes: 'A hundred bottles of beer—' "

"I was kidding, Chad."

"Oh. Of course." He sighed. "I seem to have lost my sense of humor lately. Not that there's much to smile about anymore, anyway."

"Patty would have been the first one to say not to let our"—I stopped at the sight of Kelly Birch, shuffling toward the bus, her head down. Her father gave her a wave, then drove off—"spirits sink," I said, swallowing the lump in my throat.

She was carrying skis and a boot bag, and Chad leaped at the opportunity to help her out by loading her equipment into a parent's minivan. By the time she returned to the bus, she was the last on my list and walking side by side with Chad. "Glad you could make it, Kelly," I said, feeling that this was the wrong time for saying anything substantive.

"Yeah, right," she muttered into her shoes as she stomped up the stairs of the bus.

Chad sighed and shook his head. He gestured for me to go ahead of him. "After you, Mu—Mo—, er, ma'am."

"Molly."

On that note, we were off.

Having lived in Colorado for several years, I found that this eastern ski range made for an interesting switch in terms of overall skiing experience. The steepest run on this mountain would be the bunny hill at Vail. On the other hand, at the Colorado ski resorts, they have snow. At the Adirondack resorts, they have ice. To execute a turn when skiing on ice, one must possess: a) young and strong quadriceps, b) natural grace and coordination, and c) newly tuned skis with edges sharp enough to slice through an overripe tomato. Ignoring a and b so as not to sink into depression, the trouble with c for me was that it required getting off one's fanny before *it* turned into an overripe tomato, going to a ski store, and having one's skis tuned. Mine had last been tuned in 1982—assuming that the original manufacturer had tuned them prior to shipping them to the store.

After helping the kids get their skis, poles, and boots from the rental shop at the lodge—where they did indeed have skis with actual edges—Karen, Nathan, and I got on the chairlift. This lift featured two-seater chairs, resembling slightly padded metal benches that are fastened onto a thick, continuous cable overhead. We rode up, got off without incident, and Karen waited for Nathan and me at the top of the run. When we reached her, Nathan looked at me and asked, "Ready, Mom?"

I shook my head, looking down at the illuminated ski

run. Despite the relative lack of altitude compared with the Rockies, it would be a long way to fall. If only my pants, jacket, and hat were equipped with air bags. "I'm going to start out as slow as possible. You'll have to wait for me at the bottom."

"Okay, but can I go right back up and meet you after my second run?" Nathan asked. "That'll take about the same amount of time."

"No."

He pushed off, and soon the top of his head in its bright blue helmet was all that could be seen from my vantage point as he effortlessly whooshed down the slope. I glanced over at Karen in her yellow helmet, wishing not for the first time that I had purchased one of those for myself. Which I easily could have done while having my skis tuned.

"Want to go down with me?" Karen asked. "I don't go as fast as Nathan."

"I think I'll stay up here and enjoy the view for a while. Have a nice run, and I'll see you at the bottom."

I watched her go down, till she and her yellow ski helmet were a safe distance away, then shoved off. As is often the case, I wasn't nearly as bad as I expected to be and managed to get down just fine, but I was glad to get the first run of the day behind me. Both kids were dutifully waiting for me by the ski lift.

"I'll go up one more time with you, Mom, then I'm gonna wait up for Robert," Nathan said, naming one of his closest friends.

"Gallant of you. Thanks."

Kelly was waiting in line immediately in front of our threesome, noticeably, I thought, keeping to herself, as if unable to participate in the excited voices of her peers surrounding us.

"Would you like to ride up with me, Kelly?" I asked.

She shrugged. Nathan and Karen were giving each other dirty looks at this idea, which would mean that they'd ride the lift together. They rarely argued these days, but they also avoided each other whenever possible. "How about if I ride up with you, Kelly?" Karen said sweetly.

"Okay," she said, and almost smiled. They got onto the lift.

Nathan and I had only just hopped onto the next seat on the lift when a commotion arose from Karen and Kelly's chair up ahead. The people waiting in the lift line beside us were all looking up at her.

Aghast, I saw that Kelly was hysterical, waving her arms and screaming, "Get me down! Get me down! Oh, my God! I'm going to die!"

"Stop the chair!" I yelled.

Our cries finally caught the attention of the operator, who stopped the string of chairs. By now, the two girls had to be a good fifteen feet in the air, and Nathan and I were at least six feet up. Kelly let her ski poles drop. They bounced on the hard ice and skittered down the slope, finally stopping just below my chair. I felt a little queasy at how rough the landing had been, unable to block out the thought of how much worse it would be for a person.

Kelly yanked off her mittens and hurled them down. She seemed to be clawing at her face with her bare fingers and was shrieking.

"Do something!" I hollered down to the lift operator. "Back us up!"

"Can't!" he called back.

I could tell that Karen was trying to soothe her and had one arm around her shoulder, the other, thankfully, gripping the chair itself.

Kelly was squirming so badly in her seat that the chair was swinging in a nerve-wracking manner. I was petrified, unable to look away but increasingly frightened by what I was seeing. Karen would live through a fall from such a height, but not without breaking a bone or two.

"Just stay seated, Karen, Kelly! Everything is going to be fine," I shouted.

Downwind from the girls, I doubted they could even hear me. Meanwhile, the two lift operators and a third man dressed in the red jacket for the ski patrol had rushed over underneath the girls. They were trying to talk to Kelly, who kept screaming through her tears, "Get me down!"

"Sheesh," Nathan said. "Kelly's really freaked out. I'm glad *I'm* not sitting with her."

I was too engrossed in silent prayer to comment, but I'd have given anything to have been in that chair with her instead of my precious daughter.

"Do you think Karen's going to fall?"

"No, Nathan, I don't," I snapped. "And I don't feel like talking right now, okay? I'm trying to watch!"

"You can watch and talk at the same time."

"No, I can't. I have to concentrate."

"Why?"

"So that Karen won't fall!"

Nathan, fortunately, recognized from the tone of my voice not to push me. He sat quietly, swinging his skis, which, under the circumstances, was agitating my nerves, but I managed to hold my tongue. "Cool," he said. "They're bringing a ladder."

"How are they going to get her skis off her to get her down?" I asked, not expecting an answer. Nevertheless, Nathan felt compelled to give me one, and though I was too busy holding my breath to listen, caught that his thinking was based on the theory that the ski-patrol members would have "really strong thumbs" to work the ski releases.

Meanwhile, one young man was climbing the ladder while another steadied it. Fortunately, they were both muscular. Kelly continued to sob. Karen looked back at me. Even from this distance it was obvious that she was anxious. Her eyes were wide open, and her face pale.

The man on top of the ladder managed to release each of Kelly's bindings and to hand them down to his partner. Kelly let out a piercing scream as he pulled her out of the chair, and kept a grip on one armrest so that the whole chair was tilting horribly. I bit my leather mitten to keep from crying out at the sight.

Karen managed to keep a grip on the chair herself and to stay seated. They brought Kelly down safely on the ladder. Only then did I feel as though I could breathe again.

"Should I get down, too? To keep Kelly company?" I called down to the lift attendant.

"Are you her mother?"

"No, but I'm the nearest chaperone."

He hesitated, and I knew he was weighing the thought of having to get me out of my chair and onto a ladder. He shook his head. "She'll be all right. Meet her in the lodge."

"I'll be down as soon as I can, Kelly," I shouted down to her. The chairs started once again in their squeaking, groaning ascent. "Her stepmom's here someplace," I called over the racket. "She's a ski instructor. Amber Birch."

The attendant waved, but I wasn't sure if he was signaling that he heard me or that I should shut up and let him handle things.

I returned my attention to Karen, in the seat ahead—and above—me. Would she be able to ski down safely after all of this commotion?

"That was so weird," Nathan said to me after a while. "I thought Kelly skied here all the time."

"Her mother just died, Nathan. Thankfully, neither of us knows how that feels. I think it's a good idea for you and Robert to meet up and ski together. I think I'll be spending most of my time in the lodge with Kelly."

Karen was waiting for us at the top. "Jeez, Mom. I didn't know what to do with Kelly. She seemed perfectly fine as we got into our seats. Then she, like, totally freaked."

"She's had more trauma over the last couple of days than anyone should have to handle, especially at her age."

"I offered to come down the ladder with her, but it was like she couldn't even hear me."

"I'll check on her as soon as I get down. Don't worry about it. She shouldn't have come up here tonight in the first place."

"See you at the bottom," Nathan said, clearly having grown too eager to ski to withstand any more of our chatter.

I called after him, "Meet me at the lodge at eight P.M., okay?"

"Okay," he called over his shoulder.

"I'll just join up with Anna. She's my friend Kimberly's younger sister. Okay?" Karen asked.

"Sure. Go ahead, Karen. Just be sure to meet me at eight, as well."

She, too, took off. I waited another moment, just to be sure that Karen had a good enough lead that I didn't have to worry about crashing into her. Then I aimed my ski tips downhill and let gravity do its thing.

I decided to go down along one side of the course and to go without stopping so that I could get to the lodge as quickly as possible. As is often the case when I don't try too hard, I was skiing quite well now, which reminded me how much fun skiing was. It was a shame that we didn't manage to ski more often.

All of a sudden, someone came flying at me from behind some trees on the side of the course. "Hey!" I yelled, automatically turning and getting a shoulder up to block the impact.

The skier barreled right into me and sent me flying. I managed to get one hand down to break my fall slightly. My body was spun around, and I tumbled head over skis.

My head jerked back, smacking the ice. One ski came off. I was sliding toward the evergreens at a terrifying rate. I managed to dig the heel of my ski boot into a soft patch in the ice. Thankfully, my slide toward the tree trunks stopped just in time.

I lay on the ground for a moment, waiting for a hideous pain to overtake me. None was forthcoming. I wiggled my fingers and toes and breathed a sigh of relief, glad to discover that I still had control of my extremities.

A skier stopped right beside me. "Lady, are you all right?" he asked.

"I think so."

"Oh, it's you, er . . . Mona."

I looked up to recognize Chad Martinez. His black, rectangular mustache had frost at the ends and resembled a toothbrush.

"Did you know that maniac?" he asked.

"Which maniac?" I automatically joked and tried to sit up.

"That other skier deliberately elbowed you."

"I figured he or she was just trying to clear a wide swath down the mountain."

He shook his head. "No, I saw the whole thing. I think it was a woman. Or maybe a short man. Looked about your size. Had a ski mask on. And she was just standing there looking up at the other skiers, and when she saw you, she took off after you and threw her elbow into you."

That was the impression I'd had, too, but really would have greatly preferred otherwise. I managed, with great effort, to get to my feet.

Two other skiers, who both appeared to be eighth graders from Carlton, asked if I was all right and helped me retrieve my ski, then took off again. Though it was a struggle at this angle, I eventually got my ski back on, with Chad's help.

"I'd better report this," I said to him. "What color outfit was the skier wearing?"

He shook his head. "She was pretty far away from any of the lights. I just couldn't tell, other than that she had a dark jacket and ski pants, and a dark mask on."

"I guess I'll report that much to the ski patrol."

"Lucky you didn't get knocked clear into the trees. You could've gotten killed."

"Yeah. Thanks. I think I'm calling it a night as far as the skiing goes. I'm not doing much good as a chaperone, anyway. I think I'll keep an eye on things down at the lodge instead."

"Okay. Take care, Mona."

I decided not to correct him. At least he could get the first letters of my name right.

By the time I got down, Karen and Nathan were already well on their way back up. I heard Karen yell, "Mom!" and I managed what I hoped was a happy-looking wave. No sense in putting scary ideas in their heads, or mine. They would be fine. They were better skiers than I was and were shorter and therefore closer to the ground.

I removed my skis and set them against the rack, thinking I could count on their never being stolen. Unfortunately. I found one of the men in red ski-patrol suits and told him about my "accident," and he said he'd be on the lookout and revoke the skier's pass if he could find the person.

The crash had to have been a coincidence—a case of road rage on the slopes. It couldn't have anything to do with the murder. Nonetheless, a fear niggled at me. I *could* have been killed, had I hit a tree trunk at that speed.

I entered the lodge and searched for Kelly. I finally spotted her in the corner, sitting alone at the long, picnic-table style of seating. She was sipping from a Styrofoam cup. "Hi, Kelly. Can I get you another hot chocolate?"

"No, thanks, Mrs. Masters. I've already had three."

"I meant to get down here and check on you sooner. I had a slight fall, though."

"I'm okay now. At least my mom didn't see me. She'd have been humiliated."

I didn't know what to say to that. She must have meant her stepmother, who Kelly thought would have been humiliated to have a stepdaughter with a severe fear of heights.

Just then, Amber Birch entered—her face flushed, her gait taking on that exaggerated lurch that skiers get to compensate for their inability to flex their ankles in the boots. She scanned the room and stopped at the sight of us. She rushed to our table and sat down next to her stepdaughter. "Kelly, honey, are you all right? I just heard what happened. I was out with the Lady Downhillers. I'm sorry. So, like, you got sick on the lift?"

Kelly shrugged, not looking at Amber. "I'm fine now."

"Thank goodness." Amber shifted her vision to me. "Hi. You're the . . . uh . . ." She let her voice fade and gave a quick glance at her stepdaughter, apparently not wanting to mention my having come to her door to call the police. "Amber Birch."

"Yes. Molly Masters."

"You're the, uh"—she hesitated, and I knew she was looking for an alternative to pointing out that I was the person who had barged in the night of the murder— "Veep of the PTA," she said at last.

"Right. I used to work with Patty. She was a good friend of mine."

"Yes, she was quite a person."

Kelly clicked her tongue and rolled her eyes. "Molly can just stay with me, Amber. You can get back to your class now." Kelly's voice had taken on the snide hostility that all teenagers seem to master.

Amber furrowed her eyebrows, but merely asked, "What happened?"

Kelly set her lips and didn't respond.

"She got scared on the lift," I answered for her. "They had to take her down."

"That much I heard. But scared of what?"

"The height!" Kelly snarled.

"But, Kelly, give me a break here! You've been on that very lift at least a hundred times by now. Why would you suddenly get scared of heights?"

"Gee, I don't know. Hmmm." She lifted her index finger. "My mom died three days ago." She raised a second finger. "You killed her." She raised a third finger. "You're a ski instructor here." She looked at her hand and its three raised fingers and said with a sneer, "Could it be that I've become frightened of things that remind me of you?"

Chapter 6

So __That's__ the Fax I Get?

Amber pursed her lips, got up from the table, and walked away without another word. Despite her clunky ski boots, she managed to look almost graceful as she strode out the door. I studied Kelly's features. The petite redhead was glowering at her hands in her lap, looking much younger than her fourteen years.

Quietly, my stomach in knots, I asked, "Did you see Amber . . . go over to your mother's house that night?"

Not looking at me, she answered in a growl, "She hated my mom. Just before my dad left for Japan, I overheard them arguing. Amber said my dad was still in love with her . . . and he said maybe he was."

If that was true, Amber could have had a motive. The source needed to be considered before I leaped to any conclusions, though. Kelly's version might have been colored by what she wanted to hear—and having her parents reunite had probably been at the top of her wish list. "Did you actually *see* your stepmother leave the house and go across the street?"

She grabbed the edge of the table and gave me a piercing glare. "Yes." She dragged out the "s" for emphasis.

"Did you tell the police that?"

"No . . . but I told my father. And he prob'ly told them."

I didn't know Kelly well enough to discern whether or

not she was telling the truth, but frankly, I was not convinced. Maybe it was just that her slight avoidance of direct eye contact reminded me of my own children's expression when they were being less than forthright.

As much as I didn't want to badger this poor child, I also didn't want her to be spreading very serious and perhaps completely unfounded rumors about Amber Birch. "You're certain that you saw her enter your mother's house?"

She nodded, but could not hold my gaze.

"Even if you had to stand in front of a jury to testify to that fact?"

She blinked, the color rising in her cheeks. "I'm, like, almost positive she did. I mean, I heard the door bang, so I know she left the house."

"But *I* came over to your house to use the phone. You might have just heard—"

"No, it was before that." Kelly's voice rose. "She kept looking out the window during dinner, saying how there were a lot of cars over there . . . like she didn't want any witnesses, you know? Like, she was waiting for everyone to leave."

This story was getting less and less convincing, despite Kelly's adamance. "She might be completely innocent, Kelly. Things are so bad for you right now. Please, honey, think about what you're doing here. Until the police make some real progress, convincing yourself that your father's wife—"

She slammed her fists on the table and said, "She killed my mother! I know she did!"

We were attracting an audience of other skiers in the lodge, many of whom were Kelly's classmates. All of this was giving me a sick feeling in the pit of my stomach, and I now regretted engaging her in this conversation. I spotted a public phone on the opposite wall.

"Kelly, maybe I should call your father. This is obviously not the best place for you to be right now. I'm going to see if he's home and try to arrange a ride home for you with one of the parents who drove here."

Kelly pulled a cellular phone out of the inner pocket of her ski jacket and handed it to me. "Just say 'call Dad at home' and it'll dial for you."

I thanked her and rose from the table, phone in hand.

She clicked her tongue. "You don't need to get away from me to call him. I know you're going to tell him everything I said about his stupid wife. You're going to tell him I need to see a shrink, too, but I already *am*." She got to her feet and shouted, "All I *need* is to stop having to live in the same house with my mother's murderer!"

Everyone in the room was looking at her now, most of them with their jaws agape.

I felt so sorry for Kelly that I was positively heartsick. I leaned toward her and said quietly but firmly, "Kelly, listen to me. Your step—your father's wife works here. Many people in this room know her. You *must* give her the benefit of the doubt until the police solve this thing. Nothing good can come of your insisting that she's guilty. It's not taking any of your pain away. It's just going to make whatever happens next that much harder to bear."

"What do you know about anything?!"

She had a point there. I swallowed the lump in my throat and took a few steps, feeling like Frankenstein's monster in my boots and my current role. I turned on the cell phone. "Call Dad at home." I had to struggle to keep my voice steady. One thing was certain. I was now willing to crawl on my knees to Stephanie—and to anyone else—to plead for whatever help any of us could give in getting Kelly's mother's murderer behind bars as quickly as possible.

Randy Birch answered. After identifying myself, I
said, "I'm at the ski lodge with your daughter, and she's
not doing well."

"What do you mean?" His voice was rife with alarm.
"Did she hurt herself?"

"No, but she was scared to go up the lift, and she's . . .
upset."

"Can she stay put in the lodge and come home with
my wife when she's off work?"

Kelly was peering through her bangs at me, her head
slightly turned as if to give the impression that she was
really just looking out the window. I turned my back and
said quietly, "I . . . don't know if that's such a good idea.
Kelly's made some accusations about Amber, and I don't
know how comfortable either of them would be just
now, alone together for a couple of hours in a car."

"Christ almighty," he murmured. "Amber convinced
me that this goddamned ski trip would be a good idea.
She thought it might get Kelly's mind off her loss. I never
should've listened to her. Kelly's just . . . lashing out. Can
I speak to her?"

I turned around again. Kelly was scowling at me. Her
anger and loss seemed so much bigger than she was. She
was such a tiny thing, probably the smallest student in
the eighth grade. At least her diminutive size eliminated
her from being considered a viable suspect herself.
"Kelly? Your dad wants to speak with you."

She rolled her eyes. I handed her the phone, and she
immediately snarled at her dad, "Yeah?"

Another mother of an eighth grader approached me
and offered to take her home, and we made the necessary
arrangements with Kelly's father.

Someone needed to tell Amber that Kelly was leaving.
I asked around and eventually found Amber behind the
lodge on the dimly lit wooden deck, smoking a cigarette.

In the muted lighting, she looked younger than ever. She must frequently be mistaken for the girlfriend of Kelly's college-aged brother whenever the whole family was together. She saw me and immediately stubbed out her half-smoked cigarette. "Kelly going home?"

"With Brittany's mom. I'd drive her myself, but my car's back at the school."

"She's just . . . so difficult." Amber's lip trembled slightly as she pushed some blond locks back underneath her ski cap. "She's always hated me. This is, like, the last thing we needed to have happen."

"I'm sure that's true." My voice was even, but it took effort not to scream: Of course she's *difficult*! Her mother was murdered a few days ago!

Amber clicked her tongue. "I'm making it sound like Patty's death was a mere inconvenience to me and my life. It's just that"—she stopped and searched my eyes—"I don't know what to do, you know? I remember how this felt for me. My own mother died when I was about her age." She retrieved her cigarette butt, examined it for a moment, and gave me a sad smile. "Lung cancer." She flicked it into the nearby trash can and said, "If it helps Kelly to think of me as the bad guy, I figure, fine. But I sure as hell didn't kill her mother. And I hope whoever did burns there for all eternity."

I couldn't argue with that sentiment. Furthermore, I was rapidly gaining respect for Amber, so much so that I was all but ready to cross her off my list of suspects. "Kelly seems to think you left the house before I arrived to call the police. You didn't, though. Did you?"

She pursed her lips and brushed past me, putting her ski goggles in place as she walked. " 'Scuse me. Time for me to meet up with my last class of the night."

*   *   *

Patty's memorial service was the following afternoon. Her ex-husband was there, looking extremely shaken, sitting with his daughter and his college-aged son. Amber was seated one row back. Kelly's accusations must be putting a terrible strain on their marriage. Earlier, when I'd repeated those accusations to Tommy, he was noncommittal about whether or not he'd already heard them. He did, at least, assure me that he had personally interviewed Kelly and her parents. Right before snapping at me to "Stop playing amateur cop!" Which, I assured him, I would do, just as soon as the killer was behind bars.

The funeral home was rapidly filling. Ten minutes before the start time, I would estimate that two hundred people were in the room. I was seated on the aisle. Beside me was Nathan and then Jim, with Tommy next to him and Lauren on the far side. I squirmed, uncomfortable on the hard seat. Overnight, the bruises I'd sustained in my ski accident had turned dark purple and were very painful. To show as little flesh as possible, I was wearing black leather boots and an ankle-length, long-sleeved, dark green velvet dress.

Karen had insisted on coming to pay her respects, as did Rachel, but they were both seated next to Adam Embrick in the same row as his mother. Touchingly, an entire contingent of high schoolers was present, including the four girls from the infamous tape, who were seated together to one side of us. Every time I glanced their way, I got the uncomfortable and yet acute impression that they were whispering about Karen and Adam. Even at a distance, I could tell that Karen was unnerved by them.

I caught sight of Chad Martinez, looking very somber, heading down the aisle toward us. He caught my eye and said, "Can I sit here, Mary?"

"Sure, Chip," I replied before I could stop myself.

"Chad."

"My name's Molly."

"Sorry. I'm not good with names."

"That's okay. *I'm* not good with solemn occasions." I leaned back to stop blocking the men's view of each other and said, "This is my husband, Jim."

"Hello," Jim said, shaking Chad's hand.

He glanced around before settling into his seat. "Well, I guess we're all here. All us PTA-nerds, I mean. I hear so many teachers wanted to come that they"—he cleared his throat and said in a strained tone—"they decided to hold this after three so that they could attend, too."

Someone tapped on my shoulder, startling me. It was Stephanie, seated directly behind me. When I looked back at her, she whispered in my ear, "We need to talk."

Minutes later, the service began. I had to zone out during the eulogies. I simply could not take this much sorrow.

After the service, they instructed us to leave in the standard recessional style—front rows emptying first. The four girls who'd taped us had apparently skipped out early. Too bad. I would have liked to have spoken with them, ever watchful for clues that Tommy and his men might have missed. Susan and Adam also left quickly.

As we entered the reception hall of the funeral home, I saw Karen flash a plaintive look at Rachel, who gave her a decidedly sympathetic smile. Something was going on.

"Did you know those girls from the high school who were seated together?" I asked Karen.

"Not really," she said. Her eyes were slightly averted.

My warning flags went up. "Does Adam know them?"

"Yeah, they're juniors." She pivoted and said, "Rachie, let's go get some soda."

This was not the time or place to press Karen further. Stephanie caught my eye, and we went to a quiet corner where we could talk privately. "I don't know about you," she said, "but I'm still determined to clear my good name and get the killer put away for life. Have you given any thought to my suggestion about joining forces?"

"Absolutely, and I've thought of some of Patty's former social groups we can infiltrate."

"Pardon?"

"There's a big crossover between the PTA board and these groups."

"So?"

Already annoyed, I said a bit testily, "Remember how I explained to you that the way I've been able to beat Tommy in uncovering a murderer was to spend time with the suspects?" She still had a puzzled expression on her face, so I went on. "To keep a close eye on them and learn what their true relationships with the victim were?"

"Oh, right. Well, I suppose if that's what's worked for you in the past . . . although that's no guarantee that it'll work *this* time."

"Thanks for the vote of confidence. Anyway, there's the menopause support group that she and Emily Crown spearheaded, and Chad's ballroom dance class. You should join the menopause group."

Stephanie stiffened so abruptly that she was momentarily half mannequin. "Pardon?"

"Jim and I will join the ballroom dancing group she was in with Chad."

She let out a forced-sounding chuckle, the strain evident on her features. "Molly, nobody's going to believe I'm in menopause. I mean, *look* at me!"

I did look at her in her elegant black dress, and she

was in excellent shape for a forty-two-year-old woman, which, at least to me with my insider's knowledge, was exactly how old she looked. "Menopause starts for women in their early forties all the time, and you're nearly a year older than I am."

She lifted her chin, put her hands on her hips, and attempted to glare holes in me.

I lifted my palms. "Thanks to Patty, I create faxable greetings for that group, and they already know I'm not in menopause."

"Be that as it may, I refuse to go to their group alone. We'll both join."

"Fine."

"Fine," she echoed with a haughty shake of her head. "And we'll both join the dance class, as well. Not that *I* need lessons." She whirled on a heel and marched off.

Back at home again, desperately needing time alone with my own thoughts, I escaped to my office. Jim, however, was apparently in the opposite mood. He'd decided not to return to work and soon came downstairs to join me. He stood looking over my shoulder at the cartoon I was drawing, which is something that unnerves me. I knew he just wanted to see my cartoon, but I still had to battle the impulse not to lean over and hide it against my chest.

I looked up at him and said, "Yes?"

"How were the ski conditions last night?"

I'd already told him about getting shoved by another skier and the litany of woes from poor Kelly, so this was a feeble conversation starter if there ever was one. "Okay, I guess. For eastern skiing."

"At least you all made it home from skiing in one piece," he said.

Technically, counting the kids and me, that meant three separate pieces, but I held my tongue.

He glanced around as if searching for something else to talk about. "What's that?" he asked, indicating a fax in the receiving bin.

"I don't know. I hadn't noticed it," I answered honestly, snatching it out of the tray. It was addressed to me and looked as though the original had been printed in crayon. It read:

Molly—
If you know what's good for you,
you'll mind your own business.
Unless you want to risk winding
up like Perfect Patty.

My heart sank. Why would someone send this? Why risk its being traced? Could I be closer to finding out something than I thought I was?

My typical fight-or-joke reflexes kicked into gear. "The sender didn't sign the letter. How rude."

"Dammit, Molly! You got another threatening fax. Here we go again!"

"Not necessarily. This might sincerely be a friendly warning by someone I know who's worried about me."

Jim looked again at the fax, his brow furrowed. "Sent anonymously. Mentioning a murder victim. I'm calling the police." Jim snatched the phone for my fax machine off its cradle and asked, "What's Tommy's number?"

"I don't have it memorized. Oddly."

Jim cursed under his breath as he rummaged through my messy desk for the phone book to look up the police station's nonemergency number.

Meanwhile, I looked at the sender's number in the

margin. Thinking out loud, I said, "That number seems familiar." I dialed it, using our other phone line.

"You have reached Carlton Central School," said a canned voice. "If you know the extension of the party you wish—"

I hung up. "Huh. It was sent through one of the faxes at the school. From one of the five buildings on the campus. And the dozen or so main and private offices." I looked at the time stamp. "At a little after ten A.M. During regular class hours." I waved the paper at my husband. "Now there's a great lead, hey?"

He didn't even acknowledge me, but punched in numbers on the phone. "Yes, Sergeant Newton, please." He paused. "Jim Masters."

Tommy arrived within half an hour and collected the fax as possible evidence. By then, I'd dropped all pretense of not being upset by it. Tommy was in a bad mood—surly and uncommunicative—unwilling to discuss the status of the investigation or to speculate about who might have sent me the fax.

Just after dinner, Lauren came over, and I could tell by her no-nonsense mannerisms that he'd told her about the fax. Nathan was at a sleepover, and Karen was in her room—ostensibly doing homework, but she had a phone, so that was a bit dicey these days—and Jim was entrenched in his work on his computer, which I'm sure he found easier and more pleasant than dealing with me. We'd butted heads on my tendency to get involved in murder investigations in the past, and we mostly dealt with this particular source of contention by not discussing it.

"Today is the second Thursday of the month," Lauren said as we made our way into the kitchen.

I glanced at the calendar on my wall. "So it is. That means something significant?"

"Yes." She thrust a flyer into my hands, and we both sat down on the stools at my kitchen counter. "We've been talking about doing this off and on ever since they started offering these self-defense classes. We're going. Class starts in less than half an hour."

"This is offered by the police department?" I asked, scanning the brochure.

"Tommy normally teaches it himself, but I doubt he'll be able to run this one, now that he's in charge of Patty's murder investigation."

"Speaking of his investigation, is there any progress? Forensic evidence? Solid clues from trace evidence? Matches on AFIS?"

"Not that I've heard . . . and let's face it. I usually know when he's got a lead. As far as the trace evidence goes, there was just nothing substantive either way— elimination of suspects or verification. At Patty's meeting there were . . . what? . . . eight people at the scene immediately before the crime."

"What about the weapon?"

"The knife was a total washout. The killer apparently went into Patty's kitchen, got a thick dish towel, then grabbed the knife out of one of those butcher-block–style holders on the counter. So his or her fingers weren't in contact with the handle at all."

"No telltale prints on the counter near the knife holder? Or wherever she kept the towel?"

She shook her head. "Hanging on a magnet hook on the fridge."

"What about the VCR tape? Any . . . random fingerprints that couldn't be accounted for?"

She shook her head. "Tommy says the tape was handled by way too many people prior to the meeting. He lifted a couple of clean prints, but he said they were easily explained."

"Which means they were probably Mr. Alberti's or Stephanie's. Or even Chad Martinez's."

Lauren tilted her head, a gesture that was her own personal shrug. "It looks as if, even though it was a heat-of-the-moment crime, the killer managed to be thinking clearly enough to not leave an obvious calling card." Lauren let out a sigh. "The two of us are getting like Tommy . . . taking the emotion out of a heartbreaking task."

"Kind of makes you long for the days when we used to discuss disposable diapers and baby food."

"We never discussed that."

"Didn't we?"

"No. And it's too late now."

"Thank God."

She rose. "Let's go. After all, we deserve a nice relaxing night out, right?"

"Right." I stood up as well, but slowly, straining my sore, stiff muscles. "And what could be more relaxing than a self-defense class, where we can beat up on some policemen?"

Chapter 7

Rah, Rah, Ree.
Kick Him in the Groin.

Lauren and I arrived at the class, which was in the gymnasium of one of the elementary schools on the Carlton campus, about ten minutes early. Moving gingerly, with my aching muscles from my fall getting the best of me, I had serious doubts as to how well I would hold up for a two-hour class.

There were already thirty or so students present—all women. "Do you think men think it's uncool for them to take self-defense lessons?" I asked Lauren as we surveyed the room.

"I'm sure they'd be here if this were a boxing or hand-to-hand combat class."

"Look." I lifted my chin. "There's Emily and Susan." For some reason I felt a little tense at the sight of Susan. Perhaps it was just the strangeness of having a child of mine romantically involved with someone else's child, but this was likely to be a recurring theme in my life, so I'd best adapt.

Lauren must have missed the fact that both women were suspects, for she simply said, "And there's Rachel's tennis coach. I think I'll go say hello."

Emily and Susan were standing together, pouring themselves hot water for tea from an aluminum urn. Emily appeared to be talking earnestly about something, gesturing with her pudgy arms as she spoke. Susan was so tall and lean—emphasized by that dramatic blunt cut of her black hair—that they made an odd-looking duo. I walked over to them.

They halted their conversation the moment I neared. "Emily. Susan. Hi."

"Hello, Molly," Emily said with her typical, engaging smile. A hint of color raised on her apple cheeks, which made me suspect that they'd been talking about me just now. Maybe that was just paranoia on my part, but it was hard to forget how harshly Emily had spoken about Patty when she'd thought she was having a private chat with Jane.

I glanced at the box of tea bags on the table. "Doesn't seem like they should be serving Sleepytime tea, does it? Do they really want us to fall asleep while learning self-defense? Something more along the lines of Jabbing Java, or Ragin' Raspberry would be more in keeping with the spirit of things."

"I sure would have preferred something stronger myself," Susan said, taking a sip of tea. Once again her hands were trembling. Could she be suffering from a permanent case of the shakes from alcoholism, I wondered, recalling Patty's remark about Susan's having given up drinking. She gave me a mischievous smile and winked over the brim of her white Styrofoam cup. "I've got to tell you, Molly, Adam is certainly smitten with Karen."

"Oh?"

"Mm-hmm. They've made another date for tomorrow night."

"They have?" This made two weekend dates in a row now. "I feel a bit like a mushroom these days . . . left in the dark."

She gave me a beatific smile. "Well, from everything I've heard, it sounds as though, mushroom or not, you've done a wonderful job raising your daughter."

"Thanks," I said. She was either just being nice, or she'd heard a lot more about my Karen than I had about her Adam.

There was a pause. Emily said quietly, "We heard that you're the one who found Patty the other night. Was it really . . . ?" She hesitated, as if deciding that her question was inappropriate. "Never mind. It had to have just been so horrible for you. I can't even imagine."

"No. You don't want to imagine." A shiver ran up my spine. "I just wish I could forget."

"I'm sorry. I didn't mean to dredge that up. I just wanted to tell you how very sorry I am that you went through that."

"Thanks."

"How is Kelly Birch doing?" Susan asked. "The story about her panic attack on the ski lift has been making the rounds at school."

I nodded. "It was awful to have to witness. Come to think of it, I should have called her today to find out how she was doing."

"I did, and she seems to be doing a bit better now," Emily said. "Even though I wasn't there, I'd heard what happened to her on the ski lift."

"Neither was I," Susan snapped.

Odd that she was being so defensive. Did she want to make a special point of her absence, for some reason? I had a mental flashback to the sight of the skier crashing into me and wondered if I could place Susan into that role. The lighting had been so bad and my peripheral view of the skier had been so brief that the skier could even have been Emily—an opposite body type. Besides, I reminded myself once again, odds were that the whole thing was a coincidence—a reckless skier who happened to crash into me.

"That poor, poor girl," Emily said with a sigh. "Every

time I think of her growing up without her mother, it's all I can do not to burst into tears. And that final night of Patty's life! All of that Sturm and Drang over that silly tape. In retrospect, who cares? By now we'd have forgotten all about it and gone about our business."

"You're absolutely right," Susan said. "We all reacted as if the trivial nonsense on that ridiculous tape was black-market pornography. We put Patty on the defensive, even though she was only indirectly responsible for that tape getting made. In any case, certainly she wasn't guilty of intentionally hurting anyone."

"No, she would never intentionally hurt anyone," Emily said, sounding on the verge of tears. "*She* never had a bad word to say about anyone."

Susan appeared to me to consciously bite her lip at Emily's statement.

Emily crossed her arms just below her ample bosom. "I'd have given anything to have gotten the chance to apologize to Patty. I called, instead, not five minutes after I got home. There was no answer, so I decided to wait until morning. She was probably already . . ." Emily took a deep breath to collect herself. "Patty was a really close friend, ever since she moved here. I was probably her closest friend in town, even, and I mistreated her so badly. Her best friend, and I didn't stand up for her one iota. It was all just so humiliating when those kids caught me putting her down like that. I mean, I've never done that before. I loved her like a sister. That was the one and only time I ever bad-mouthed her."

She seemed to be warming her way into one of her long speeches, but then she looked at Susan as if for reassurance. Susan nodded and said, "Everyone realized that you were just caught on film at a bad moment. We *all* were."

Lauren had stepped up behind me to join us, and Emily dabbed at her eyes. "I didn't really mean what I said on that tape, you know, Molly. I was just letting off a little steam. I'd had a bad day, and Patty just happened to be in the way."

"I was equally bad," Susan said, "and I'm sure Patty understood that we all say things in anger that we don't really mean. I knew Patty for much longer than you, Emily, and I assure you, Patty understood and forgave you."

"I didn't realize that you and Patty went way back," I said.

"Our husbands used to work together in Michigan," Susan explained. "In fact, my husband is the one who transferred Randy Birch out here."

Lauren said, "You know, Emily, I saw the tape, too— Tommy showed it to me—and since I'm not on it myself, I can be objective. It truly was not cause for anyone to get that upset about."

"Yet somebody must have been," I muttered.

Emily blanched, and her eyes flew open wide as she stared at me. "You don't think it was . . . one of us at the meeting, do you? Who killed Patty, I mean?" She glanced nervously at all of us. "Some madman could have coincidentally broken into the house that night. Maybe during the meeting, even, and was waiting for our meeting to break up so that . . ." Emily let her voice fade. "I'm creeping myself out."

I kept silent, but wished that I believed that the killer was an unknown assailant. Ironic to find comfort in the thought that there was a homicidal maniac roaming the streets of Carlton who breaks into women's houses and stabs them to death. Still, that was better than thinking one of my fellow PTA board members was a murderer. The bottom line, however, was that a killer acting at random wouldn't have sent me a threatening fax.

A baby-faced, uniformed officer entered the room,

walking swiftly and sporting a big smile. "Sorry I'm late, ladies," he said. He did a double take and gave me a slight nod, letting me know that he recognized me. I remembered meeting him a few times before, but couldn't recall his name. "Some of you were expecting my boss, Sergeant Newton, to instruct this class, but the demands on his time got to be too great."

"Which is why so many of us are here," Susan said.

The officer looked at her and promptly lost his smile. "Right. Self-defense is a serious matter. My name's Bob, and although this is just an introductory lesson, I can teach you the basics of how to protect yourself." He spotted Lauren then, and the color rose in his cheeks. It must have been a bit unsettling to realize that the wife of the boss who normally taught this class was a student. He cleared his throat. "First, I'm going to put you in pairs and have you take turns as attacker and attackee."

We paired up as instructed. Bob teamed me with Susan, and Lauren with Emily. This was good, because I couldn't see myself pretending to try to injure my best friend. On the other hand, Karen would be furious with me if I accidentally injured the mother of her new boyfriend. Karen's boyfriend. Yikes! I would never get used to that thought!

"We're going to start with facial attacks," Bob said. "The face is an especially sensitive, vulnerable part of the anatomy. Effective counterstrikes are a thrust to the chin." Bob thrust the heel of his hand into the air as if at an unseen chin. "Or a chop to the Adam's apple." He demonstrated a partially closed hand chop to an invisible neck. "Also, a thumb or thumbs to the eyes. And a real showstopper, clawing the assailant's nostrils." These he let speak for themselves with no visual aids.

"Darn it all!" I said. "I knew I shouldn't have invested in that manicure right before class!"

Everyone laughed, but I had an unpleasant sense of déjà vu and glanced around for any teenagers carrying large purses where a video camera could be hidden. It occurred to me that, with my gargantuan nostrils, I was going to have one heck of a time if Susan decided to practice this one on me.

Officer Bob said, "The eyes and nose are extremely sensitive and can cause intense pain when struck. You jab your fingernail into the flesh in some creep's nostril and, believe me, you get his full attention. His focus instantly shifts away from attacking you, and toward protecting himself."

We worked on our facial attacks in slow motion. Both Susan and I were squeamish and cautious with the thumbs to the eyes. The "nostril rake," even in slow motion, *especially* in slow motion, was out of the question. After we'd switched roles a couple of times, Bob asked, "Questions?"

I raised my hand.

"Molly?"

"I can't imagine myself being able to gouge out someone's eye. I mean . . . yikes! Can't I just buy some pepper spray or something?"

"Sure," the young officer said. "But what if you can't get to your pepper spray? What if it's in the car and you and your assailant are two blocks away, on the sidewalk?"

Why in God's name would I be stupid enough to be two blocks away from the safety of my car? But that wasn't his point, and I conceded that it was a good one. "Then . . . I'm screwed."

"*Then* you poke him in the eyes."

I nodded, thinking that, in theory, at least, I might be able to manage this, as long as I was merely reacting to the threat and had no time to think about what I was actually doing.

"The first thing we're going to assume is that your attacker is stronger than you are. That means you have to attack his weakest areas. The places where it hurts the most." He called into the hallway, "We're ready for you."

A man waddled through the door. At least, I assumed the waddler was a man, but in the protective fencing mask and padding underneath the sweat suit, it was impossible to tell. Talk about a stuffed shirt, I thought, but kept silent, thinking that would be embarrassing to say out loud, even without a camera recording the moment.

"Now, ladies, I'd like you to meet Mr. Would-Be Attacker. This is the role I normally play in Sergeant Newton's class, by the way, so I'm happy to shed the costume for tonight." He gave a little smile and nod to Lauren as he said this.

As he continued with his instructions, my thoughts again drifted to my concerns about being in a self-defense class while bruised and with aching muscles. I tuned in again as Bob was saying, "You do whatever it takes to get free, then you run. Say the assailant grabs you from behind. You stomp back on his instep. Turn and knee him in the groin. Sharp upward thrust into his chin." He demonstrated this in slow motion with the poor guy in the sweat suit. "If you're not already free of him, you go for the face, especially the eyes. Easiest and best way is to claw the face as hard as possible. Start at the forehead, and rake your fingers downward toward the chin. The assailant will involuntarily close his eyes, and probably even cover his eyes. You immobilize him now with a knee to the groin or a blow to the throat, with a sharp, strong punch to the base of the neck."

Even in slow motion, this looked grisly.

"In summary, you strike with your strongest areas to his weakest . . . heel of hand to the chin, fist to the trachea, stomp-kick to the instep, knee to the groin, thumb to the eyeball." He released our Stuffed Sweat Suit, and turned to face us with a smile. "Who wants to be our first volunteer?"

Nobody raised their hands. I'd become queasy. Had he asked, "Who wants to be our first vomiter?" I might have raised my hand.

"Molly? How about you?"

I shook my head. "I'm feeling a little sick to my stomach."

"Let's work through that."

Easy for him to say. He wasn't the one who was nauseated. "Is vomiting on your assailant an effective deterrent?"

"Possibly, but I wouldn't want you to stake your life on it." He gestured at me. "Step forward on the mat and start walking toward the door."

I did as instructed, and after a brief, unpleasant verbal confrontation with Stuffed Man, I had the much *more* unpleasant sensation of being crushed against his chest, his arm around my throat.

I wriggled and was soon pushed to the ground. The man in the stuffed suit had pinned my shoulders, and I couldn't do a thing to stop him, despite Bob's instructions to "go for his eyes" or "knee him in the groin."

At length, Bob said, "Let her up," and shook his head at me. "That's just not strong enough to fight off a grown man. A sick fish, perhaps, but not a grown man."

"There's just no way I can do this. I don't want to hurt anybody."

"Exactly." He turned to the class. "You hear that? She doesn't want to hurt anybody. Which is why your attacker has the advantage on you. Because, I guarantee it, ladies, he *does* want to hurt *you*."

"Pretend he's going through you to get at Nathan or Karen," Lauren called out to me.

We tried it again, and I did as Lauren suggested. A strange sensation overcame me. I had a vision, almost as though in a walking nightmare, in which I could see Patty's lifeless body. In a blink of an eye, I was Patty, alive and confronted by my attacker. I felt myself getting grabbed on the shoulder, and suddenly I turned into a whirling dervish, barely conscious of what I was doing, except to know that I was punching and kicking with all my strength, throwing elbows and knees as if my life depended on it.

"Okay, good. That's enough! Stop!"

I heard the voice, but didn't let it register that he was speaking to me. I had the man down on the mat by now, and was still pounding on him.

"Hey!" my assailant cried. "You're hurting me, lady!"

My head cleared, and I stopped, realizing finally where I was. Instantly I was horribly embarrassed. "Oh, God. I'm sorry! I must have gotten a little carried away."

"I'm just glad you didn't rip off my arm and start beating me with it," he grumbled as he got to his feet.

"Let's take a break," Officer Bob said.

My fellow classmates clustered into conversation groups that seemed to exclude me. At length, Lauren came over and patted me on the shoulder. "My advice worked a little too well."

"Teacher's pet," Susan said to me with a wink and a grin as she made her way past us and over to the makeshift snack bar.

"Just what I always wanted to learn about myself, hey? That I can turn into a violent, crazed maniac."

"This is news?" Lauren joshed.

"Officer?" Emily Crown asked in a loud voice over the din of conversation. "After our break, can you teach us how to fend off someone with a knife?"

"Absolutely," he called back.

Some people poured themselves a cup of tea, and some went to the women's room—probably the tea drinkers at the start of the class. Then Bob declared our break over, and my classmates had their chance to do their own Battle with the Bulge. He then gave us some demonstrations of what to do if the assailant was carrying a knife, which in this case was a mangled Styrofoam cup.

The first step, according to Officer Bob, was to predict which way the assailant was going to move the knife, based on how it was being held, then move out of its predicted path. Then Bob showed us how he could twist out of the path and yet into the bad guy's body. Bob wound up being able to lock the guy's knife arm over his shoulder such that he had to drop the knife to concentrate on getting his arm free before Bob broke it at the elbow.

Spoilsport that I sometimes am, I raised my hand and asked, "Isn't all of this rather in contrast with our first assumption, though, that our assailant is probably stronger than we are?"

Bob frowned. "Yes, but at least the assailant is not going to expect you to strike back. You have the element of surprise in your favor."

"I'd rather have the element of an armed bodyguard in my favor," I murmured.

Nevertheless, as we continued the class, Bob got us comfortable with the concept of "changing fear into anger." We learned to shout "No!" and be the ones to throw the first blow, making sure that this "blow" was one that could immobilize the assailants long enough to allow us to get away. By the time Lauren and I left, I was very glad we'd taken the class.

As we drove home, however, an irony occurred to me. If either Emily or—God forbid—Susan was the killer, she had just learned about "surprise" defensive tactics herself. This whole self-defense effort could be nothing more than supplying tactics and weapons to the enemy.

Chapter 8

Unable to Handle the Tooth

The moment I got home after class, I called upstairs to Karen, who yelled back through her closed door, "Yeah?"

"I want to talk to you for a moment."

She opened her door and, leaning through the doorway, said again, "Yeah?"

"Are you free tomorrow night?"

"No, I kind of have another date with Adam tomorrow. Okay?"

I put my hands on my hips. "That's what I thought. I found out from Adam's mother. She was at the self-defense class I took."

She blushed a little. "Yeah, Adam says his mom is really nosy. I'm sure glad *you're* not."

"Oh, I can be big-time nosy when I need to be. Think about it. If I were you, I'd consider circumventing that curiosity of mine by keeping me better informed from here on out."

She blinked twice, then said brightly, "Mom? I have a date tomorrow night with Adam."

"Oh, really? That's great, hon. Where are you going?"

"There's a basketball game after school that starts at five. Then we're going out for dinner. Probably just for pizza or something. I'll definitely be home before midnight."

"That sounds like fun. Thanks for keeping me informed."

"No problem." She gave me a little wave, then shut her door.

"So, everything must be going really well, hey, Karen?" I said to myself. "Oh, absolutely, Mom. I'm having the time of my life in high school."

When I turned around, Jim was standing in the doorway, watching me, his brow furrowed. "Are you okay, Molly?"

"Sure. All things being relative. But I could use a hug."

"Me, too," he said, and pulled me into his arms.

"Oh, and guess what. You're taking me dancing tomorrow night. And tonight I learned how to do an eye gouge and a nostril rake, so don't even think about saying no."

The next evening, Jim came home from work in time for us to grab a quick dinner before our ballroom dance class. Afterward he said he needed to change clothes, then failed to do so, instead sitting on the couch and reading the newspaper while pulling on his mustache. Stephanie, I knew, was not one to patiently wait for others and would flip out if we weren't ready to go the moment she arrived.

Seeking to hasten things along, I dropped into the seat beside him and said, "Honey, look at my last two cartoons here and tell me if you think I'm losing my sense of humor."

This was my personal version of a loaded does-this-dress-make-me-look-fat? question, and he knew it. He reluctantly set down his paper, took the drawings from me, and looked at them. He forced a chuckle as he looked at that morning's creation. A group of people in a museum were staring warily at a man in a uniform who

says, "This next exhibit is from a prehistoric saber-
toothed tiger. Look for as long as you wish, but remember,
YOU CAN'T *HANDLE* THE TOOTH!" The caption
read: Having worked as museum curator for many years
now, Arnold Tuttle found subtle ways to amuse himself.

Jim then looked at the second cartoon, which I'd
drawn the day before yesterday. Not even able to force a
chuckle at that one, he said, " 'A different drummer,' eh?
Very clever. And funny." He patted my knee and stood
up. "I'd better get ready for the big dance."

"Okay. Thanks, dear." Worked like a charm. The doorbell rang, which brought BC, as ever, racing into the
room to bark at the door. "Stephanie's early," I murmured. She was going to be even less thrilled at the pros-
pect of putting up with BC barking at her than she would
at having to wait for us. "Could you take the dog with
you?"

He grimaced slightly. "I'll just be a minute," he said,
dragging BC upstairs as I opened the door.

Stephanie was dressed to the nines . . . or was that the
tens? Eights? Never having understood the expression, it
was hard for me to remember. In any case, she was wearing a formal dress—a scarlet taffeta gown that, at least,
wasn't floor-length. I bit my tongue rather than ask her if
she intended to serve as a bridesmaid after our class.

"Hi, Stephanie. Come on in. Jim's changing and will
be ready in a minute."

"Don't you need to get dressed yourself?" Stephanie
asked, eyeing my khakis and white T-shirt.

"Get dressed?" I repeated, and looked down at my attire, checking for perhaps a stain down the front. "My
clothes aren't invisible, are they?"

She widened her eyes at me. "*That's* what you're wearing tonight?"

I clenched my jaw, but then said pleasantly, "No, Jim

is. He and I are swapping outfits in the car." I called up-stairs, "Hey, Jim. What am I wearing tonight, anyway?"

"Pardon?" he called back.

Stephanie rewarded me with an eye roll. "Well, Molly, at least you set to rest that old cliché about being able to dress someone up but not take her anyplace. *You* can't even get dressed up."

"I can. I just choose not to put on my formal attire for a class." If only I hadn't whisked away our would-have-been-barking-at-her dog or passed up delivering my crack about her bridesmaid dress. Too late now. Adopting Stephanie's arms-akimbo posture as I scanned her attire, I asked, "You're wearing an evening gown? For a class?"

"Of course. It's one of my personal rules . . . the right attire for the right occasion. Dance is all about elegance." She did a little pirouette as a visual aid. "What good does it do someone to learn how to do something in the wrong clothes? Tell me something, Molly. Do you remember your rehearsal for your wedding?"

"Barely." I did remember that we'd held it in Colorado, and that Stephanie had not been invited.

"Let me guess. You wore something casual to it, right?"

"Yes. And I was comfortable and at ease throughout." This was going to be a long evening. I was already getting so annoyed as to hope that she would get too close on the dance floor tonight and I could "accidentally" smack her one in the face.

"And did you have any stairs to climb for the wedding processional?"

I sighed. "Point taken. I hadn't practiced being in a floor-length gown while carrying a bouquet so, yes, I stepped on the hem of my dress on each stair and was practically on my knees when I made it to the altar."

Stephanie gave me a smug smile.

"Nevertheless, Stephanie, I assure you that I have no intention of ever entering into a ballroom dance competition, or climbing stairs whilst dancing, so it would be a waste of my good clothes to wear anything fancier tonight."

"Suit yourself," Stephanie said, giving her blond tresses a haughty toss.

The dog came racing down the stairs, barking fiercely at Stephanie—hurray—and Jim came down the stairs a moment later. He hesitated on the bottom step, looking at Stephanie in her gown. He turned to me. "Am I supposed to be wearing a suit?"

"No, Jim. You see, Stephanie's dress tonight is the equivalent of the doughnut weights that baseball players use during warm-ups in the batter's box."

For some reason, BC lost interest in barking and trotted off to rejoin Nathan in the family room. Thankfully, Jim cut short the conversation by asking, "Am I driving? We can go out through the garage."

Knowing how greatly she preferred to travel in her classy BMW, I answered, "We're taking Stephanie's car. Her thighs are allergic to cloth seats."

Stephanie laughed, redeeming herself a little in my estimation. "Tell you what," she said. "Before we go, why don't I show you a couple of steps so that you don't make total asses of yourselves?"

I said to Jim, "I don't know about you, dear, but I was rather looking forward to being a total ass tonight. I could be the left cheek, and you could be the right. Or would that be ass-backward?" I turned to Stephanie. "Which cheek leads when dancing?"

Jim said quietly, "A few pre-class instructions wouldn't hurt anything."

My jaw dropped. Jim knew Stephanie well enough to

practice avoidance. He must *really* be self-conscious about his dancing to opt for an initial lesson from her.

Leaping to the task, Stephanie said, "We'll go to your family room. It's the only area in your house with enough open floor space." She led the way through our living and dining rooms and down the few steps into our family room.

Nathan was watching television, which Stephanie immediately shut off. "Nathan, help your father move that couch back against the fireplace, and put the dog outside. Your parents are going to dance."

"They *are*?" Nathan asked with the same incredulity as if she'd announced that we'd sprouted wings and were going to soar along the ceiling. He single-handedly moved the furniture, unceremoniously shoved Betty Cocker out the back door, then sat down on the top step to watch us.

"The floor surface in here is all wrong, of course," Stephanie said. "The whole point of ballroom dancing is the glide, the effortless movement of the feet across the floor. You don't want carpeting."

"Then why is dancing called 'cutting the rug'?" Jim asked. Which was such a good question that Stephanie ignored him completely.

"As long as you can do reasonably well with the forward walk and backward walk, as well as with your basic alignment and positioning, you'll be fine." Humming to herself, she did little dance movements in the center of our family room.

The first dance step simply amounted to taking a long stride with knees slightly flexed. Having used the old-standby posture improver of walking with a dictionary on my head as a teen, I knew how to do this, and Jim, too, did reasonably well. She then showed us how to do the dictionary-on-head walk backward and had us try this side by side.

Watching us, Nathan laughed wholeheartedly. In one sense, we had lucked out—had Karen been home, she would be wearing her omigod-my-parents-are-doofuses expression.

"Jim," Stephanie said, "you're doing a duckwalk. Glide. Don't arch your back or bend your knees quite so far. Very good, Molly."

She then ran us through some of the standard positions, most of which were self-explanatory. Jim cut her short by saying, "Shouldn't we go?" Clearly, he'd been annoyed by Stephanie's duckwalk reference and had lost interest in her private lessons.

We moved the furniture back in place, said good-bye to Nathan, then left. As Stephanie drove, she lectured us on techniques and terminology. I remembered the promenade from my old hideous square-dancing days in school. A male voice with a Texan accent, twanging out the phrase "Now promenade your partner" kept running through my head, which drowned out Stephanie's words.

When she paused for a breath, I said, "Thanks for the help, Stephanie, but let's not forget our primary purpose tonight . . . to see if we can find information about Patty's murder."

"Of course," Stephanie said. "But what if there are no Carlton PTA board members here?"

"There will be at least one—Chad Martinez. He had the hots for Patty and could have killed her in his rage when she rejected him."

Jim said, "I never can get why you do this, Molly. Why not let Tom do his job and find out on his own if Chad killed Patty in a rage?"

"Because he's a policeman, working in an official capacity. People don't open up to him the way they do to somebody who happens to be in their social circles. We're far more likely to hear the rumblings of what was really going on than Tommy is."

Jim sighed and said nothing. He'd long ago vowed that "if you can't beat 'em, join 'em" when it came to my poking into Tommy's cases, but Jim also forever held on to the hope that I'd desert the amateur sleuthing someday. Nothing would make me happier, because that would mean that nobody I knew had been murdered.

We pulled into the parking lot of Chad's dance school, which was located in a strip mall not far from the school campus. Where, come to think of it, at this very minute, my daughter and Adam Embrick were currently watching a basketball game . . . I hoped.

Stephanie lingered at the door for some reason, and a moment later it was clear that she was waiting for Jim to open it for her, which he did. Stephanie then strutted into the studio ahead of us as a diva might walk onto the stage.

The room was unexceptional, large and square with a parquet floor. Straight-backed chairs lined the walls. Chad had about twenty students here, mostly elderly women, and they were gathered in three distinct clusters.

Loath as I was to admit it, Stephanie had been right about my choice of attire. All of the women were wearing dresses, although considerably less formal than Stephanie's. Ah, well. If Jim and I had to make a run for it, our pants and tennis shoes would make for a quick— and quiet—escape. Then again, it'd be a long, cold trek; Stephanie had driven us.

Chad left one of those clusters and came over to us. He was dressed in a white silk shirt and shiny, tight-fitting black slacks. He gave me a big smile, which seemed to spread to his little Hitler-ish mustache, and said, "Hi . . .

there," clearly having forgotten my name once again. He shook Jim's hand, saying, "Good to see you again," then shifted his focus to Stephanie. "Well, well, if it isn't Stephanie Saunders."

What *was* this? Could the man only remember the names of blondes?

Continuing to lavish his attention on Stephanie, he said, "My, my, I never thought you would need instructions from me."

"Please. Chad, you and I both know that I could teach this class myself."

"Then by all means, be my assistant this evening." He turned, clapped his hands sharply twice, and announced to the room at large, "It's time to begin. We're fortunate tonight to have as our guest a very experienced dancer whom I'm sure you already know—Ms. Stephanie Saunders."

She gave a little curtsy and lowered her gaze as if embarrassed by the attention.

"Oh, please!" I grumbled to Jim. If the folks here did know Stephanie, they sure as heck wouldn't believe her shrinking-violet routine.

Chad continued, "Tonight we'll be moving into the rhythm style of ballroom dance and will work on the cha-cha and the rumba. Ms. Saunders and I are going to demonstrate these marvelous dances for you. Pay close attention."

Stephanie took Chad's arm and strode to the center of the floor with her nose in the air. I whispered to Jim, "At least my jaw muscles will get good exercise tonight as I grit my teeth."

Chad nodded to a preteen girl who, if I wasn't mistaken, was his daughter, and music started. I was distracted when I spotted a familiar face across the room. "Oh, Mr. Alberti's in this class. I didn't realize that."

"Another suspect?" Jim asked.

"Yes, anyone who was present at the board meeting is. We'll have to switch partners at some point tonight. I should chat with him for a while." I carefully surveyed the remaining faces. "It's just Chad and Al who were there that night. Somehow I'd gotten the impression that Chad had recruited a couple other board members to this class, but I guess I was mistaken."

Meanwhile, Stephanie maintained her Amazing Plastic Smile as she danced, beautifully of course, with Chad. After the demonstration, Chad ordered us to "form couples. Ladies, you can either dance together or sit this first one out."

A few of them promptly sat down, but others stayed on the dance floor. Maybe they would take turns leading, as we did in attacker/attackee in last night's self-defense class. "Try to emulate Stephanie and me," he further advised.

The thought of emulating Stephanie gave me some pause.

After giving us time to spread out, the music—some salsa-sounding instrumental—began again. Jim took my right hand and put his other hand on the small of my back as we assumed a slow-dance position. I had to say that this made me smile. Not counting our earlier attempts in our family room, we hadn't danced together in a long time.

I had to fight off the giggles as we instantly mangled the cha-cha. We were bumping knees. Jim shuffled his weight foot-to-foot in time with the music, and I did my Webster's-on-the-head forward and backward steps.

"Somehow it looked more graceful when Chad and Stephanie were cha-cha-ing."

"Aha," Jim said, "there's our problem right there. I'm doing the rumba."

"Show me your cha-cha."

"Molly," he said, giving me a sly grin. "Watch yourself. We're in public."

I laughed and saw Chad glance our way. "Let's just try to keep out of Chad's line of sight, shall we? Keep other couples between us."

We spent the rest of the song doing forward and backward walks according to however we could best escape the instructor's gaze, with me battling the giggles throughout. Fortunately, Chad's attention was mostly focused on his own dance with Stephanie. He seemed to occasionally give one-word instructions to those couples nearest him. At least this meant that Stephanie was granted ample time to engage him in conversation.

From the corner of my vision, I saw a late-arrival enter the room. I looked at her. "Jim, we're in luck. Jane Daly just came in. As soon as this song ends, I'm going to go talk with her."

"That *is* lucky. I have to pee."

I feigned a contented sigh. "I love the way you whisper sweet nothings in my ear when we dance."

"I'm a born romantic," he said with a smile.

Moments later the song stopped, and I immediately went over to Jane Daly and said hello. She was still stashing her things below a chair.

"Molly, hi. I'm glad to see you're still up and moving. I heard that somebody bashed into you on the ski slope the other night."

" 'Fraid so. It was a hit-and-ski. Whoever crashed into me didn't stop. Probably just some out-of-control kid."

"Are you all right?" she asked.

I flexed my shoulder muscles, the question reminding me that my back and left hip were indeed still hurting a little. "I'm a bit sore, but I always am after I ski, and I'm no more so than usual."

"That's lucky. Chad said it could have been much worse."

The incident seemed a strange thing for Chad to have mentioned to her. The two of them didn't seem all that close, and he gave *me* so little thought that he couldn't even remember my name for five minutes. I peered at her rather unattractive face, weighing the possibility that she was lying. Could she actually have known about my minor accident because she herself was the kamikaze skier? Perhaps my reputation had preceded me, so she realized that I was looking into the murder. She knew I'd be up there that night, because she had called me herself. She could have donned a dark ski mask and intentionally tried to wipe me out.

As casually as I could despite my thought pattern, I said, "I'm flattered that Chad remembered my name for once."

She grinned and watched Chad across the room. "Oh, well, he didn't, I'm afraid. He called you Mona, but I eventually figured out who he meant."

I chuckled, relieved that she wasn't lying; he *had* been calling me Mona that night, so Jane had heard about my mishap secondhand from Chad. "Figures. At least he cared enough to tell you about what happened to me."

"Maybe now that you're enrolled in his class, he'll make an effort to remember you."

"This is just a drop-in visit. I doubt we'll come back. I don't think ballroom dancing is for us."

"Us?"

"My husband, Jim, is here, too."

She frowned. "I'd have given anything to get my husband here. I just love dancing. But he refuses to join me. Half the time, I have to dance with other women."

"Well, tonight at least, Jim would be happy to dance

with you. I'm sure he'd like to have a partner who knows what she's doing for a change."

He returned to the room and joined us. I introduced them. After minimal hinting, Jim asked her to dance just as Stephanie decided to sit one out. She sashayed over to me. "What a wonderful dancer that man is," she intoned with a sigh, watching Chad across the room.

"Did you learn anything?"

"Of course not. As I told you already, Molly, I could teach this class."

"I *meant,* have you learned anything about Chad as a suspect in the murder?"

"Oh, that. Well, let's see. Chad is prickly when it comes to his relationship with Patty. I asked him if the two of them ever dated and got the impression that she always turned him down. Also that he blamed Al, not Patty, for the tape, and has yet to forgive him."

"I wonder if that's just a cover . . . pretending to have had a beef with someone other than his victim. Next time you dance with him, find out if he had an alibi for the time from when he left Patty's place till I returned there myself."

She gave her head a little shake. "I think it's your turn to sleuth from here on out. Chad told me that after the first few dances, he insists that everyone switch partners." She looked around the room. "Not that there's much to pick from. Although Jim's quite handsome, in a down-home sort of way."

I had no idea what she meant by "down-home handsome," but before I could decide if I wanted to know, she asked under her breath, "How's your marriage going?"

Testily, I said, "Just fine. Spending a lot of time down-home. Why? Are you on the market?"

"Of course not. I'm no home-wrecker. I only ask because Emily Crown is a marriage counselor."

That surprised me. Emily was so much more talkative than the prototypical good-listener therapist.

Stephanie continued, "If you're willing to learn how to dance just to talk with Chad, you might be willing to seek therapy from her."

"What a shame none of the suspects are surgeons. I could have an elective appendectomy. Bet I could get all kinds of clues while I'm on the table."

She gave me a long look. "It was just a suggestion, Molly. You needn't get snippy."

She was right, but I didn't feel gracious enough to acknowledge that. "I guess I should dance with Chad, then," I said, watching as Chad came over to us. His eyes, however, were squarely on Stephanie.

An elderly woman said, "You two have danced together long enough," and stepped in front of Stephanie and me to grab Chad's arm. "They're playing our song."

Chad obliged, and a handful of couples found space on the floor to cut the nonexistent rug. I looked around for Jim. He was still dancing with Jane.

Stephanie said, "Just like our old square-dancing days." She giggled a little. "Remember back in junior high, Molly? Nobody would pick you, and you'd be stuck sitting there like the proverbial wallflower?"

Imitating her phony voice and phony smile, I said, "Yes, I remember, Stephanie. But, for one thing, that was true for several of us, not just me, and, for another thing, shut up."

"Oops. I hit a nerve, didn't I? I always felt sorry for you then. But you grew out of all of your awkwardness. Or most of it, at any rate."

"Stephanie, I'm curious about something. Do you ever stop to think how you would feel if someone were to say to you what you say to others?"

She arched her eyebrows and looked thoughtful for a

moment. "Nobody can say that I wasn't asked to dance or that I'm dressed inappropriately, because that's never the case. But if I hurt your feelings, I'm sorry."

These types of discussions with Stephanie were so much wasted breath. "That's all right. I'm going back to work, as it were." I made my way over to Mr. Alberti and asked if his dance card was full.

"I'd be delighted to dance with you," he said with a slight, gracious bow. We began to dance, or a reasonable facsimile thereof on my part, although Al was quite good. "My palms sweat a little. I'm sorry."

"Everybody's do, and I hadn't noticed at all." Till he brought it up, that is, which was now all I could think about. Suddenly my hands felt as if they were getting waterlogged. Desperate for a subject change, I followed his gaze to an attractive, dark-haired woman in the corner and asked, "Is that your wife?"

"Yes. We didn't realize when we first signed up for this class that Chad would force us to change dance partners so frequently." Al swung me out for some sort of dance step to the side. Not knowing what else to do, I gestured into the air with my left hand and kicked my left foot out. He swung me back toward him.

"Jim and I are just here on a trial basis. And I think we've been found guilty."

"Guilty?" Al repeated.

"In the trial. It was a stupid pun."

"Ah." Again, he released one of my hands to swing me to his side. This time I did a little John Travolta *Saturday Night Fever* point at the ceiling, then swung back.

My lame joke had brought our conversation to a screeching halt. Al was doing some sort of tango step. Mine was more like a severe-bladder-problem strut. After a while, he asked, "You discovered Patty's body, I hear."

"Yes. Did you know her well?"

"Not really. She came into my classroom a half dozen times to help out. She was a terrific parent. If they were all like that, teaching would be a breeze."

Chad and his partner, a smitten-looking woman in her late fifties or so, had pulled up beside us. With my inept dancing we were lucky that, so far, we'd avoided crashing into other couples. I smiled at him, but he shook his head and said, "Watch your balance and alignment during your contra positioning, Mallory."

"People have been telling me that my whole life," I replied. Though they usually call me Molly, I added to myself. As we stepped away, I said to Al, "I guess therein lies the appeal for you men. Some of those terms are fairly male-oriented . . . 'balance,' 'alignment,' 'contra.' You could be working on a car, or staging a coup in a jungle."

He merely shrugged. "I got into ballroom dance the old-fashioned way. My wife made me."

"I wonder how Chad got into this . . . running a dance school."

"The studio used to be his and his ex-wife's. She got the house. He got the business."

"Sounds like he 'got the business,' all right."

The song ended, and Al was soon swept off by a woman I'd never seen before. Jim, too, was dancing with a stranger. I made my way over to Al's wife and introduced myself.

We made small talk, then I said, "Everyone at high school must be stunned by what happened. Especially in your husband's class that taped our PTA in action. How are his students handling everything?"

"He hasn't mentioned them. He's pretty depressed these days, and not saying much about anything. That's why I insisted we come tonight . . . to get him out of the house and get his mind on something else for a while."

I'm sure my presence here and questions are hardly helping things, I thought. Could Al have had much more involvement with Patty than he claims? Could that be why he's depressed? "Did you know Patty Birch at all?"

She raised an eyebrow. "Even to a teacher's spouse, she was hard to miss. A great mother and PTA president I'm sure, but she was a gadfly at the high school. She was even starting to usurp the authority of the teachers at times. It got to be a joke among them. Someone would ask if they could get the vending machine repaired, and a teacher would crack, 'Have you checked with Patty?' "

To encourage her to keep talking, I nodded and said, "They had quite the controversy over that tape of the PTA. We never knew if it was really Patty who gave the students the idea for filming us in action like that."

She frowned. "Oh, it was her idea, all right. She came to Kevin at the start of the year. He told her he wasn't comfortable with the idea, and thought that was the end of it, but she must have talked to the students themselves."

"Really?" That was hard to believe. It was one thing for her to have simply *suggested* the project; she couldn't have known how badly it would backfire. But to spearhead the notion? Surely Patty would have realized that she risked—at the very least—the rancor of her fellow PTA officers. "I wonder why on earth she would have done that."

"Maybe she honestly believed she was doing such a bang-up job as PTA president that she wanted her reign captured on film. More likely she just wanted to keep up her self-image as being someone high school students thought was cool. Some parents seem to need—"

Chad called out, "Change partners." Mrs. Alberti

promptly excused herself to join her husband on the floor, and Jane came over to stand beside me, awaiting a new partner. Stephanie, too, was partnerless, and seemed none too happy about it.

I heard Jane gasp as a fortyish man in a dark suit entered the studio. "My God," Jane cried. "That's my husband. What's he doing here?"

Beaming, he came up to her and bowed. "May I have this dance, Mrs. Daly?"

Still breathless, she said, "What do you mean? I've been trying to get you to dance for years. But you've always refused."

"I was just embarrassed. I needed to gain some ground on you, so I've been taking lessons on the sly."

Her jaw dropped. "You *have*?"

He grinned. "Surprise."

"Oh, Aaron! I'm so touched! Thank you." She curtsied to him and had to dab away the tears as they crossed the floor together.

I, too, felt a catch in my throat at witnessing Jane's delight. "Well," I said to Stephanie. "That was worth the price of admission."

"I suppose so," she replied in a bored voice.

Just then, my vision happened to focus on Chad. Though he quickly looked away, he had clearly been listening. For some reason, he was now staring at the Dalys with a look of pure malevolence.

Chapter 9

Run for Your Life!

We had another uneventful weekend. Nathan wrote a report about the giant squid that had been assigned three weeks ago and was due Monday; he started it Saturday morning. Karen spent a lot of time on the phone with Adam—or with Rachel to recount the previous phone conversation she'd just had with Adam. Karen was a straight-A student, and it would have been premature to get on her case about her social life interfering—unless and until it actually *did* interfere. As for parental duties, both Jim and I put in a couple of hours with her behind the wheel. The lessons were going reasonably well, despite her tendency to announce each time she got into the driver's seat, "Don't be surprised if we crash into something."

On Monday afternoon, Nathan was unusually quiet. He went straight to his room after school without looking for me or stopping into the kitchen for snacks. Knowing my son as I do and having once been in junior high myself, I played immediate host to gut-wrenching worries.

I knocked on his door. His subsequent "Yeah?" was an octave lower than it was when he felt cheerful.

"Can I come in?"

"I guess."

I opened his door. He was lying facedown on his bed.

The sight made me flash back to so many other times when I'd stood here, just inside his doorway, breathing in my child's unique scent while he lay, distraught but dry-eyed, on his bed. "Rough day?" I asked.

No answer.

"Me, too." Needing to draw him into conversation, I went on: "My cartoons have gotten really stupid lately. Today I drew a batch of terrified nuns running down the street and shouting, 'Run for your life! The hills are alive with the sound of music!' And in the background there's a pair of enormous hills that have sprouted arms and legs and are dancing."

No reaction. Normally such a silly cartoon appealed to his sense of humor.

Hoping that the cause of his sadness concerned the least worrisome aspect I could come up with, I asked, "Did you have trouble on a math quiz, or with some other schoolwork?"

"No. It doesn't matter. I'm fine. I'm just tired."

My stomach knotted. He was obviously far from fine, and if he wasn't having academics troubles, he must be having social ones. I took a seat at his desk chair. "I remember my experiences at Carlton. One of the things that stands out was all the teasing I had to put up with. Especially from the older guys in the school."

Nathan stiffened, and I could tell he was listening. I went on, "There was this one class I had to get to in another part of the building. There was no way to get to class except down this one hall, and a group of boys would stand there and make fun of me. Every day. Mornings, I'd sit in class just dreading having to make that walk. It ruined my life for a while. I wouldn't tell anybody about it, not even my friends, because it was too embarrassing." I paused.

"What did you do?" Nathan asked into his pillow, still not looking at me.

"One day, one of the boys said something really awful to me . . . I don't even remember exactly what . . . but I stopped walking. I looked straight into his eyes and didn't say a word. Finally, he looked away, so I started walking again. And, of course, the guys with him teased me about that . . . 'Whoa. She's giving us the evil eye.' Junk like that. But the next day and from then on, they didn't say a word when I walked by them."

Nathan boosted himself on one elbow and looked around at me. "They quit teasing you? Just because you looked at one of them?"

"Yes. I guess they figured that it wasn't fun anymore if their victim was going to stop and look them straight in the eye. But do you want to hear about something much worse that happened, and that bugs me to this day?"

He shrugged as if indifferent, but also sat up.

"It happened during my sophomore year, a year or two after the teasing from those boys in the hall. There was this girl who rode our school bus. She was a little plump, but not at all fat or unattractive. She was just a normal-looking girl, a junior in the high school. A really nice-looking boy lived in our neighborhood, and we all thought he was really cool. He started teasing that one girl just . . . hideously . . . *way* worse than what those guys had said to me. And some of his buddies joined in, showing off to their ringleader. It went on like this for a couple of weeks. One day, they made her cry. She was just . . . sobbing as she got off the bus. The rest of that year, she never rode the bus again. Not even once. You know *why* that bugs me so badly, Nathan?"

"Because she cried?"

"Because I never said a word to tell them to stop picking on her. I never told the bus driver what was going on.

That would have been so easy, but it didn't even occur to me. And you know why I didn't?"

He just looked at me.

"Because I was just so relieved that it was somebody else getting picked on, and not me. I'd bet anything that's what more than ninety percent of kids think when they see someone get teased. 'Thank goodness it's her, not me. If I try to help her out, it will be me.' "

"It would have been, if you'd said something."

"Maybe so, but I'd have survived. And you know what, Nathan? That was some twenty-five years ago. Nowadays, I almost never think about how I'd been teased by those guys in the hall. Yet I think about that girl on the bus a lot, wishing I'd spoken up."

I paused, weighing my words, not wanting my advice to make matters worse for him. "I know it's rough, Nathan, but we're all only in junior high and high school for a few years in what we hope will be a long, happy life. It just feels like it'll never end when you're a student."

He flopped back down on his bed. "I'll say. I'm too skinny. I'm a wimp."

"Who's teasing you?"

"A whole group of guys. I don't know. Some guy named Raine is their leader."

"For what it's worth, Nathan, the experts say that the thing to do is to ask for help. To say to the bully, 'I don't like what you say to me, and if you don't stop, I'll get help.' "

"I'd feel like a dork if I said that."

"And what do you feel like when you're being teased?" Nathan didn't answer, so I prompted, "Would feeling like a dork be any worse?"

He grabbed hold of a textbook and set his jaw, making it clear that the discussion was over.

"You *will* gain weight, you know. And when you do,

you'll still have all the qualities you do now. You'll be smart and funny and have a great heart and care about other people, and all the things that really matter in this world."

He pretended not to hear me.

I left, closing the door behind me, wishing that I could be taking his pain with me. Because that wasn't possible, I went straight to the desk in the kitchen and rummaged through the messy drawers until I found the school directory. Even in a class of three-hundred-plus, there couldn't be that many Raines in the junior high. Plus, the boy had to be in the eighth grade. A younger boy was unlikely to tease an older one in this manner.

I discovered one boy named Raine and searched through every name to be sure there was no mistake. Indeed there was only one: Raine Embrick, the younger brother of Adam, my daughter's new love interest, and whose mother was Susan Embrick, the secretary/treasurer of the PTA.

"Dammit!" I muttered. I hated it when my life started to digress into downward spirals.

I would probably see Susan at the menopause support group tonight. At least I had a couple of hours to try to come up with a tactful way of telling her that one of her sons was getting himself into some deep doo-doo where I was concerned.

Later that evening, Stephanie was my unwilling passenger as we drove to Emily Crown's house. Stephanie must have found the concept of going to this particular group so humiliating, she might as well slum it and travel there in my inexpensive car.

"I'll have you know that I did a little preliminary research," Stephanie said at length, breaking what had been a gloomy silence.

"About menopause?"

"Heavens no. About the group. Three people are going to be there that we know from the infamous PTA board meeting. Emily Crown, of course, since it's at her house, but also Jane Daly and Susan Embrick."

I winced involuntarily at this last name.

"Don't you find *that* suspicious?" she asked.

"Which part?"

"That there is such a big crossover between the PTA board and this other group?"

"Not especially. One group was probably recruited from the other."

Stephanie scoffed. "As in, 'You're obviously having hot flashes from hormonal imbalance. Why don't you come join the PTA?' "

I chuckled and didn't reply. We pulled into Emily's driveway. Her home was a tri-level, on a quarter-acre or so of nicely manicured lawns. I hadn't realized—or had forgotten—how close she lived to Patty's house. It was just around the corner.

Emily greeted us warmly, but her usual spark seemed absent. Stephanie and I were a couple of minutes late. Even the habitually tardy Jane Daly was already there. Emily told us to join the dozen or so women seated in a circle of hard-backed chairs in her living room. We did so, and Emily introduced us to everyone, but I instantly lapsed into memory overload. I said hello to Jane and Susan, but avoided Susan's gaze, not ready to broach the subject of Nathan's troubles with Raine. The mood in the room was somber.

"I'm sorry I'm not fully up to my hostess duties tonight," Emily said, partly to me and partly to the group at large. "This is the first time we've met since . . . Patty left us. I was going to cancel, but was just having such a rough time that I thought some company would do me good."

"We understand," Jane said in sympathetic tones. "All of us were Patty's friends, too, but you two were so close. Did something happen today that especially set you off?"

She nodded and sighed, her eyes averted as she fidgeted with a tissue. "This morning I saw the ad for the annual craft show."

Emily's words reminded me that, as a cartoonist who sometimes helped out in high school art classes, I had been tapped to judge the "youth" category this year. I also immediately remembered the event's significance: Patty had won "Best in Show" for the last two years, deposing Jane Daly's stranglehold on the contest. In fact, Jane's facial expression soured at the mention of the fair.

Emily continued, "I actually picked up the phone to call Patty to ask what she was entering in the contest this year." She shuddered. "The reality of Patty's death hit me like a sledgehammer."

An uncomfortable silence ensued, and I sensed that Emily needed someone else to talk for a while. "How long ago did Patty get the idea to form this group?" I asked Jane.

To my surprise, though, it was Emily who immediately answered. "It *wasn't* her idea. It was mine. It became Patty's group as time went on, the way *all* of my ideas eventually . . ." She gave me a sheepish smile. "I'm a marriage counselor, and a wife's menopause can be a stressful time for marriages. By the time I went through menopause myself, I had accumulated so much information from my own research and my patients, I decided to form a support group. Patty was perimenopausal herself then, and so she . . . took over the membership."

We again lapsed into silence. I'd run out of ideas for

conversation starters. What was I supposed to say? Have you heard the one about the menopausal woman who goes into a bar . . . ? I didn't know the majority of women here, although they'd bought my cartoons for their newsletter and to share with friends. I glanced over at Stephanie, but she was in a total frump. She sat in the circle of chairs with her arms tightly folded, her eyes downcast and the corners of her lips down-turned.

A thin, fiftyish woman leaned closer to Stephanie in the circle and peered at her face. "I must say that your complexion is really remarkable."

"Thank you," she replied, instantly brightening.

"That's what the HRT does for you," the woman said with a knowing nod.

"HRT?"

"Hormone Replacement Therapy. Estrogen works wonders for the skin."

Stephanie straightened and said in a partial growl, "It won't be able to work any wonders on *mine*, because I'm not *on* estrogen."

"Too bad. It also improves one's disposition," the woman retorted.

Stephanie pursed her lips and shot a fiery glare at the woman, then at me.

"All right, then," Emily said. "Let's get the meeting started." She gestured at Stephanie and me. "I already introduced everyone to our new members."

"*Visitors,*" Stephanie corrected. "Drop-in visitors."

"What did you say your name was again?" the woman who'd had the prickly exchange with Stephanie asked me.

"Molly Masters."

She grinned. "You're the one who does those adorable cartoons for us!"

"Yes, I am, and thank you. This group sure saved my business, let me tell you."

Stephanie felt the need to interject, "Molly needed emotional support to come to the group today, so that's why I'm here."

The thin woman leaned forward again, patted Stephanie's knee, and asked kindly, "In denial, honey?"

"Absolutely not! I assure you, whoever you are, that I understand and appreciate that menopause is a natural stage of a woman's life, and when I'm old enough—*many* years from now, I might add—I will face up to it with my head held high."

The woman scoffed, and a couple of other women in the circle snickered. "Yeah, right," the dyed redhead seated directly across from me said. "A woman like you could *proudly* sweat through her dress till it was soaking wet, have handfuls of hair fall out, and watch her complexion go to hell."

Stephanie stared at the woman in horror. In barely audible tones, she asked, "Your hair falls out?"

"Only in thirty percent of the women. Mostly just happens to the bleached blondes."

"Carla!" Emily chastised. "You know that's not true."

She laughed openly. "Sorry. Just teasing." She returned her attention to Stephanie. "How old are you, anyway? Forty-three? Forty-four?"

"Thirty-nine!" Stephanie retorted with all due indignation.

Carla chuckled. "For how many years now?"

Determined not to laugh at Stephanie's plight, I avoided everyone's gaze by riffling through my purse, as if in search of a pen and notepad. If this was a support group, I would hate to be in a nonsupportive one. After a long pause, Stephanie quietly answered, "Three."

"And you've never once had the boob sweats?" Susan Embrick asked.

"Pardon?"

Jane added, "You know, Steph. Boob sweats. Where they were itching and sweating so badly, you wanted to rip your blouse and bra off and do a chest-press into a snowbank?"

Stephanie lifted her chin and said evenly, "That's only happened to me once. Despite your colorful analogy, I'm quite certain that was because I forgot to add fabric softener to my whites."

Emily said gently, "Stephanie, it's an undeniable fact that, even though we might be unconscious of our hormonal changes, every woman's body undergoes drastic changes from her late thirties until actual menopause occurs."

"Well, isn't that just . . . ducky," Stephanie said, giving me another glare.

"The thought of a woman raging out of control emotionally because of her menopause is a gross exaggeration, though, right?" I asked, picturing the scenario of a menopausal woman attacking Patty with a knife.

"Ha!" a woman cried. "Tell that to my husband. One time when my hormones were raging, I dumped all his things out the window." She focused on Stephanie and asked, "Want to know what he'd done to set me off?"

Stephanie said, "I suppose so."

"He left the toilet seat up."

"That *is* annoying," I said.

"At the time, I swore up and down the fact that I'd been having hot flashes every hour on the hour all that day had nothing to do with it. Now, of course, I know differently."

Jeez. Maybe I was on the right track, infiltrating this group to investigate the murder. "What about you, Emily?" I asked, wondering if she felt a hormonal imbalance had caused the embarrassingly harsh, recorded conversation that she'd later blamed on a bad day. "Has your temperament been affected much?"

"No, but then my husband never forgets to put the seat down." Everyone chuckled, then she said, "Seriously, no. I'm more inclined to get weepy than angry when I'm hormonal."

I glanced at Susan's and Jane's faces for signs that they were especially uncomfortable with the subject matter, but they didn't appear to be. It was strange that Jane Daly was even *in* this group, at her age. "Jane, you look quite a bit younger than I am. Aren't you still in your thirties?"

"Yes, but I had a hysterectomy last year."

"They automatically give hormones then, don't they?" I asked.

"Yes, and they truly do work wonders, just as Lynne was saying," Jane replied.

Lynne must be the name of the thin woman who'd gotten Stephanie's goat earlier. Now she said to Jane, "That's not what you said about your HRT last month. Remember? You were talking about how you completely lost control at your daughter's birthday party?"

Jane blushed. "Oh. Well, in retrospect, I think that was just . . . the sleep deprivation from the slumber party."

"Sleep troubles," Susan said, nodding. "Tell me about it."

"No, no, I mean it," Jane said. "That was just a . . . onetime thing. My HRT works wonders."

"So you didn't talk to your doctor about changing your levels after all?" Emily sounded incredulous.

Jane hesitated for just a moment. "Oh, that's right. I spoke to her about that already. Right after our last meeting. I'd forgotten."

"Memory loss is another symptom," the redhead commented.

"Gosh, but this menopause does sound like fun," Stephanie said in a deadpan voice. "I'm just tickled pink that you brought me here, Molly. And, apparently, in the near future, I'll not only be pink, but perspiring profusely."

"Don't mention it," I said, narrowing my eyes at her. We were at long last making a little progress in our investigation, and I didn't want Stephanie to alienate everyone. Jane, for one, had acted so defensively about her problem temper that she'd fibbed about how her HRT was affecting her mood swings.

Emily said in an authoritative voice, "Last meeting, as you all recall, I asked Mary Beth and Sarah to do some comparison research on calcium-supplement products."

"Hey zah!" Stephanie muttered under her breath. I was beginning to deeply regret bringing her, but then again, her attitude might just test Emily's and Jane's supposition that they had no trouble with losing their tempers.

Emily, sitting beside Stephanie, raised an eyebrow and said to her, "You need to hear this report, Stephanie. Bone loss in menopausal women results in life-threatening debilitation in more than ten percent of women. Even if you're fortunate enough to beat those odds, there's a significant reduction in bone density to the overwhelming majority of women over the age of fifty."

I grew increasingly alarmed as the women presented their findings. Eventually I chose to listen with only one ear—and that ear decided that I was going to have to start taking calcium citrate myself—but I didn't want to lose sight of the real reason I was here.

After the two women gave their formal presentations, the group decided to take a coffee break. Stephanie, still in a funk, opted to remain in her chair alone in the living room. I, however, went into the kitchen with the others.

Here, the mood was very different. One rather overweight woman was saying through her laughter, "I swear, ever since menopause, it's like my butt went completely flat, and my tummy went completely round. Stark naked, I can stash the contents of an entire Maybelline cosmetic counter between my tummy and my breasts."

"And what department store security guard wouldn't want to write up *that* report?" I interjected before I could stop myself. Fortunately, everyone laughed, including the woman, who took no offense.

As conversation continued, I took the opportunity to mosey up to Emily, who was standing next to Susan. "Is this everyone in your group? They're all here tonight?"

"Yes. Full attendance." She added sadly, "Everyone's here but Patty."

"That's pretty remarkable." To keep the subject matter at least loosely focused on Patty, I said, "I'm impressed by any group of a dozen people that has full attendance. It's not always this way, is it? Even back when you were meeting at Patty's house?"

"No."

"You know what?" Susan interrupted, her voice on edge. "Could we please just not talk about Patty anymore tonight? I'm already having nightmares, and I just don't want her name brought up. Okay?"

Emily's bowlike lips parted in surprise, and the color rose a little on her round cheeks. "Absolutely. Of course."

Susan held my gaze for a long, uncomfortable moment. "Is that all right with you, for once, Molly?"

"Absolutely," I said, my cheeks warm.

"Good. Excuse me for a minute. I have to take a cigarette break." She marched out of the room.

"I thought you quit," Emily called to Susan's retreating form.

"I did. Unfortunately, I started up again last week." She fetched her purse from the living room and went out the front door.

Chapter 10

I've Seen Skye and I've Seen Raine

Susan's abrupt departure brought a halt to all conversation in the kitchen. "She's going to freeze out there," Jane said, shaking her head.

"I'll go bring her her coat," I said, and promptly headed into the living room to grab her jacket while I still had a clear recollection of where she'd been seated in the circle. We'd all simply hung our coats over the backs of our chairs. Even though I was willing to honor Susan's request not to even mention Patty's name—effectively ending my evening's investigation—I still needed to talk to Susan about the troubles between her son and mine.

Alone in the living room, Stephanie stared glumly out the window, paying no attention as I snatched Susan's gray, wool jacket off the chair.

"Steph? Are you okay?"

She shook her head. "I'm getting old, Molly. I know you are, too, but you have less riding on your looks than I do."

After giving a glance at the kitchen entrance to ensure nobody could overhear, I said quietly in her ear, "We're here to learn more about our possible suspects. Not to obsess about the Cycle of Life having run roughshod over our bodies."

She continued to stare into space.

Some partner *she* was turning out to be. Ordinarily,

because she hadn't overheard Susan's request not to talk about Patty, Stephanie would have been in the best position to dig further. This was just like virtually every team project I'd been assigned to in school. "I'm going outside to chat with Susan Embrick. Keep up the good work."

I put on my own coat, went outside, and handed Susan hers. She was just outside the door, shivering terribly but sucking on her cigarette as if it were giving her sustenance. "Thanks," she said, then studied my features for a moment. "Pay no attention to my little outburst a moment ago. It was a nicotine craving, for the most part. Though it does upset me when all anyone wants to talk about is Patty Birch." She scoffed and shook her head. "It's so weird, really. All of us on the PTA board suspect one another, and none of us has the balls to admit that."

I shrugged. "I do."

She chuckled and ran her hand through her short, black hair. "And we know how you fancy yourself as a premenopausal Nancy Drew." She held my gaze for a moment. "Do you think *I* did it? Is that why you came out here?"

I leaned back against the wood railing. "No, I came out here to chat with you about your son in junior high."

"Raine? What about him?"

"He and my son, Nathan, have apparently had some unpleasant run-ins lately."

She furrowed her brow. "Do they even know each other? I didn't think they were in any of the same classes. Except maybe phys ed."

"They aren't, and that's probably part of the problem. I don't think they *do* know each other, but he's been teasing my son. Apparently with a group of cronies."

"Damn it." She stomped her foot. "The old playground bully crap again." She took a drag on her cigarette, then let out an indignant puff of smoke. "I'm truly sorry to near that, Molly. We've had this problem off and on with Raine for the last few years. I honestly don't know what to do about it."

"I know of a really good counselor . . . someone Nathan's seen in the past. I could give you his name."

While slowly blowing out more smoke, she shook her head adamantly. "Finances are way too tight to burn money on self-proclaimed childhood experts. I'll just have to threaten to humiliate him by hanging out at the junior high all day with him if this doesn't stop instantly."

I grinned at the thought of how any teenager would react to that particular threat. "That will probably bring some quick *short*-term results, at any rate."

She dropped her cigarette butt on the concrete porch and crushed it with the ball of her foot. "This is interesting, Molly. We've got our oldest children dating each other, and our next two fighting. We've got quite the tangled family webs here, don't we?"

"Apparently."

She bent down, retrieved her now flattened cigarette remains, then opened the door, grumbling, "I sure hope you didn't murder Patty. It'd be just my luck to have my kid fall head over heels for a murderer's kid."

"My sentiments exactly."

She froze and looked back at me. "*I* certainly did not kill Patty."

"Neither did I."

She arched an eyebrow, but held the door for me. We rejoined the group, which had apparently deteriorated into a gripe session about how hard menopause was to endure while living in a society that doesn't respect its elders. I'm sure the venting was healthy, but it didn't make for especially enjoyable listening.

During the drive home, Stephanie was still glum and

silent. I asked, "Where is little Mike these days? I haven't seen him in a couple of weeks."

"Didn't I tell you? He's with his grandparents in Europe. They're on a four-week sight-seeing trip."

"Wow. He's missing school all that time?"

She shrugged. "It's only second grade, after all. He'll catch up. They brought his textbooks, and they're going to lots of museums."

"Your house must seem awfully quiet."

She clicked her tongue and gave me a long look. "Whatever are you thinking? Molly, my daughter is away at college. My little boy, the light of my life, is gone for a month. I'm already depressed. Do you want me to be suicidal?"

"Sorry."

She turned back around in her seat and crossed her arms. "We're not getting anywhere in our prime objective, Molly."

"I realize that."

"We've gotten to know Chad, Emily, Jane, Susan, and, to some extent, Al. That's everybody who was there that night, not counting you and me. No one seems to be coming up to us and begging for us to listen to their confession. What good does all of this socializing with these people's pathetic little groupings do us if nobody reveals anything?"

"None at all."

She threw up both hands in a gesture of exasperation. "This was all your idea. You've done this before. You've got to *think* of something now that will force the killer to reveal some evidence here."

"I'm working on it," I murmured, deep in thought. I wasn't quite as ready to declare our entire investigation thus far fruitless. Still, there was another possibility we might have mostly overlooked. Maybe it wasn't a PTA ɔoard member after all. There was one other suspect who had been in the neighborhood that night—Amber Birch.

"Do you ski, Stephanie?"

"No. And I've got to tell you honestly that your communication skills would be vastly improved if you didn't change topics at random."

"Speaking of which, I recently learned how to gouge a person's eyes when being attacked."

Stephanie pursed her lips and remained silent for the rest of the drive.

After school on Tuesday, BC started barking so vehemently out the front window that I finally looked out myself. One of the camera girls from the videotape was standing on our front porch. Even at this distance, it was obvious that she'd been crying. I opened the door and asked, "Can I help you?"

She looked at me. Though she was clearly a bit startled by my opening the door before she'd even rung the bell, she said, "Yeah. My name's Skye. Skye Smith." She had a defiant set to her jaw and voice, as if the name should surely mean something of great significance to me, which it didn't.

"Hello, Skye. It's nice to meet you. My name's Molly. I recognize you from your frequent attempts to get funding for the VCR camera."

"Oh, right. Yeah." She peered past my shoulder and shuffled her feet a little, but said nothing.

"Is there something I can do for you?" I again prompted.

She scoffed and rolled her eyes. "Is Karen here?"

"No, she's at a friend's house, studying."

Again, she let out a derisive puff of air and muttered, "Yeah, right. Bet she's with Adam, and that they're studying *biology*."

I clenched my teeth. "Trigonometry, actually." She was at a girlfriend's house, not Adam's, but her whereabouts was not Skye's business. The reasoning behind her unexpected visit and surly attitude was now becoming clear—if bizarre. "Is there a message you'd like me to give my daughter, Skye?"

She started crying, but said harshly, "Yeah, you can tell her that her new squeeze is gonna dump her the same way he did me when things get bad. You can tell her that he knew full well somebody broke into my house and some of my stuff got stolen last week, and that I was all freaked out. He just dumped me 'cuz I was unhappy. All he cares about is having fun. He doesn't even give a—" She stopped and swiped at her tears. She yelled, "Tell 'em both that my life bites, and I hope they're happy!"

She was reconstructing the cause and effect to best suit her wounded psyche. Karen had said that Adam had broken up with his girlfriend a couple of months ago. "Skye, I'm sorry you're hurt and going through a bad time right now. I assure you, my daughter is not the cause of your problems."

"Yeah, right. Whatever." She turned on a heel and walked away.

I closed the door, then looked down at BC. "A lot of good you did," I complained to Betty, who was wagging her little tail, thinking she deserved a treat for not barking at Skye. I knelt and petted her. "What should I do, Betty? I have zero experience with this kind of thing. There's not a whole wealth of information on handling your daughter's boyfriend's . . . unstable ex-girlfriend."

Although BC didn't answer, I realized that, at the very least, Karen needed to be informed. I called the girl's house where Karen said she'd be, and she was, indeed, there. She greeted me with, "What's up, Mom?"

"Nothing major. I just wanted you to know that you got a visit just now. Do you know Skye Smith?"

There was a moment's hesitation. "Yeah. She's Adam's ex-girlfriend. What did she want?"

"I think she was actually looking for Adam, but she wanted to spread her misery around a little. She was pretty upset. Has she been bugging you at school?"

"Kinda. She's a junior. We're not in any classes together or anything. It's no big deal."

No big deal? Her intonations told me otherwise. "Are you almost done studying? Do you need a ride home?"

"Yeah, but Kate will give me one."

"And she's had her license for how long?"

"Eight months, Mom. And she lives just across from the Grand Union. It's like . . . two miles! Jeez!"

"All right. I'll see you in a few minutes. Okay?"

She hung up on me. I sighed and looked down at my little dog, who'd followed me to the phone and was now looking at me with please-give-me-a-treat eyes. "That went well. Thanks for the advice."

Karen arrived home a few minutes later. She, like her brother had done yesterday, tried to head straight to her room. This time I was prepared and called out, "Would you like a fruit smoothie?" This was a shameless ploy, but I reasoned that making it obvious that I'd made an effort was half the battle.

Already halfway up the stairs, she hesitated, then said, "Sure," sloughed down the stairs, and flopped into a seat at the kitchen table. In the process, she'd ignored her beloved dog, which was a very bad sign. I worked silently—not counting the noisy blender—and brought her the concoction a minute or two later. She took a spoonful—my "smoothies" being "lumpies" and therefore not sip-worthy—then said, "I don't want to talk about Skye."

"Okay." I sat down next to her and wracked my brain for any stories of my high school days that might be appropriate, the tactic having worked reasonably well with her brother. My mind was a blank, unfortunately. I just looked at her, hoping I could will her to open up to me.

"What!? Are you just going to sit there and stare at me?"

"How was school today?"

"Jeez, Mom!" She crossed her arms, pouted for a moment, then apparently broke her resolve. "Here's the four-one-one. Skye and a couple of her friends are just sort of giving me a twenty-four/seven freeze-out. That's all. My friends are still on my side, and it's no big deal. Okay?"

"Why is she giving you a hard time? Does she think she'll win Adam back this way?"

"I don't know. I mean, he broke up with her just after New Year's, but she claims she already bought her dress for the prom, so they're, like . . ." She took another bite of her smoothie, then pushed it away. "It's no big deal. I've got to go study for my test." Her voice had wavered a little. She rose and headed for the stairs.

The phrase "no big deal" had suddenly become my very least favorite part of Karen's frequently used lingo. "Don't you want the rest of this?" I said, holding out her glass.

"Not hungry. Thanks, though, Mom." She trotted up the stairs, shutting the door behind her.

BC had gone with her, so I didn't even have the dog to talk to. Nathan had been in the basement for a while now and must have been deeply involved in a computer game to have missed all the stomping of feet and slamming of doors.

"I'm not smart enough to be a mother," I murmured. I recalled Amber Birch's plaintive "I don't know what to do" when we'd spoken about her stepdaughter at the lodge. At least I didn't have it as tough as she did.

Could she have killed her arch-rival? Or was it Emily, who seemed to have a lot of not-so-deeply buried resentments toward her supposed best friend. Then there was the lovesick Chad. And there was something about Jane's personality that, I had to say, I just didn't like. But then, I didn't know her very well.

I started stacking the newspaper sections that had been strewn across the table, and my vision fell on a small advertisement. I snatched it up and reread it, double-checking, as it seemed so serendipitous. Indeed, tomorrow morning Jane Daly was teaching a little arts-and-crafts class at the store where she worked. This would be a fine opportunity to get to know her better. Against my better judgment, but deciding to honor my agreement to let her help whenever possible, I called Stephanie Saunders and left a message about the class.

Bright and early the next day, armed with a glue gun, Popsicle sticks, and tongue depressors, I was about to learn how to be artsy-craftsy. Although there was plenty of reason to think that this wasn't going to be the case. Such as forty-plus years of experience with living in my own skin.

I toyed with my glue gun, pulling its trigger, trying to see if I could come up with a cartoon. In my mind's eye, a dapper, James Bond–type man is pointing a glue gun at a criminal who is feverishly trying to pull his hands apart while eyeing a machine gun on the floor. With a smug look on his face, the man with the glue gun says, "Bond. Glue bond."

There are times when my cartoon ideas are so obviously not going to work out that I don't even bother to draw them. This was one such idea. "Bond. Erasable bond," I muttered to myself.

There were just two of us students so far. I didn't know the other woman at the table beside me. Five minutes after class was supposed to begin, Jane looked up at me and smiled. "Well, this is going to be a small class today, but we're honored by the presence of a professional artist."

I turned to see if this artist was standing behind me, then realized that Jane meant me.

"Oh, my!" the elderly woman beside me cried. "Are you a professional artist, dear?"

"In a manner of speaking. I'm a cartoonist."

"Oh, my!" the woman cried again. "You're not by any chance the creator of Gary Larson's *Far Side* cartoons, are you?"

"Um . . . no, Gary Larson is. And he retired a few years ago."

"Oh, did he? I noticed I haven't seen any of those cartoons in a long time. Maybe since he's retired, you could jump right in there and do a cartoon panel called *The All New Far Side*."

"I don't think his copyright lawyers would appreciate my doing that." Besides which, my hunch was that Gary Larson never once considered arming James Bond with a glue gun. He might have armed a *cow*, perhaps, but not James Bond himself.

The class was held at the Craft and Hobby Shop in what was loosely referred to as downtown Carlton. Through the glass doors, I'd seen Stephanie Saunders walk past twice already. She knew she was supposed to join me, and she was clearly having a hard time shoring herself up for the job.

With a shudder perceptible even at this distance, Stephanie at last stepped inside the store. Jane whirled around to look at her as she neared. "Stephanie, good morning. Are you joining our class?"

"Is this what you call a class? Molly and one other person?"

"It's a small group, certainly, but we might get some more drop-ins later."

"I rather doubt it." Stephanie grabbed a seat to the other side of the elderly woman. " 'Fun With Glue' sounds like a preschool class, and you're holding it mid-morning on a Wednesday. The three-year-olds are in day care."

"We *are* going to have fun, however." Understandably, Jane's voice had taken on an edge. "In fact, why don't we make this more interesting?" She had a glint in her eye that made me nervous. She retrieved a bright yellow slip of paper from a drawer and held it up to show us. "I have a ten-dollar gift certificate here to the store, which I'll give to the person who creates the best craft item today."

I looked at my bag of wooden sticks and said, "A person could probably buy a whole lot of tongue depressors for ten dollars, right?"

The elderly woman next to Stephanie said to her, "I hate it when they make competitions out of what should just be a fun learning experience. Don't you?"

Stephanie examined her glue gun as though it were an Uzi automatic, and she were preparing for battle. "You're asking the wrong person. I thrive under competition."

Jane began again: "Now, while you work, I'm going to be demonstrating some techniques and showing some craft ideas you might want to take a look at. In the middle of the table here, you will see that I've given you quite an assortment of goodies to choose from. Just help yourselves, and don't be afraid to ask me for help and suggestions. That's what I'm here for."

"I'm going to need a miter box and some safety-goggles," Stephanie said, sketching an elaborate blue-print on the paper that covered the table.

"Planning on making a model of the Guggenheim Museum, Stephanie?" I asked.

"Just the witch's candy cottage from 'Hansel and Gretel,' if you must know," she replied.

That sounded a lot more ambitious than anything I could come up with on my own. "Let's do a joint project, while we're at it, and if we win, you can keep the ten. I'll get started on the cauldron." Jane was scowling at me, so I asked, "Do you have any dry ice? And an Ivory soap bar I can carve terrified little children from?"

"You're on your own, Molly," Stephanie said, already beginning her task.

"Don't forget the bread crumbs," the elderly woman added. "Now as for me, I'm just doing star-shaped drink coasters." She set two triangles of Popsicle sticks to-gether in a Star of David formation. Pushing down the corners, she said, "Nah. Too wobbly. It's going to be tri-angular drink coasters, instead." She grinned and held up her handiwork. "Look, everybody. I've already got two done."

"Possibly you could decorate those a little," Jane sug-gested. "I've got all sorts of spangles and lace and color-ful little beads here."

I decided that I might as well make something that one of my family members would enjoy, and Nathan seemed the easiest to please in this regard. I decided to make a catapult for him, powered by a rubber band.

Jane tried to do a minilecture on the versatility of the tongue depressor and various gluing and decorating tips, but it was obvious that no one was listening. After a while, she rounded the table to sit next to me.

"How are you doing?" I asked her.

"I'm okay." She sighed. "The store will probably have trouble staying in business, now that our best customer is gone."

It was an odd comment, and I didn't know quite how to respond. "I'm sure Patty would be doing something more creative than a catapult, were she here now. Though maybe Stephanie's cottage could have given her a run for her money."

Jane snorted. "Patty's cottage would have been totally edible and featured working windows, doors, chimney, and a drawbridge."

Stephanie looked as though she was about to object, but then hesitated and looked at her work with a furrowed brow. "You're right. That woman never took second place in any contest."

"You must be talking about Patty Birch," the elderly woman said. "Now *that* was a truly talented woman. You talk about good with a glue gun. That young lady could glue a robin's egg back together."

"If only Humpty Dumpty had known," Jane grumbled. All of us stopped working and looked at her. She held up her hands. "I'm just kidding. You're absolutely right. She was a truly talented woman."

Our fellow classmate said, "Her entries at the fair were really amazing. Every year."

"Yes, they sure were," Jane said with, I thought, a hint of envy in her voice. "She'd donate them to the store sometimes."

At times, I too had envied Perfect Patty, but I was never tempted to kill her. Jane might not have been tempted, either, though she did seem to have had a sizable chip on her shoulder. Stephanie, meanwhile, had gone into hyperdrive with her glue gun, apparently forgetting all about our getting to know Jane better by being here.

"She must have cost you your blue ribbons the last couple of years," I prompted.

"Not to mention students from your little classes," the woman beside me said with a laugh. "I remember the day she came in for a class that you were teaching on mosaics. She wound up having to show you how to do it. Remember?"

"That's not true," Jane replied in clipped tones. "She just had an alternative method. I still believe my own is superior."

"The judges at the crafts fair sure agreed with Patty, then." She showed me one of her triangular coasters. "What do you think?"

"Nice," I replied.

She nodded. "I'll make each of you a set," the woman said with a smile.

I glanced over at Stephanie and Jane to see if they appeared to be as unenthused about this offer as I did. Stephanie was so involved with her project that I doubted she'd heard. Jane was staring out the window, her face set in a hideous scowl as she broke a Popsicle stick into little pieces.

Chapter 11

Bottom's Up

Having stashed our craft projects in our respective cars, Stephanie and I walked across the parking lot to a small coffee shop where we'd decided to have a state-of-the-investigation discussion.

We got our steaming beverages—Stephanie insisting on paying for both—then sat down at a round, wood table in one corner. "What are your thoughts so far?" she asked. Ever since we'd snapped at each other in the car the other day, she'd been on her best behavior.

"The only thing that surprises me is that Patty's faults seem to have been more obvious to others than they were to me. Apparently she was nowhere near as popular as I'd thought she was."

"I could have told you that," Stephanie said, stirring sweetener into her coffee and taking a sip. She pursed her lips as if dissatisfied with the flavor.

"Jane is certainly jealous of Patty for taking her arts-and-crafts queen crown."

Stephanie shook a second packet of sweetener into her coffee. "Yes, but that would hardly be reason for killing a person."

I took a sip of my chai, which was delicious, the creamy brown liquid perfectly spiced. "It's as good a reason as anything else."

Stephanie smirked. "Come now, Molly. My cottage

was superior to your catapult. Are you going to kill me for my ten-dollar gift certificate?"

"Not over that, no."

She peered at me over the brim of her coffee cup. "Are you seriously trying to tell me that Jane might have killed Patty just so that she could get a blue ribbon rather than a red one this year?"

"We're not talking about ribbons so much as a person's self-image, Stephanie. Some people seem to think that's all they've got . . . if they can no longer see themselves in the one exact role they're comfortable with, that they're nothing. They don't know any way to exist other than how they've been up to that point."

Although Stephanie had listened to my theory patiently, she set down her cup and said in biting tones, "Your point, then, is that Jane Daly was accustomed to being the best glue gunner on the block, till Patty arrived. According to your theory, it must have been seeing the leprechaun on Patty's door that pushed Jane over the top."

Put in those terms, my suggestion sounded ludicrous, but she'd annoyed me into obstinacy. "Maybe so."

Stephanie scoffed and returned her attention to her coffee, which she stirred rabidly with a little wooden stick between sips. Come to think of it, Jane Daly should have provided the stirrers as caulking for the Popsicle sticks and tongue depressors.

"Let's look at this from your angle, Stephanie. You're always perfectly dressed, your makeup flawless, not a hair on your head out of place."

"Thank you."

"My point is, why do you care so much about your appearance? Wouldn't you be the same person if you threw on jeans and an old sweatshirt sometime and, for example, went bowling?"

"I don't even *own* a sweatshirt, so I couldn't very well throw on an *old* one."

"But would you even recognize yourself if you did wear one? Plus leave your house with your hair unkempt and sans makeup?"

She tossed her perfectly coiffed blond hair back from her shoulders in disgust. "Of course I'd recognize myself. Not that I would want to."

"Aha! That's because you value your self-image as this well-dressed, sophisticated, classy woman. And if someone were to take that image away from you, wouldn't you hate that person?"

She sipped her coffee without answering, which I took to mean that I'd made my point. Then, however, she met my gaze and said, "Are you referring to yourself, Molly?"

Her response threw me for a loop. "Huh? Me? No! I'm referring to Patty . . . in the case of Jane. That maybe what gave Jane her self-image and sense of worth was her inimitable crafts skills. I don't even . . . why would you think I meant me?"

"Because you *do* take away my sense of worth. You mock me and make fun of my values."

I was momentarily speechless. "If I do that . . . how horrible of me. I'm sorry. But I really . . ." I let my voice fade. My cheeks felt red-hot now, and I felt truly miserable. "Stephanie, I don't want to confront some personality flaw of mine right now. I'm just trying to help catch a killer."

Kindly allowing me to change subjects, Stephanie said, "A pursuit in which we haven't ruled out a single suspect, and we haven't made any significant discoveries."

"Right. We're spinning our wheels. But at least now, thanks to the menopause workshop, I know to be more concerned with calcium intake. Plus I got me a real nifty catapult."

Stephanie gave no response. At length, she said, "I'm getting a refill," and returned to the counter.

I sipped my chai, reflecting on this new revelation from Stephanie. Had I been mocking her values all these years? It hadn't felt that way. Sometimes I went on the offensive when responding to her cracks about me. Perhaps from her perspective, she was only doing the same.

Stephanie returned to the table, just as Jane came into the shop. She did a little double take at seeing us there. All charm, Stephanie cried, "Jane, hi. Let me buy you a cup of coffee, in appreciation for my unexpected gift certificate."

Jane took Stephanie up on her offer and joined us, but kept fidgeting with her sandy-blond hair. She explained that she was just on a short break and could only stay for a couple of minutes.

"How did you first get interested in crafts projects, Jane?" I asked.

She raised an eyebrow. "Why ask me? You're an artist yourself," she said with a laugh.

"My artistic pursuits are limited to cartooning, though. I can't think three-dimensionally. I barely scraped by with a B in sculpture and was a total bust in pottery. Plus I've never made any kind of decoration in my life of my own volition. I'm terrible at that sort of thing."

"That's true," Stephanie chimed in.

Jane said, "My background sounds polar opposite to yours. I started doing crafts projects when I was twelve, making finger puppets to sell. I needed the money. My family was poor. We all had to pull our own weight."

"You supported yourself from the time you were twelve?" Stephanie asked in horror.

Sipping her coffee, Jane gave a small nod. "I took on

any kind of sewing and knitting work I could. And I'd make things with the scraps. Little catnip mouses . . . all kinds of little items."

"My God," Stephanie cried. "How . . . unimaginably harrowing that must have been!"

"Oh, I don't want to paint too stark a picture. We always managed to keep food on the table. It just wasn't much of a table. Or much of a meal, for that matter." She leaned back and spread her arms. "But look at me now."

In her ordinary and inexpensive-looking cotton dress and denim jacket, her plain features unadorned with makeup, it was hard to follow Jane's logic. Maybe she meant that she was no longer half starved.

Stephanie snorted and replied, "No offense, dear, but this is hardly the Ritz."

Jane lifted her chin. "How you look at things is all a matter of your frame of reference. When I was growing up, I'd have been thrown out of a place like this. I never dreamed I'd have a nice house, a loving husband, my own car, two healthy children. I've done very well for myself, considering how far I've had to come."

I said honestly, "I've always looked at arts and crafts as a luxury. It's remarkable to think that at one point, those skills helped you to survive."

She chuckled. "That should be the subject of my next class . . . Making Money at Crafts."

"Now *that* would draw folks into the store in droves," Stephanie said.

"Yes. It probably would. And would drive them *away* in droves when I got to the section entitled, Garbage Picking for Materials." She stood up and motioned with her coffee cup as if in a toast to Stephanie. "Thanks again for the coffee. I hope to see you both at a future class of mine."

"Thanks," Stephanie and I said in unison.

Jane left.

"Jeez. Another lesson in humility," I said watching her through the glass. "I'm always forgetting how lucky I am."

"It's amazing, all right," Stephanie murmured. "You might actually be right, Molly. She *does* look at arts and crafts as a matter of life and death."

Despite Stephanie's words, during my short drive home, I admitted to myself that I didn't really put that much stock in the notion that Jane had killed Patty because she was better at crafts. I'd felt cornered into defending the theory, but secretly agreed with Stephanie's first impulse that it was too flimsy a motive for anyone to have actually resorted to taking another human being's life.

Once home, my thoughts turned to my children. Was Raine Embrick still teasing Nathan? Nathan had seemed his usual self when he came home from school yesterday. That was a major relief, but nowadays my worry was almost equally divided. Karen was also getting hassled by a fellow student—Adam's former girlfriend. Karen had reached that time of life where she was selective about sharing her worries with me. She was certainly getting harassed, but to what extent and how greatly that was affecting her was not information to which I was privy.

Maybe Susan Embrick would know. She, at least, knew about her son and my daughter's second date. I called her and said that I'd like to talk some more about our kids, then offered to take her to lunch at the restaurant of her choice. She agreed and named a place that I'd never heard of but that she said was near her home. Even so, I arrived first. The restaurant was a bit dark and claustrophobic for my tastes, but the menu prices were reasonable. Having plenty of time to read the menu while waiting, I decided to go with the "Lunchtime Classic!" Otherwise known as soup and a sandwich.

Susan was nicely dressed in a cream-colored blouse and black slacks that matched her hair. She waved at me as she came inside, ordering coffee before she'd even pulled out her chair. The waitress came over with a pot of coffee and poured a cup for Susan, then offered one to me, which I declined. Susan then said she needed a few minutes to look at the menu. Already tapping a cigarette out of her pack, she asked me, "Do you mind if I smoke?"

I did, but said no, and after a few false starts with her lighter, she took a long, languid drag on her cigarette, which she washed down with coffee. Susan's hands were shaking so badly that the coffee was sloshing over the lip of her cup as she tried to set it into the saucer.

As she tamped up the drops with her napkin, she muttered, "God, I hate this."

"The coffee?"

She met my eyes for a moment, but gave no answer. She fanned away the smoke as she speed-read her menu. "The salads here aren't very good. I'm going to go with the soup-and-sandwich combo."

"Me, too."

"Which we could have made for ourselves at home for one-tenth the cost."

"Yes, but we're paying for the ambience and the service."

She chuckled, managing to breathe smoke out her nostrils and her mouth simultaneously, looking a bit draconian in the process. She glanced around the unexceptional room. "This *is* nice."

We gave the waitress our order. She asked if I'd like anything besides water to drink, which I didn't. "How about you, ma'am?" she asked, shifting her vision to Susan, who was staring at the small wine list on our table as if mesmerized. The waitress picked up on it and asked, "Something from the bar?"

"No. Just coffee is fine," she said with a sigh. The moment the waitress left, Susan asked me, "Has Nathan said anything more to you about his having trouble with Raine?"

"No, he hasn't. And he was in a good mood after school yesterday. I'm hoping that, between us, we can help keep it that way."

"Absolutely," Susan replied. "Don't hesitate to let me know if you think anything could be starting up again. I told Raine this, and I fully intend to stick with it, but if I have to get special permission to shadow him all day, that's what I'll do."

"You said that you've had trouble with him before, right?"

She nodded. "At his school in Michigan, before we moved. Of course, I was drinking for part of that period, and I assumed he was just acting out."

So she had indeed had a problem with alcohol. I'd begun to suspect as much. Asking her to expound on that subject was too nosy, even for me. So I changed subjects slightly and asked, "Were Raine and Kelly Birch friends back in Michigan?"

"No, they've always had very different interests. Even when we'd get them together as toddlers, they could never find something they both wanted to play."

"Your two families *do* go way back, then." I wondered when Amber had first arrived on the scene. I had visions of her having been their children's baby-sitter. "Did you know Amber, as well? She must have lived in the same town at some point, too, right?"

"Randy and Amber met on one of his business trips

to Colorado. I didn't meet her till he and Patty had divorced, and Amber suddenly moved in with him."

"That must have caused quite the upset. Talk about grist for the rumor mill . . . Patty's husband having an affair, Patty moves out, and he remarries."

Blowing out another puff of foul-smelling smoke, she shook her head. "It wasn't like that at all, Molly. Randy hung on far longer than most men could have. You should have known Patty back then. You'd have barely recognized her."

"She'd changed that much?"

Susan nodded. "On the surface, she sure did. It was Patty's drinking habits that led to Randy's developing a roaming eye. How would *you* like to be coming home to a drunk every night? God knows how *my* husband stuck with me all those years."

"Patty was a recovering alcoholic . . . too?"

"Yes, although not a very good one." Under her breath, she added, "Not that I'm much of one to talk, though." She stubbed out her cigarette. "I was doing much better, up until she moved here. With her in the same town as me again . . ." She curled her lip and didn't complete the thought.

"I see."

"No, you don't," she said with a low chuckle. "I'm ashamed of my weakness for the bottle. Part of the reason I joined the PTA three years ago was to keep myself busy. It's much easier that way . . . keeping your mind occupied with some sort of volunteer effort so you don't have to remember the horrid things you've done to your loved ones. My drinking woes were part of why we left, in fact. To get me a clean start on things."

"You're sober now, though, right?"

She frowned and shrugged. "For three months and

four days. And, before that, six months and eighteen days."

She'd slipped up back in mid-December, then. "Patty's moving here was like your past catching up to you. Is that what you're saying?"

She grimaced. "You could call it that, yes. When Randy approached my husband for a job, Mike felt that he couldn't turn Randy down, though I begged him to. I knew Patty would come, too, and what that would do to me."

"You got back into drinking because your old drinking buddy came back into your life?"

She answered through clenched teeth, "She was the one who pushed me off the wagon. And then threw the wagon into reverse and drove right over my face."

"In what sense?"

Susan gritted her teeth. In barely contained fury, she said, "She slipped a shot of vodka into my orange juice."

That was a startling accusation—unfathomable from my perception of the generous, kind-spirited person I'd believed Patty to have been. Was Susan lying to me? "Why? Why would she do that?"

"She was a very odd person . . . wonderful on the outside—charming, gracious, and giving. But her childhood was no bed of roses. Her mother had been the town drunk, and Patty had been overcompensating all her life. She once told me that what put her over the edge was when she had a miscarriage. She started drinking."

"I had a miscarriage myself. It's definitely hard to endure."

"Of course it is," Susan said in clipped tones. "So are a lot of things."

"And hard times are not an excuse or explanation for why she would give you a glass of juice with vodka in it."

Susan lifted her hand a little from the table, as if in concurrence. "She denied having done it, of course."

"Why do you think Susan spiked your drink? I mean, it's . . . sick to give a recovering alcoholic a shot of vodka without her knowledge."

"She must have thought it would give me loose lips. And she was probably right."

"She was plying you with alcohol to get some secret out of you?"

"She was trying to recruit me to help her get her husband back. My husband is Randy's boss and makes out his travel assignments. Patty's plan was to *accidentally* be at Randy's next hotel. Her thought was that she lost him to Amber on one of his sales trips. She intended to make herself his next . . . dalliance, so to speak. And since I'm the de facto travel agent for my husband's department, I'm the one who knew when and where her ex was going."

I rubbed at my forehead, wishing this was all making more sense than it was. "Why would she have had to get you drunk to get that information from you? Did she know you wouldn't have told her of your own volition?"

"As a general rule, I only give the travel arrangements to my husband and to the travelers themselves. It would be unprofessional of me to do otherwise."

Our food arrived, but I'd lost my appetite. I simply did not want to accept this picture of Patty as an underhanded, self-centered woman who would trick a recovering alcoholic into having a shot of vodka to advance her own selfish pursuits. With the waitress once again out of earshot, I asked, "Are you sure it wasn't an accident? Couldn't she have given it to you by mistake? That she'd meant to spike her own drink?"

"That's what I'd thought, too, till I saw Adam's tape.

He happened to have been fiddling with Skye's camera at our house that day, and he showed it to me afterward."

I did my best to disguise my reaction to this mention of the person I worried might be making my daughter's life miserable of late. "She's one of the girls who put that tape together. And his former girlfriend, right?"

"Yes, and, unbeknownst to me, Adam helped them edit the tape."

"He *did*?"

She nodded grimly. "He mentioned that to me when he saw me testing our own camcorder the other day, so that I'd be able to film the All-Cultures Day for the junior high on Friday."

"You're taping that?"

She made a face and nodded. "Patty had extended my role as PTA secretary to include videotaping all of the special PTA-funded events. We talked about that at the first meeting back in September. Remember?"

"Not really. My attention wanders quite a bit during meetings." If Adam had edited the tape, Susan could know a lot more about the killer's motive than she was letting on. I tried to make my voice sound casual as I asked, "Did Adam show you the outtakes of the tape?"

"No, he didn't have them. Skye was in charge of the project and she kept all of the camcorder cassettes at her house. Adam told me that, last winter, he'd shown the girls how to pick and choose which portions of the camcorder cassettes to put on the final tape."

"Do you still have the recording of Patty spiking your orange juice, though?"

She shrugged and turned her attention to her food. "I think so."

"You've got to turn it into the police, Susan. There could be a reason behind . . ." I let my voice fade, lost in thought. "My God. I hope the two things aren't connected."

"What two things?"

"Skye came to see Karen, all in tears yesterday. Fortunately Karen wasn't home. Skye told me that her house had been burglarized last week."

Had the police allowed evidence that could have revealed the killer's motive to slip through their hands?

Chapter 12

Stirring Up Trouble

Susan interrupted my silent reverie by saying, "I'm sorry to hear that Skye's harassing Karen. Maybe you should talk to her parents. They're divorced and both remarried. I've got their phone numbers in my address book at home, if you need them."

"Thanks. I'll let you know if it comes to that."

"I can't tell you how relieved I am that Adam gave her the heave-ho. She always struck me as petulant and self-obsessed."

"That was my impression, too," I murmured.

The news of Patty's duplicities and the unedited tape perhaps being in the killer's hands had so unnerved me that I no longer felt like tapping Susan for information about Skye. We finished our lunch, not discussing anything of consequence.

After Susan had pulled out of the restaurant parking lot, I snatched my cell phone out of the glove box and called Tommy at the police station. As soon as he was on the line I said, "Tommy, I just wanted to double-check something. Have you looked into a recent burglary of a Carlton home?"

"I've been rather busy with a murder investigation, Molly."

"I know, but the crimes might be related. The burglary was at Skye Smith's house, one of the four girls who made the tape about the PTA. At one point that night, Mr. Alberti had said that the embarrassing sections were left on the cutting room floor, so I was just—" I stopped. The truth was that I was calling to make sure Tommy was aware of the connection, but I needed to be more tactful. "I was wondering if the whole thing was connected."

"Prob'ly not. Hate to disillusion you, Molly, but we do get a number of burglaries in this town every year. Anyways, if it makes you feel any better, I'll look into it."

"You did already ask those girls to give you everything they'd filmed, right?"

Tommy hesitated. "I'm sure we did."

"So you might not have? I would have thought that was one of the very first things you would do. I mean, you knew there were supposedly embarrassing outtakes."

"Yeah, but—"

"Tommy, what if the kids recorded something that would have been the one piece of evidence that identified the killer? And what if that evidence has since been stolen in this seemingly random burglary?"

"Come off it, Molly! Just what do you think could have been on that tape? Someone saying, 'I'm planning on killing the PTA president in March, so don't count on me for any volunteer work that month!'?"

"No, but what if someone was caught in a compromising position? What if Patty had found out that someone . . . bought themselves a new car with the PTA's money? And what if the kids recorded their argument?"

"Like I said, Molly, I'll look into it. Is there anything else?"

"No, just . . . could you keep me posted?"

"Of course, Molly. Just as soon as you get hired as my superior officer, I'll be sure 'n' fill you right in on every little detail of my investigation." He hung up.

I stared at the phone as I turned it off, then returned it to the glove box. Maybe my side of the conversation hadn't been a lesson in civility and tact. Still, what an outrageous oversight if Tommy truly hadn't immediately collected the camcorder cassettes from those students.

I drove straight to the high school, ostensibly to give Karen a ride home and spare her from a bus ride. My plan, however, was to try to find out what part of the building Skye Smith would be in during the last period. I could camp out near that exit and perhaps talk to her.

To my frustration, I arrived a few minutes late. Classes had already let out for the day, and my chances now of catching her were greatly reduced. Nevertheless, like a salmon swimming upstream against the torrent of students leaving the building, I made my way into the lobby. Where I ran smack into Karen and Adam, walking arm in arm.

She stopped dead in her tracks, as did Adam, the three of us forming a little eddy in the traffic pattern. "Mom! What are you doing here?"

"I'm . . . giving you a driving lesson. Thought I'd see if you were up for driving home."

She narrowed her eyes at me, but said, "You remember my mom, right, Adam?"

"Yo," he said with a nod.

"Nice to see you again, Adam."

Karen and Adam made a nice-looking couple, all right, and I trusted her, but I sure didn't know him well enough to trust him. And I wished he would drop the "yo" from his vocabulary. I was always tempted to respond, "Skoal," but didn't actually know what that word meant.

"In fact," I said, "I'm really glad we ran into each other. I just had lunch with your mother, and she mentioned that you helped edit the tape that some students put together in Mr. Alberti's government class."

"Yeah, that's true."

"Those tapes are kind of important, considering what happened to Patty Birch. Did you see anything when you were editing them that somebody might have wanted to make sure nobody else saw? Maybe that you deliberately left out because it was so embarrassing?"

He shrugged. "Those tapes were mostly lame, you know? Moms and teachers talking on and on about nothing."

"That's what I thought you'd say." I waited, hoping he'd elaborate, but no such luck. I cleared my throat. "Skye came over to our home the other day and mentioned that their house was burglarized. Do you happen to know what was stolen?"

"Just like . . . their VCR and stuff."

"By stuff, do you mean their tapes? Including the ones of the PTA? Or did you keep the original tapes?"

"No, I gave them back to Skye." He had no trouble meeting and holding my gaze.

"Do you know how I could find Skye, to ask her about them?"

"Haven't seen her much today." He had stiffened, and Karen was giving me the evil eye.

Time for me to exit and give them time alone so as to appear to be less the prying, nervous parent than I actually was. Al might have seen an earlier version of the tape, or discussed the content of the outtakes with his students. Besides, he was another person with opportunity to have killed Patty. Maybe he had some motive that I'd yet to uncover. "I've got to talk to Mr. Alberti about some PTA business. How about meeting me in the parking lot, Karen? I'll be there in fifteen minutes."

"Yeah, okay. Thanks, Mom." Her tone was anything but thankful, however.

On the lookout for Skye or her cronies, I made my way toward the wing where Al's classroom was located. From there it would just be a matter of poking my head into the ten or so rooms till I found him.

After looking in four doorways, I spotted Al. He was alone, reading something on his desk, his shiny pate aimed in my direction. I leaned into the room. "Hi, Al. Have you got a minute?"

He smiled. "Of course. Is this about ballroom dancing?"

"No, 'fraid I've hung up the old dance shoes for good." I closed the door behind me. "It's about that video your students made. It appears that the original recording might have been stolen from Skye's house during a burglary."

He furrowed his brow. "She mentioned last Friday that now she really did need a camcorder from the PTA . . . that hers had been stolen."

"Did she say anything about the tapes, or whether she'd given them to the police?"

"No, it was all off-topic, and we were having a quiz that day."

"Did you ever see the tape yourself?" He was shaking his head, so I went on, "Or did the kids ever tell you what happened in scenes they decided to cut?"

" 'Fraid not. Why do you ask?"

"Just . . . being a concerned citizen, hoping that this crime gets solved sooner rather than later."

"We can all get behind you on that point."

I hesitated, wishing there were an easy way to find out how badly Skye Smith and her cronies were harassing my daughter. But Karen was not even in Mr. Alberti's class, and it was a large school.

"You still look puzzled. Is there anything else on your mind?"

"Always. Just nothing especially interesting."

He started erasing the blackboard. "You know what we teachers like to say about asking questions . . . that the only stupid question is the one you don't ask."

"There *is* one thing. Skye Smith came over to my house, asking for my daughter and being generally unpleasant about Karen's newly begun relationship with Adam Embrick. The incident made me worry about the likelihood of friction between them during school."

He turned around again and faced me. "Skye's a good kid, but overly dramatic and impetuous. My hunch is, by next week she'll have found somebody new and forgotten all about Mr. Embrick and your daughter."

I smiled, glad that he was willing to tell me what I so wanted to hear. "Thanks. I'll see you at a future PTA function, I'm sure."

He went back to his blackboard. "Take care."

The hallways had already pretty much emptied out as I made my way down the hall. I found Karen sitting in her fiercest demeanor in the driver's seat of the car.

"Thanks a lot for embarrassing me half to death with Adam," she said the moment I sat down beside her.

"If what little I said in the lobby embarrassed you half to death, you're going to have one heck of a hard time surviving the next few years. I mean, I wasn't even trying. Are you *daring* me to shock you in front of your new beau?"

She gave me the triple whammy—indignant sigh, tongue click, and eye roll—but started the car. She drove to our neighborhood in silence.

"How's the homework situation tonight?" I finally asked.

"Easy, for once."

"Let's see if Lauren and Rachel are home."

"Okay." I knew I wouldn't have to twist her arm on

that one. She pulled into their cul-de-sac. Rachel appeared to have just gotten home from the bus. Her backpack was beside her as she sat on the porch, her now-ancient cat, Misty, in her lap. As we got out of the car, Karen gave Rachel a significant look, which I knew meant: Wait till you hear the awful thing my mother did *now*! The two of them went inside the house where they would no doubt escape to Rachel's room before I could even get in the door.

I glanced at my parents' house as I climbed Lauren's front steps. It had been fortunate for me that my parents were in Florida when all hell had broken loose here in Carlton. They were not due to return for another month, but when they did, my mother, and probably my father, too, would resent the fact that I hadn't told them about the murder. They would want to return now if they knew about it, somehow assuming that their presence would make things safer for me, despite prior evidence to the contrary.

Lauren was all smiles at our unannounced visit. She and I sat at her faux-wood-grain Formica counter and sipped peach-flavored tea. Cutting right to the chase, I said, "I think I really ruffled your husband's feathers earlier this afternoon."

"So what else is new?" Lauren said with a grin.

"I got on his case because it's possible that he never collected the unedited version of the videotape that we saw at Patty's house. Now it looks as though someone broke into one of the girls' homes and may have stolen the tapes."

"Ouch. So you . . . pointed out to him what a major screwup that was?"

"Something like that."

"Well, you were right. Not that that helps. I can only imagine how heads are going to roll if that's really the case . . . if they let a big piece of evidence slip through their fingers like that."

"I know." I feigned a big sigh. "You'd think sooner or later he'd just face facts and make me his consultant, wouldn't you?"

She knew I was joking and chuckled. "Really. So how's the sleuthing going?"

"In circles. Lately, though, I've heard from a couple of people that Patty was trying to win her ex-husband back. That makes Amber Birch a more credible suspect."

Lauren tilted her head. "Amber isn't even on the tape, though, right?"

"No, she isn't."

"So if these tapes were stolen by the killer, she's off the hook, right?"

I considered the matter. "Not necessarily. She could have had reason to think she was in the outtakes. I'm starting to think that Patty was a lot more underhanded than she ever appeared to be. Maybe Amber came over after the meeting broke up, and Patty lied and told Amber that she'd been filmed by Skye Smith doing something that would cause Randy to leave her. Then Amber became so enraged, she murdered Patty. Afterward, Amber stole the tapes to destroy the evidence."

Lauren said, "I guess that's possible. Have you gotten to know her at all?"

"Not well enough." An idea hit me. "I just thought of the perfect excuse for going to see her tomorrow morning. She works part-time at that sports equipment store downtown. Or rather, the place that would be downtown if Carlton actually had a downtown."

"You're going to buy sports equipment?"

"No, just finally get my skis tuned. Thanks for being my sounding board, Lauren."

"My pleasure."

Just then there was a considerable racket as Rachel and Karen came trotting down the stairs. Rachel was saying, "This is going to be so cool. I'm glad you asked me to help."

"Help with what?" I asked.

"Shopping," Rachel replied.

Karen said, "Adam asked me to the junior prom."

"Oh, that's wonderful," I said automatically, but needed a moment to accept the news. Having not been asked to my own prom, this would be my first time shopping for one.

It really would be quite terrific to be able to play formal-attire dress-up with Karen, to take photographs, to see her date in a tuxedo, all without having to actually spend an evening in all that uncomfortable clothing myself. I could do this. I could be a prom mother.

"So can I have two hundred dollars?" Karen asked me.

"*How* much?"

"Two hundred. I need a prom dress, and Rachel and I are going to go pick one out next week."

"Hey, for that kind of money, you shop with me."

She shrugged. "You can come if you want."

Well. So much for vicarious prom experiences.

Jim had to work late, which was badly timed, because the phone rang three different times with the caller hanging up the moment I answered. It was really getting on my nerves. A fourth time, Karen happened to pick up. She hung up the phone a few seconds later, but her twisted facial expression told me what had happened. "Was that Skye calling?" I asked.

"Yeah. She just called to say she hates my guts. Like I haven't figured that out already."

"That does it," I snapped, reaching for the phone.

"I'm going to dial star-six-nine and get her back on the line, then I'm—"

"Don't, Mom," Karen cried. "Please. You'll just make things worse."

I frowned and hung up the phone. "Okay, but I've got a real short fuse on this. We'll see if Skye can get a handle on herself by the end of the week. If not, I'm talking to her parents."

Karen grimaced, but said nothing.

The following morning, after calling to verify that Amber was there, I grabbed my skis, stuffed them into the Honda CRV, and headed off in search of Amber. I had to fight off three different sales clerks till I located her in the ski department.

"Molly. Hi. Looking for a trade-in on some new skis?"

"Actually, I thought I'd just have these old ones tuned."

She took them from me and studied them with a deep scowl on her attractive features. "No offense, but these look older than I am."

"That's because they probably are."

"Have you ever tried parabolic skis?" She gestured at the rows of shiny skis that lined the wall. "They are much, much easier to control. They practically turn by themselves."

"So do mine. It's just that they sometimes do so when I'm trying to go straight."

"Let me just show you what I've got in stock, for future reference, if you ever decide you want to upgrade. All right?"

Twenty minutes or so later, I was trying to calculate the exact moment when things had gone awry for me. It was probably the blue screen—a high-tech device that made it look as though I was actually on the slope, skiing like a scene out of an old James Bond movie.

In any case, I had just spent more money on new skis than Karen expected to spend on her prom dress. I put my foot down, literally, and insisted that the bindings merely be transferred from my old skis to the new ones and that my old boots were fine. The unfortunate aspect—probably only one of many that I'd yet to consider—was that all I had to show as I completed my transaction was a receipt. The skis themselves would not be ready for pickup until the end of the week.

As with the other strip mall, where Jane's crafts store was located, this sporting goods store was near a chain coffee shop. "Now that you've sold me new skis, can I buy you a cup of coffee?" I asked Amber.

She smiled. "Tell you what. I'll part with a couple bucks of my commission and buy you one, okay?"

"Deal," I said, though my heart sank a little. There was an evil part of my heart that didn't want to start to like Amber. Yet I was liking her more and more each time we spoke. We made our way to the coffee shop on the opposite side of the parking lot.

I ordered a chai and Amber got a latte, and we settled into chairs. As a conversation starter, I said, "It's too bad my son gave up karate and is no longer into the Asian disciplines. I always thought it would be neat to drink chai tea while watching tai chi."

On second thought, not much of a conversation starter, that. Amber had nothing whatsoever to say in response. After a pause, she said, "This is a special occasion. After more than two years in this town, this is the first time I've done something social with another mother. I mean, people at work like me and accept me, both at the ski shop and the slope. Just no one who's in the all-important Carlton PTA."

"That's Carlton for you. I grew up here. Our slow-to-warm-up climate doesn't just refer to the weather. There's no welcoming or greeting committees for people moving into this town."

"Till now. Patty started up some groups. She, of course, noticed the absence."

"Oh, that's right. I remember hearing about that." She'd asked me to join, but I'd declined, being too much a product of this town myself.

Amber frowned. "Let's get real, here. Even if this place brought fruit baskets to new families, I'd have received the pits and rinds. I'm the 'other woman' who all married women see as the enemy."

"Maybe so."

"Definitely so. Randy and I bought our house and moved in two months before Patty did. Yet everyone treated *me* like the intruder and welcomed Patty with open arms."

I shrugged, uncomfortable and unwilling to admit to some of the ugly truths, even though I'd thought them myself. "We got to know her quicker because she stepped in to take over as PTA president when Stephanie needed someone to volunteer. Maybe a lot of the PTA'ers . . . felt it would be disloyal somehow to befriend you. And, yes, like you say, when you get older, you still feel young, and yet you come to realize that society doesn't agree. You do worry about the cliché of your husband having a midlife crisis and dumping you for a younger woman. It happens all the time. How often do you see a fifty-year-old woman dumping her husband for a twenty-year-old stud muffin? It angers us aging women, and the wrong person gets blamed. After all, it's not you young women who left their spouses and children."

"No, my husband was the one who did that . . . but *I* betrayed the sisterhood."

"Well, maybe not you specifically. Only if you look at it in symbolic terms and generalize like I just did."

Amber pursed her lips. "I'll tell you something, Molly. There are days when the very hardest thing for me to believe is that anybody could possibly be jealous of me. Sometimes I envy everybody else, just because they don't have to be me."

"I think everyone feels that way at times. But I'm sure it was really hard to be in your particular triangle, living right across the street from Patty."

"*I'll* say. God. That woman was like . . ." She gestured in the air as if seeking divine inspiration. "Nothing that I did could ever come close to being good enough. I'm not much of a cook. I get bored easily and can't stand being cooped up in the house. I just . . . want to be outside, climbing mountains or throwing Frisbees or having fun, you know? I can't stand all those interminable meetings at school, or all that artsy-fartsy junk Patty was into. So if you Carlton moms want to hate me, sorry, but why should I care? Screw all of you." She paused and gave me a sheepish smile. "I mean . . . it's not that I hate you and your friends, Molly. It's that you all hate me without knowing me."

My cheeks were warming. "I can understand how that must feel."

"It's Kelly that gets hurt. I mean, it was bad with Randy's son, too, but he was only around for a year after Randy and I got married, and now he's off at Harvard, so it's not so rough on him." She gestured as she spoke. The coffee was making her animated, or maybe that was just the effect of her finally feeling free to unburden herself to one of us who'd made her life so hard.

I murmured, "It's obvious what a tough time you're having with Kelly."

"I can't be like her mom was. All that feathering-of-the-nest stuff. I'm just not into it, but I felt so inferior. And I do want to make Kelly feel welcome . . . like it's a real home for her. I know that's what she's used to, so I try my best, and that just makes Kelly hate me all the more. I see the disdain on her face every time she looks at me."

"A lot of that goes with the territory of having a teenager, you know."

"Sure. As you no doubt are thinking, I was a teenager myself just eight years ago, so I remember how it is. But this stuff with Kelly is way worse."

"Is Kelly's counseling helping at all?"

She spread her arms wide. "How can it be? The kid thinks I killed her mom!"

"Maybe that's just an act. Maybe in her heart of hearts she knows you're innocent." Though I hated myself, I was determined to check for her reaction to the rumors. "I think she wants to believe that you and Randy were in trouble . . . that he was considering going back to her mother."

She froze for a moment, then took a sip of her coffee. "That's what this is about? You invited me for a cup of coffee because you're trying to figure out who killed your friend, and you think I did it?"

"No. To be completely honest, I don't think you did it. But, yes, I am desperate to find the killer, largely for Kelly's sake. She's a sweet kid, and she deserves better than this."

Amber held my gaze. "Kelly's right about her father. It's hard to say if he'd still be with me, had this not happened to her mother. Now I'm hanging on to my marriage by my fingernails. I didn't kill her, though."

"You were right across the street. Are you sure you didn't see or hear anything? A car pulling into her driveway? Raised voices?"

She combed her fingers through her blond hair. "I wish I had, but I didn't." She took another sip. "My break time's over, and I've got to get back to work." She widened her eyes as she rose from her seat and said jokingly, "Nice talking to you."

"Amber, maybe when this is all over with, you and I could get Kelly and Nathan together. Maybe go out for lunch some weekend or—" I broke off my words as I caught sight of who was coming in the door.

Skye Smith and one other camera girl had come into the coffee shop.

Chapter 13

Rearview Mirrors

Amber followed my gaze, then turned back toward me. "What?"

I ducked behind her a little, not wanting Skye to see me yet. "Some of my daughter's friends must be cutting classes today. I think I'll go nag them about that."

She nodded, taking my words at face value. "I'll talk to you again in a couple of days, when your new skis are ready."

I thanked her and watched her leave. She never looked back, or gave a second glance to Skye and her friend who, in turn, were too engaged in their own animated conversation to notice anyone else in the room. Another indication that Amber was either innocent or an astoundingly good actress. If Amber had actually seen that tape at some point, she'd have recognized Skye and her friend.

The girls purchased frothy drinks at the counter and sat down at a table across the room from me. Skye was doing most of the talking, tossing her bleached hair back from her shoulders every few seconds and speaking in what—to my biased ear—sounded like a perpetual whine. Her friend, who wore glasses and had thick dark hair, appeared to be nodding sympathetically. Bringing what was left of my chai, I walked over to them.

Skye was saying, "So then she said, 'That's got nothing to do with—' "

Skye's companion's eyes widened, and she elbowed Skye, who broke off midsentence to stare at me.

"Hello, Skye. Mind if I join you?"

"Umm . . ."

I pulled up a seat and sat down. I looked at her friend. She had neither Skye's perfect nose nor her flawless complexion, but behind her lenses, her dark eyes sparkled appealingly. "I'm Molly Masters. We spoke once at a PTA meeting, but I don't remember your name."

She jutted out her chin and murmured, "Heather." In the time it took me to sit down, her demeanor had shifted from caught-red-handed to defiant.

"Cutting classes?" I asked.

"Just study hall," Heather said with a shrug.

That was what kids always claimed when caught off-campus during school hours. I nodded and turned toward Skye. "Have the police had any luck catching your burglar?"

"I dunno," Skye said through gritted teeth. "I don't know what you—"

"Were the original recordings that you girls made of the PTA stolen, or had the police already taken that as evidence?"

"They were stolen," Skye said, her voice haughty and derisive. "Along with our camcorder, VCR, and DVD player. Which were, like, worth a lot more than the stupid tapes."

Not to the killer, I said to myself. "Mr. Alberti says that you told him you cut the really embarrassing parts that you recorded. Can you describe those sections to me?"

The girls exchanged glances. "Nothing having to do with *you*," Skye answered in a you-are-such-an-idiot tone of voice that was difficult for me to endure.

"I figured that much, but I'm asking because I think those tapes might have contained a major clue that could identify Patty Birch's killer."

Again, Heather gave a glance to her friend and then replied, "We went over this with the police last night."

"You did? Good."

"Yeah," Skye said. "And, anyways, you can ask Adam Embrick. I'm sure you see *him* all the time. He was the one who wouldn't let us put in the parts about his mom, the alcoholic."

"Did you film her drinking liquor at a school function?" I asked, keeping my voice steady to mask my discomfort at the implication. If the killer *had* to turn out to be a fellow PTA board member, Susan Embrick would be my very last choice.

"I dunno." Skye shrugged. "We axed the stuff about her. I was just trying to be respectful of Adam. A lot of good it did me."

"Were there any other deleted scenes?"

Heather said, "Like we already told the police, we taped that guy with the dumb-looking mustache when he was talking to some other guy about Patty. The mustached guy wanted to know how to, like, make the moves on her 'cuz she wouldn't give him the time of day."

The man with the dumb-looking mustache was obviously Chad Martinez. "What other guy?"

"I don't know. It was just some middle-aged guy."

"When did this conversation take place?"

"After school one day, I guess."

Strange. Could the second man have been Randy Birch? Chad might have approached him to ask about her. Then again, Randy was not one to come to school very often. "Do you remember what he looked like?"

"No, and it was nothing, like, major. We just took it

out because it was so pathetic . . . one old guy asking another old guy for dating tips. I mean, sheesh!"

"Anything else?" I asked Heather.

"No," Skye said, "and besides, you're kind of interrupting an important conversation."

"Okay, I'll let you get back to it in a second. I remember a couple of times in the film where Patty seemed to be a bit upset. One time she was kind of . . . glaring at someone. It was right when you both came up to her and asked if you could get on the agenda for the next meeting. Remember?"

They both stared at me with blank faces and said no.

"Another time it looked as though one of you had come into a room to speak to Patty just as someone else might have been yelling at her. A door slammed, and Patty said something like, 'a friendly face at last.' It was right before she kind of winked at the camera, and you ended the film."

"Oh, yeah," Heather said, as if recalling this for the first time. "That was me. Some woman had been shouting at her. She kind of stormed out just after I came in. I didn't catch any of it on the camera, though, and I didn't overhear anything."

"Not even a few words?"

Heather shrugged. "Not that I remember."

"Was she a member of the PTA?"

"Yeah. I'm pretty sure she was one of the ones we taped dissing Patty that time in the cafeteria."

Aha! Now I was getting someplace! "Was it Emily Crown or Jane Daly?"

Again, a blank face, so I prompted, "The one with dark hair who's a little heavy, or the one with lighter hair . . . who sometimes wears a red knit cap?"

"I don't remember. Just that I'm pretty sure it was one of them. I mean, sheesh. It's not like I knew at the time

Patty was gonna get . . . I'm sorry I can't help you and the police, but nothing we taped you guys saying seemed important enough for me to remember. You know?"

"Adam helped edit the tape, right? Could he have made a copy or shown it to his mother?"

"No way," both girls said in unison. Skye continued, "He just helped us a little in the beginning. But I had all the camcorder cassettes, and I made the final video myself."

"There were never any copies of the video?"

"Just one. I made it and kept it myself. Adam never even saw the tape."

That my daughter's boyfriend wasn't involved in this PTA-video mess was a relief to me. "Okay. Thanks for your time." I gave the girls a smile and started to rise.

"Yeah, right," Skye mumbled. "Like we had nothing better to do. You can sure tell Karen's your daughter . . . barging in on other people's lives."

That stopped me in my tracks. I glared at her. Skye was pretty, all right, but she was sadly lacking in social graces. "One last thing, Skye. My daughter's an eminently capable person and can handle her own problems. But don't make any more harassing phone calls or visits, because it's *my* home, too, and that makes your behavior *my* problem. I advise you strongly to stop and think how it must look to the guys at Carlton High when they learn how desperate and vindictive you're acting." I got up. Skye was now staring at her cup, her cheeks bright red. "It was nice meeting you, Heather."

Some of my bravura deserted me during my drive home. Had I only made things worse for Karen? I hoped not. In any case, it was too late to take back my words now.

Susan Embrick might have been lying through her teeth to me. If Skye truly had seen her imbibing, Susan was unlikely to have been sober as long as she had claimed to be. That, in turn, cast doubt on her tale of Patty's having slipped her vodka. But why lie about that?

Come to think of it, of the four girls, Skye never seemed to have been the one to talk to Susan about getting the camera. So then, when exactly had Skye managed to catch Susan drinking? Or was Skye really only referring to the time that Adam was supposedly fooling around with Skye's camera, and he caught the vodka-in-the-juice incident? Each scenario was perhaps equally likely.

The girls' account of the deleted scenes also cast a bit more suspicion on Chad, who'd forever chased Patty in vain. Also, either Emily or Jane had had a serious argument with Patty at the end of the tape. That struck me as potentially significant, because it took place within only a week or two of the murder. But how to find out which of the two women had fought with her? As Tommy would no doubt want to point out to me, if that argument had, in fact, led to murder, the killer was not about to say, "Oh, yes, Molly. Come to think of it, I was telling Patty her days were numbered right when that kid with the camera interrupted us."

I decided to let my subconscious work on the problem for a while. Once back home, I dropped into my chair in the living room with BC at my feet and doodled. I started thinking about how the women in Emily's group had joked about the changes in their physical appearance. I drew an elderly woman trying on a swimsuit, staring over one shoulder at the mirror behind her. She calls over the fitting-room partition, "Mabel, we need to go to the Lost and Found right away. My rear end is missing."

After my drawing was complete, I realized that this cartoon could give me an excuse to talk to Emily Crown. Every month, Emily published one of my cartoons in the newsletter that she faxed or e-mailed to members of her menopause group. The deadline for my next cartoon was fast approaching. My usual procedure had been to fax the sample cartoons to Patty, who gave me the okay and brought them to Emily. Because that was no longer an option, it would be reasonable to show this in person to Emily. I called her, and on the fourth ring, just as I was about to hang up, she answered.

"Hi, Emily. This is Molly Masters. I wasn't sure you'd be home today. I'd just been thinking that you were probably in your office."

"I work irregular hours. How are you?"

"Fine. After going to your menopause meeting, I thought of a—"

"The support group," she corrected. "That's what we call it. Menopause meeting sounds rather daunting."

"Okay." Not that it seemed at all less daunting to me to have a support group as opposed to a meeting, but whatever. "I have a cartoon for your next newsletter, but I'm not completely sure how well it'll go over."

"Oh?"

"I wanted to show it to you in person, because I'm not sure if I should scrap this one and try again. Do you have a few minutes free today, by any chance?"

She said she did and suggested that it would be easiest for her if I just came by her place now. I hopped into the car, with my roughed-out cartoon as my excuse for dropping in on her.

When I showed her the cartoon, she laughed and said she "couldn't imagine anyone finding it offensive." Then she invited me to stay and chat for a while. After a minute of parenting-related conversation, I said in a true anecdote, "Last night I had a nightmare about Karen, that she was the one filming Patty in that last piece of the tape, when Patty revealed that she knew she was being filmed."

"You dreamed about it?" Emily asked, leaning forward in her seat on the couch a little.

"Yes, but it took place in my own living room," I fibbed. "Where was that conversation actually recorded? Do you remember?"

"In a room at the high school."

"That's right. I remember now. But what was Patty doing in a room at school by herself?"

"As of last month, the principal was letting her use a room at the high school that used to be one of the counselors' rooms. Before the latest budget cut cost us a counselor, that is."

"Oh, yeah. I remember Patty telling me that she had her own key to the building."

"The room is available for use by all the PTA board members. I'm surprised she didn't tell you that."

"She probably did, but it must have slipped my mind." Though this conversation felt more forced by the minute, I pressed on. "When exactly do you think that conversation was recorded? I didn't notice the time stamp on the tape. Did you?"

"No idea."

I waited, but she didn't go on. Emily was being nowhere near as loquacious as she normally was. "When Stephanie and I first arrived at the . . . support group the other night, you said something about Patty. About how she took credit for other people's ideas. Remember?"

She furrowed her brow. "I doubt that was my exact wording."

"How would you word it?"

"That she took credit for *my* ideas," she replied with a sarcastic chuckle.

"Did she really? How infuriating that must have been for you."

"Not infuriating, really, just annoying at times. It wasn't all that important who got the credit, after all, and I truly believe Patty never realized when she did that."

"But that would have made it all the worse, in a way. One time someone stole a cartoon of mine and presented it as his own. At least I knew that *he* knew he'd gotten credit for something of mine. If he'd unknowingly plagiarized it, I wouldn't have even had that sense of . . . validation."

"True, but you thought a whole lot less of this man for his deliberate theft, right? If he'd unknowingly plagiarized your cartoon, you wouldn't have felt so violated, I'm sure."

"True. So that's how you could still be friends with Patty," I said, completing the thought for her. "But, knowingly or not, why would she consistently take your ideas?"

Emily lifted her hand as if to dismiss the matter. "That was Patty. She was a whirlwind of energy, who didn't always know in which direction she should take that energy."

At the support group, Emily had claimed "all" of Patty's ideas came from her originally. How literal had she been? "What about the idea for Al's students to make that video? Was that your idea?"

She froze for a moment. Her cheeks turned red, and she averted her eyes. "Guilty as charged, I'm afraid."

"Why did you suggest such a thing? When Patty was taking the heat over her supposedly suggesting it, why didn't you say it was originally your idea?"

"Molly, I've felt horrible about that. And, I guess I'm glad you're calling me on the carpet, as they say."

She didn't go on, so I prompted, "So . . . what

happened? Did you suggest it to Patty in passing or something?"

"Yes. Just before school started this year, Patty happened to say that Al's class had been her son's favorite in high school. I mentioned, half jokingly, what a great project it would have been for him to have surreptitiously taped our PTA meetings. We got to talking about other things after that, and I never dreamed the results would be that . . . damned tape."

I nodded. "Apparently, Patty went directly to Mr. Alberti's students and suggested the project to them."

Emily's mouth opened slightly in surprise. "She did?"

"According to Al's wife. She thought Patty might have done that to show off or something . . . to demonstrate to the kids how cool she still was."

Emily's face fell. "Oh, dear. Poor Patty."

"You knew Patty better than I did. Does that make any sense to you?"

Emily looked truly miserable. "Yes, Patty could be desperately insecure at times. She knew a couple of those camera girls through her son. Helping them out by suggesting a topic for a class assignment would have made her day."

"Don't you think she should have realized that—"

"Let's just drop the subject. Okay?"

"Okay." She must have not wanted to cast aspersions on her late friend. "Well, I've got to say that, of all people, Patty Birch had the least reason of anyone I know to feel insecure. I mean, the woman was nicknamed Perfect Patty, for heaven sakes."

Emily furrowed her brow.

"Sorry. I'm not very good at dropping subjects once I've got a good hold on them."

"We all have our faults. And none of us enjoy having them exposed for the world to see."

I nodded. "I guess, in that respect, we're all like the joke about the old, ugly stripper . . . in which the crowd starts yelling, 'Put it back on!' "

She smiled a little, but that quickly turned to a frown. "Molly, everyone knows you're the self-appointed murder investigator in this town. Do you really think this is the way to go about it?"

"What do you mean?"

"Confronting people like this? Asking them what they were thinking when they made negative comments about Patty? You're just stirring up trouble, aren't you?"

"I suppose so. I'm sorry. I didn't mean to imply that I thought you were guilty of anything. You've been really close to Patty, ever since she moved here. Literally, too. You're all of—what?—two blocks away?" Which also meant that she probably didn't drive that night, either, I told myself.

"Yes, we used to go for walks together, every morning. Good prevention for osteoporosis, by the way." She narrowed her eyes at me. "Do you even have the slightest interest in menopause, or did you join the group just to garner evidence against us?"

"Of *course* I'm sincerely interested in learning about menopause. What woman in her forties can afford not to be?" I couldn't resist adding, "Though I came mostly for Stephanie's sake."

Emily nodded thoughtfully. "She's got a lot of perimenopause signs, now that I think about it." She glanced at her watch, and I took the hint and said that I needed to get going. She walked me to the door, but then stopped and touched my sleeve. When our eyes met, she said gently, "Molly, I'd hate to see you become a second victim. Let the police do their jobs. If I were you, I'd stay out of this entirely."

"So would most rational human beings."

Too bad I wasn't one of them, I thought as I stepped outside into the brisk afternoon air.

Despite some of the things I'd recently heard about Patty, I knew one wonderful thing about her: She was absolutely the type of person who, had it been me instead of her, would have done anything and everything to help my children.

I also knew beyond any doubt that the only way that I, or anyone else, could help Kelly Birch was to see to it that her mother's murderer was brought to justice.

Chapter 14

Chia Cheese Pets

After school, Nathan had gone to a friend's house on the opposite side of our development. Blessed with some extra time on my hands, I gave Karen another driving lesson. She was doing well as we navigated down a congested main road. Up ahead of us was a sign for the highway, and Karen asked, "Can I please go on the Northway? Just for one exit?"

For some reason my mouth short-circuited my brain, and I heard myself say, "Okay."

"Thanks, Mom!"

Already I was getting a major case of nerves. "We'll have you stick in the right lane no matter what, and we'll get off at the next exit. I just hope I'll be able to remember how to get us home on the back roads."

My heart was racing, and I dug my fingers into the armrests. I tried to silently reassure myself. Karen truly had been making great strides in her driving, and there was nothing innately challenging about being on the Northway, except for the high speeds, increased traffic, and additional lanes. "Karen, on second thought . . ." Too late. She'd started to veer onto the ramp.

"What?!"

"Nothing. It's fine. We'll be fine." We're fully insured, and we have air bags. At least this was early enough in the day that we weren't dealing with rush hour.

I held my breath and prayed for the Saint of Traffic and Driving Conditions to intervene on our behalf. Mercifully, as we sped onto the highway, we were indeed blessed by a nice, empty slow lane. In gratitude, I silently swore that I'd obey all speed limits for a month.

Breathing once again, I said, "Okay. No cars. Just put your left blinker on, accelerate, and pull into the traffic lane."

She did so, more or less, and I complimented her. In truth, however, she had yet to master the skill of merging smoothly into a lane, seeming to believe that she could make the car hop lanes by jerking the wheel. My standards were lower these days. Any drive accomplished without being in imminent and real fear for our very lives was a good one.

We got up to the speed limit without incident. Nevertheless, I continued to feel as though we were running the rapids atop barrels of nitroglycerin. All the while, I continued to tell Karen how well she was doing and give little tidbits of instruction about highway driving.

With just a mile or two to go till the exit, we caught up with the car in front of us. "Slow down and we'll just follow this car," I said.

"This guy isn't even going fifty! Can't I pass him?"

"No! Changing lanes is for a future lesson, way down the road. So to speak."

Karen protested, but slowed down. My attention was diverted to the car ahead of us. "Hey, that's Chad Martinez driving, and it looks like his passenger is Susan Embrick."

"Adam's mom?"

"Yes."

"Should I tail them? Find out where they're going?"

"No. Like I said before, simply follow them until we reach the next exit."

Karen stayed a reasonable distance behind their bumper. They were certainly engrossed in their conversation. What could they be discussing so earnestly? They turned off at the next exit, and we followed.

"You know what, Karen? Since I never go this way and don't really know how to get back, tailing them for a while isn't such a bad idea. Just kind of lag back a bit and keep following them till I can pick up on some street names."

"Cool! I feel like a secret agent!"

"Well, don't get too attached to the notion. We're just doing this till I get my bearings, then we're trading places. This has been a long enough lesson for one day. I don't want you to overload."

Chad had put on his signal to pull into the parking lot of a grocery store.

"This is perfect, Karen. Just follow them into the parking lot. This will be a good place for us to swap drivers."

We pulled in behind them and found a section with three empty parking spaces, which was roughly the amount of open space Karen needed to park without incident. Chad, however, stopped directly in front of the grocery store. Susan got out of the car and went into the drugstore next door, while Chad left his car in the no-parking zone and dashed into the grocery store.

"Are we switching drivers now?" Karen asked as I opened my door.

"Yes, but I'll be right back. I'm going to ask Susan how to get back on a less-busy road than the Northway."

"Okay, but don't bring her out here. I don't want Adam's mom to think we're, like, weird or something."

"Oh, no chance of that." I trotted into the drugstore and found her in the indigestion-products aisle, examining some small box.

"Susan, hi."

Her eyes widened in surprise. "Molly. I didn't expect to see *you* here."

"It is somewhat off my usual beaten path. I was giving Karen a driving lesson and happened to spot you and Chad. Thought I'd ask if there was a direct route back, or if we should turn around and head back up the Northway."

"If I were you, I'd just head up to Ballston Lake Road."

"Does that intersect with this road?"

She furrowed her brow. "Yes, just a couple of miles up ahead. Haven't you lived here for something like . . . ten years now?"

"Seven or eight. Plus, I grew up here. The thing is, though, I have no sense of direction whatsoever."

"That must be a challenge."

"It is." I hesitated, curious about her being with Chad. "So, what brought *you* out this way?"

"Chad's thinking of opening another studio and wanted a second opinion . . . normally the type of thing he'd ask Patty to do, but I took classes from him when we first moved here, and he seems to think I'm outspoken with my opinions." She fluffed up her black hair and widened her eyes jokingly. "No idea where he got such an outlandish idea."

"He's thinking of putting a second studio right here?"

"No, farther south. I'd just been feeling a bit under-the-weather and asked him to pull in here."

"Hope you feel better soon. Well, have a nice evening. And thanks for the directions. I'd better get back to my car before my daughter gets bored and tries to take off without me."

"See you later." She went back to examining the box of medicine in her hands.

As I walked, I idly considered whether it would be worth my while to track down Chad and chat with him, too. All thoughts of additional sleuthing flew from my head the moment I stepped outside and saw what was happening in the parking lot.

Karen had gotten out of the car—probably to switch to the passenger seat—and pushed toward the rack a grocery cart that a shopper had deserted. The cart had a gimpy wheel and, instead of going into the rack, it headed toward Chad's car, which was just a few yards away from this storefront.

It was as if everything were taking place in slow motion, and yet my reactions were operating at an even slower speed. Karen gasped and put both hands to her face. I tried to dart around Chad's gold-colored Toyota to catch the cart. Meanwhile, someone came out of the grocery store and yelled, "No-o-o-o," as he ran. Both of us arrived at the point of impact a second too late. The car door was dented and scratched.

"Oh, my God!" Karen cried.

Chad shoved the cart away, ran his hand over the slight dent, then pivoted, his face beet red. "You idiot! Look what you've done to my car!" He rolled up a newspaper he was carrying, and I had a vision of him beating my daughter over the head with it.

"Hey!" I shouted. "It was an accident. The damage is already done. Name-calling and temper tantrums aren't going to change that."

Showing no signs of softening his temper, Chad whirled to face me. "Easy for you to say when it's not your car!" He focused again at poor Karen, who was already in tears. "You have nothing better to do than to stand out in parking lots, shoving carts into people's cars? What's the matter with you?"

"There's nothing the matter with my daughter, Chad! She had a minor lapse of judgment that led to a small scratch on your car, which—"

"What happened?" Susan cried as she ran toward us down the sidewalk.

"I scratched his car," Karen said in whimper. "It was my fault." She looked desperately at me. "Someone left the shopping cart in a handicapped space, and I thought I could just give it a little shove into the rack."

"Why didn't you keep hold of the handle? This wouldn't have happened if you'd pushed the cart all the way into the rack!" Chad cried.

"And it wouldn't have happened if your car hadn't been parked illegally in the fire lane," Susan said calmly.

"I was only going to be here for a minute! I was just buying a newspaper!" He lifted the paper rolled in his fist as if to demonstrate.

The man had a ridiculous temper. The damage was very minor, and I was having to struggle to keep my own temper at bay for his getting so carried away at my daughter. "Chad, get the damage appraised, and I'll pay for it."

"You bet you'll pay." He glared at Susan. "Let's get out of here. Now."

"Don't feel bad, Karen," Susan said. Eyeing Chad, she said evenly, "This is truly not a big deal."

"Chad, my husband's name is James Masters. Susan can help you remember that. We're in the phone book. Just call me as soon as you get an estimate." My teeth were clenched so tight, it was lucky they didn't break as I threw my door open. Karen was crying softly as she handed me the keys and we got into the car.

I tried to count to ten to calm myself. "Some people put a whole lot of importance into their cars. But it was just a little scratch. Don't worry about it, Karen. As I told Mr. Martinez, your father and I will pay for the repairs." I started the engine, and we pulled out of the lot, leaving Susan and Chad behind.

"I feel awful. It was my fault. And it would have to happen to the car Adam's mother, of all people, was riding in. I should be the one to pay for it."

"You don't have any money. You can pay me back by driving the speed limit and obeying your curfew, and using good judgment at all times. That and doing the dishes for the next two weeks."

Karen sighed, but was otherwise silent for a minute or two. Finally she said, "Can't I just give you an IOU?"

The minute we got home, Karen went straight to her room and closed her door. I picked up Nathan who, to his credit, promptly began his homework in his favorite spot: seated on the living room floor with his books on the coffee table. I called Jim, telling him about our impending auto-body bill at such great length that he moved from anger at Karen to anger at Chad and then all the way into complacency. Finally, I hung up and started working on a cartoon.

Betty, meanwhile, was being especially emphatic about wanting more dinner. She carried her food dish into the living room and then dropped it right on my foot.

Mulling the benefits of owning plants rather than animals, my subsequent doodles were of a Chia Pet. Eventually I wound up drawing a couple of men in white lab coats studying a piece of scuzzy-looking, moldy Swiss cheese. The one scientist is saying to the other: "Maybe we could try cutting it into the shape of a mouse." The caption reads: The inventors of Chia Pets work to expand their product line.

I glanced over at Nathan and thought about showing him the cartoon, but decided not to risk rejection right now. "How's Kelly seem to be doing?"

"We had a test in algebra today, and right in the

middle of it, she started crying and said she had to go to the nurse."

My heart lurched. "Did she say she felt sick?"

"No, just that she couldn't remember anything she'd studied last night and that she had to go to the nurse."

"Did she come back to class?"

"I don't think so. I tried to find her at lunchtime, but couldn't. It's weird, though. She was always really good in math."

Tears started to well in my eyes. I tried to find a distraction in my drawings, not wanting Nathan to see me cry.

"Do you think I could make her a card?" Nathan asked. "We're kind of friends, and I wish she wasn't so sad."

"I do, too. I think a card would be nice."

That evening, Karen hated the dinner I'd prepared, which meant that Nathan liked it. My children believe in taking opposite stances whenever possible. I told Karen, "You know, you're old enough to cook dinner yourself. Laura Ingalls Wilder was already a professional teacher and working for a living when she was your age."

"Oh, good argument, Mom." She rolled her eyes. Apparently she'd recovered her sense of sarcasm in the wake of her shopping-cart incident.

The phone rang. Both Jim and Nathan were mid-bite and Karen was mid-scowl, so I answered.

It was Stephanie. "Molly, get . . . spiffed up. We're going to a dance competition tonight."

"We are?"

"There isn't much time. It starts in an hour."

"An hour from now? And we're just finding out about it now?"

"I've known for a couple of days, but kept forgetting to call you." She paused. "That's not quite accurate. I kept assuming I wouldn't have to be the one to call you. I thought you'd call *me* to send me off on another wild-goose chase with you. Then you never did."

"I think I'm going to have to pass, Stephanie." I added jokingly, "I just don't think I'm up for competing tonight."

"Not you. Me."

"You're going to be *in* the competition?"

"Yes, but it's not much of a competition, in the classic sense of the word. More of a publicity stunt to get more students. Three of the dance schools in the immediate area are showing off what their students have learned so far. Chad Martinez has asked me to be his partner to fill in for Patty."

While Stephanie was talking, I wandered out of the dining room with the cordless phone. I said quietly, "That's nice, Stephanie, but Karen's in a volatile mood, and the last person in the world I want to see right now is Chad Martinez. I was giving Karen a driving lesson to-day, and—"

"Molly, we're wasting time here. This is a golden op-portunity to talk to most of the suspects. Not only will Chad be there, but so will Emily Crown, Jane Daly, and Kevin Alberti. I will be too busy dancing to look for clues."

"Emily is in Chad's class?"

"I think so. I don't know. Chad told me something about her, but I wasn't listening."

After getting the particulars and hanging up, I rejoined my family at the dinner table. "Anybody feel like going to watch an amateur adult ballroom dance competition in the high school gymnasium tonight?"

I was greeted with silence and shudders.

"That's what I thought."

                    *   *   *

I arrived at the gym roughly on time. Emily Crown and Jane Daly were seated in the audience and were wearing slacks, like me—although my slacks were technically blue jeans. There was only one section of bleachers set up, and even those were sparsely occupied.

Jane and Emily were seated together. I said hello and took a seat next to Emily. "Stephanie told me you two would be here, but I assumed you'd both be dancing tonight."

"No, we're here as cheerleaders." Emily twirled a finger in the air. "Rah."

Jane explained, "Chad chose the dancers, and we didn't make the cut."

"Jane's being modest," Emily said. "She and her husband, Aaron, would have made the cut with no problem. Chad had a bee in his bonnet about Aaron's eligibility, however."

"Oh?"

Jane nodded. "Chad felt Aaron couldn't compete because he wasn't a student of his. This competition is only for students of the three studios competing tonight."

"But Stephanie's competing, isn't she?" I asked Jane. "She wasn't Chad's student, either. As far as I know, she only went that one time when Jim and I went. And your husband was there that one time for almost as long as Stephanie was."

"Tell me about it," Jane said.

"Chad's just jealous because Aaron got private dance lessons on the sly." Emily pointed at Jane with her chin. "Now he's making the Dalys pay for it by disallowing them."

"So . . . Chad's upset because your husband went to someone other than him for dance lessons?"

"Yes," Jane replied. By her body language she made it clear that the subject was now closed.

"Oh, look!" Emily exclaimed, indicating the gym entrance with a tip of her head. "Here comes Susan. She said she might come watch tonight."

She joined us and gave me a warm hello. Our row had filled in while we talked. I squished against the railing at the end of the bleachers to give her room between Emily and me. Susan was the best dressed of any of us, wearing a mid-calf–length shift and leather boots. "I didn't realize you were a ballroom dance fan, Molly," Susan said.

"Neither did I."

"Chad calmed down considerably after we left the parking lot this afternoon, by the way."

"That's nice," I grumbled, still resenting the scene he'd thrown too greatly to be civil.

We lapsed into silence for a moment. Stephanie had been right: Nearly everyone who'd been at the meeting at Patty's that night was now here. "What about Mr. Alberti and his wife?" I asked Emily. "Are they competing tonight?"

"Yes."

"Where are they now, then? I don't even see Stephanie or Chad. I'd like to wish all of them luck." Or rather, three of those four. I'd just as soon dent Chad's thick forehead and try to knock some sense into him.

Emily gestured in the direction of the railing that pressed against my shoulder. "Just around the corner behind us. The back hall is serving as a warm-up room. Just remember to say, 'break a leg,' and not 'good luck.' Chad's very superstitious."

I stood up, but found myself nearly face-to-face with Chad. Technically, though, with the added height of the risers, I was tall enough to bop him on the head. I sat back down before the temptation to do so grew too strong.

"Hello, everyone," Chad said, beaming. "Thought I heard someone say my name."

"We were just discussing how much we'd all like to see you break your leg," I said.

Chad merely smiled and replied, "Thank you. I must warn you that the instructors and their partners are going last, so it'll be a while yet."

And, indeed, a while it was. Al and his wife were one of the first couples to dance. They did a rumba, according to the announcer. They looked terrific to me, but apparently not to the judges, who awarded ribbons to the top three couples, which meant all but two won—the Albertis and a very overweight twosome from another studio. Afterward, they joined our cheering section. I congratulated them and told them that, in my opinion, they were robbed. Al just threw up a hand and said cheerfully, "Ah, this is just for fun."

Chad and Stephanie sat with us periodically, both doing running commentaries on the quality of dancers we were seeing. By the time two hours had passed, all of us were feeling restless and making excuses to leave our seats on the hard bleachers.

Al and his wife left for good, with apologies, before the instructors danced. I was thinking that I might just have to follow suit when the announcer said, "And now, in our final event, the studio teachers will perform."

The three couples danced three times apiece. As wonderful and graceful as all of them were, I was practically nodding out. Not wanting to injure myself if I actually did fall asleep and topple over the side of the bleachers, I excused myself and watched the last dance while standing against a gymnasium wall.

Afterward, I went over to them. Stephanie and Chad took second place in the contest, and seemed very pleased.

"I thought you two did really well. Especially considering that you were here without your regular partner and really didn't even practice together."

"Thanks, but I've got to admit that Stephanie filled in for Patty more than admirably. In fact, I'm certain Patty and I wouldn't have scored as high."

"Really?" I asked, surprised that Chad would admit to anything less than perfection from his former dance partner.

"Patty was an excellent dancer, but she lacked Stephanie's experience and style."

Stephanie released a trilling laugh. "Actually, Molly, Chad and I have been practicing every available minute ever since you dragged me to class with you that night. Besides, ballroom dancing is like riding a bike."

"Oh, yeah. Bike riding. I keep forgetting how to do that," I teased.

"Well, Stephanie," Chad said, bowing to her. "Thank you for being such a divine partner."

"Thank *you*, Chad. It was my pleasure." She gave him a curtsy.

He searched my face for a moment, then grinned. "It's Molly, right?"

"Yes, Chad."

He nodded. "I'm a little overly protective of my car. I took another look at that dent your daughter put into my car door and decided it really wasn't worth repairing."

"I'd really rather not feel indebted to you for—"

He waved off my words. "I mean it. Don't give the little dent a second thought." He gave me a little bow. "If you ladies will excuse me, I'd best go chat with my fellow instructors." He crossed the room.

Stephanie maintained her smile till he was out of sight. Then she grimaced. "We took second place out of three competitors, and he's acting as though we won a national event." She shook her head, then marched off. I rounded the bleachers and saw to my disappointment that Jane, Emily, and Susan had left, and that my coat was the only one still there.

I put my coat on. It was chilly out as I walked to my car. I put my hands in my pockets and touched what felt like a paper towel. Perhaps I'd stuck it there without remembering. I pulled it out to see what it was.

In block, handwritten letters were written the words: THIS IS YOUR LAST WARNING. BACK OFF!!!

Chapter 15

At the End
of the Food Line

In his minuscule office at the police station, Tommy rubbed his forehead and sat for a long moment with his elbows on his desk and his head in his hands. He looked both exhausted and slightly ill. He had already collected the note from me and had sent it on to the lab for analysis. "Let me see if I've got this straight. Your coat was on the bleachers, unattended. Everyone who was at Patty's house the night of the murder was there, at one point or another."

"Right."

"And it was written on a paper towel, which could have come from the men's or the women's bathroom."

"Right. What do you think the chances are for your getting a fingerprint?"

"Off a paper towel? Zilch."

Tommy looked so tired and forlorn that I found myself wanting to cheer him up. "At least this lets Amber Birch off the hook. She didn't come to the dance competition at all tonight."

"Uh-huh."

"So that cuts the suspects down to Jane, Emily, Susan, Chad, and Mr. Alberti."

"You said Stephanie was there, too."

"That doesn't count. She's not a suspect."

"She still had motive, means, and opportunity."

"Yeah, but . . . come on."

He leaned forward and looked straight in my eyes. "Molly, at this point *you* are, technically, still a suspect."

Offended, I retorted, "Well, then . . . so are you. Do *you* have an alibi?" Not exactly my wittiest comeback, but I was tired, and, anyway, we can't all be Dorothy Parker.

"Yes. I was home with my wife and family. Which is where I wish I were right now!"

"Well, gee, Tommy. What can I say?" I got to my feet. "Sorry if my quasi death threat has ruined your evening!" I stormed out of his office and drove home.

The next morning dawned damp and colorless. I hadn't slept well, Tommy's words to me wreaking havoc with my nerves. Nevertheless, I was determined to put some spring back into my step. Today was going to be a nostalgic trip down memory lane, or at least down the school cafeteria line. The PTA was sponsoring a special lunchtime celebration at the junior high. This was an "All-Cultures Day." Nathan was hoping this meant chips and salsa.

Just as I drove into the junior high building's parking lot, I saw Amber Birch parking her car and waited for her. She nodded at me and said, "Hello, Molly."

"Hi. Joining Kelly for lunch today?"

"Oh, you betcha." She looked less than thrilled with the idea. "Tell me something. Whose stupid idea was this?"

"To tell you the truth, I can't remember. The PTA has had it in the works for a couple of months now. I think it was one of those collective stupid ideas that spontaneously generate from committees."

"That would explain it."

"Do you object to the luncheon in particular, or to the idea of All-Cultures Day?"

She shrugged. "Oh, I don't know. But let me ask you something . . . do you suppose that in Mexico and Cuba they have North America Day and serve hot dogs, soda pop, and macaroni-and-cheese from little blue boxes?"

I grinned at the analogy. "No, I rather doubt that they do. Some of the celebrate-diversity programs at schools are a bit silly, but when I was growing up in this town, we didn't have any of that. We just lived in our own white, middle-class community, largely unaware of other cultures and peoples."

She held the door for me, and an unbidden "Age before beauty" popped into my head. "Yeah," she said, "but that's kind of the problem. It's like we're doing this to appease our guilt for being members of the privileged class."

"Maybe so. The whole issue of cultural representation strikes me as one of those damned-if-you-do-damned-if-you-don't scenarios. If you've got any suggestions, I know the PTA would love to hear them. I remember what you said about hating meetings, but so do I. Why don't you come to the PTA meetings, anyway?"

"Maybe I will." We headed into the lunchroom in tacit agreement that the discussion was over.

I found my son in the cafeteria, waiting in line with a tray. Several parents before me had butted in line to join their children, so I did as well. Mustering all my enthusiasm, I said brightly, "Hi, Nathan. This is really terrific."

"It'd be better if they just served macaroni-and-cheese," he grumbled.

"That wouldn't be representative of the many cultures of the world."

He shrugged. "The cheese could have come from a foreign cow."

I laughed in spite of myself. "That wouldn't count."

"Whenever we do All-Cultures Day, we leave out America. We're a culture, too."

"This is supposed to be a special occasion. We can hardly have Welcome to Another Day in America."

"Why not?"

"How would we be able to tell it apart from any other day?"

"I *like* that. I don't *want* things to be different. I like macaroni-and-cheese for lunch. What's wrong with that?"

"Nutritionally, a lot. Plus, as they say, variety is the spice of life."

"I hate spicy foods," he muttered.

We were far enough in the line to see our servers. To my surprise, the usual grim-faced cafeteria workers were absent. Instead, Mr. Alberti and Chad Martinez were wielding the serving spoons. Al wore a matador's hat, and Chad a sombrero.

Al winked when our eyes met. I said, "Hi, Mr. Alberti. You're really a jack-of-all-trades at school, hey?"

"Indeed, I am." He grinned, swept off his hat, and gave a little bow, revealing the protective shower cap that covered his ring of hair. "Actually, I've got a substitute handling my class for this period. Patty Birch had asked me to do this a full month ago . . . to help us get into the spirit of All-Cultures Day."

Chad was smiling at me as we spoke. I said, "Nice sombrero, Chad."

"Thank you."

"I must say you both make very handsome cafeteria ladies."

"What can I get for you, señor?" Chad said to Nathan.

"Two tacos without any meat, lettuce, or tomatoes."

"Just the cheese and the shells?" Chad asked.

Nathan nodded, and Al complied without comment.

"And for you, signora?" Al asked me.

Wanting to make up for my son's finicky order, I said, "How about a small serving of everything?"

As we left the line, Kelly was sitting alone at the end of a table, looking despondent and picking at her food. I glanced behind me and saw to my chagrin that, although we'd entered the cafeteria at approximately the same time, Amber had dutifully gone to the end of the line.

"Let's go sit next to Kelly Birch," I suggested to Nathan.

"Okay. But the girls have their own tables, usually."

"We'll start a new trend of bipartisanship along gender lines."

"Huh?"

I reached her table and said, "Hi, Kelly. May we join you?"

"Sure," she said. Nathan was looking a bit embarrassed, so I quickly opted to appease him and sat next to Kelly. He sat directly across from me.

Neither child said anything to each other. I said, "I was hoping to see you here, Kelly. How are you doing?"

She shrugged. "I'm okay, I guess."

"Good." I wracked my brain to come up with another topic of conversation. "Are you entering any of your artwork in the crafts fair this weekend?"

"I dunno." She shrugged and stirred her spaghetti with her fork.

"Why wouldn't you?" Nathan asked. "You're the best artist in the whole school."

She smiled shyly. "I'm not really. But thanks."

By now, Amber Birch had gotten her food and started to head toward us. Kelly mumbled, "Oh, jeez! Who told her she could come!"

Thankfully, Amber didn't seem to hear the remark and

maintained her smile as she approached our table. "Hi, Kelly. Your dad got tied up at work, I'm afraid, so I offered to take his place."

"Lucky me," Kelly said, her vision riveted to her plate.

"Have a seat," I said to Amber, gesturing at the spot beside Nathan and across from Kelly. "The food's not half bad." Which was not to say that I'd decided which half was good.

Nathan said to Kelly, "My mom's judging the youth competition at the fair. You're sure to win."

I hastened to add, "I did this last year, too, and, just so you know, I never look at the names of the contestants until after I've made my decision. But Nathan's right that you really should enter." I turned to Amber and explained, "We're talking about the arts and crafts fair."

"What about entering one or two of your watercolors, Kelly?" Amber asked. "That one you did for your mom, of the daffodils, remember? That's just stunning."

Still avoiding her stepmother's eyes, Kelly said, "I can't show that one. It was Mom's. It belongs in her house."

An awkward silence fell over us, and we all pretended to be too concerned with eating to talk. Amber said, "I wish they had a multicultural salad here."

"Me, too," I said. Instead, my plate was an international incident waiting to happen to my stomach—Chinese egg rolls, tacos, Spanish rice, spaghetti, French bread.

Nathan said, "Hey, Kelly. Listen to this." Nathan forced a burp. "That's a multicultural burp."

To my surprise, Kelly laughed, as did Amber. Amber started chatting about the troubles she'd recently had trying to use a snowboard for the first time.

"I'm gonna go outside," Kelly interrupted. "See you later."

"Bye, Kelly," Amber said. She sighed and met my eyes.

We couldn't talk freely with Nathan here. She looked at him and said, "Nathan, I got the chance to watch your skiing last week. You're really good."

"Thanks!" Nathan beamed.

She turned to me. "Your son's a natural on the slopes. Has he ever thought about joining a ski team?"

"Yeah, right," Nathan grumbled.

"He's got the wrong parents for that, I'm afraid. Neither Jim nor I are enough into skiing to fork over the money for season tickets, and I just can't see driving him round-trip two-plus hours a few times a week for training."

"I could drive him myself when I go up. Or we could all go. You could take some lessons from me."

"Maybe," I said, not meaning it.

Al, who'd been replaced behind the counter, came over to our table. He said to us, "It all seems to be going well, don't you think?"

"Absolutely. I'd say it was a success."

He looked around the room. "Yes. And it's nice for me to get a peek at my future students."

"My son, Nathan, is in the eighth grade."

"Ah." He rocked on his heels and smiled at Nathan. "Do you enjoy studying history, Nathan?"

He shrugged. "I guess."

Al's gaze shifted to Amber, and he snapped his fingers. "I just placed your face. We bumped into each other at the school last night. At the dance competition."

My heart quickened. Was it my imagination, or had Amber blanched? "You were there, too?" I asked.

"Just for a minute. I'd been speaking to a counselor at the junior high, saw a poster advertising the dance, and decided to peek in on it before I went home."

Nathan got to his feet. "Save my seat, Mom. I'm gonna go back and get another taco."

Amber rose, as well, but said to Mr. Alberti, "Why don't you take my seat?"

"No, thanks. I'd better get back to the high school. Good seeing you again, Molly, and meeting your son."

"Sure thing," I muttered to Al, too unnerved at the realization that Amber, too, had been at that blasted competition and could have left me that note.

She said, "I'll give serious thought to becoming active in the PTA. It might just be the best thing for me, to get out of my rut in this town."

"Great." I watched her leave, then pushed my tray away. My stomach was suddenly feeling a bit queasy. No wonder someone had taken the ludicrous risk of writing me a threatening note. None of the suspects had been eliminated, and whoever wrote it was successfully messing with my head!

Just as Nathan returned with his second helping, Susan Embrick arrived at the cafeteria, camcorder in hand. I waved. She came over to our table, gesturing for a large boy a couple of tables down from ours to come with her. Undoubtedly this was Raine Embrick. He made a face, grumbled something to the three other oversized boys at his table, then obliged, carrying his tray of dirty dishes. Although some of his facial characteristics resembled Adam's, Raine was not as handsome and, to my best estimate, must outweigh him, despite being three grade levels behind.

Susan gave her son a pat on the shoulder. "This is my son, Raine. This is my friend, Molly Masters, and her son, Nathan."

He nodded and said, "Hello," in barely audible tones, not looking at either of us.

"You two know each other, right?" I said to Nathan, urging him with my eyes to say hello.

"Yeah. Hi."

"Hi."

Nathan stood up and grabbed his tray. "I've got to get to class."

"Yeah," Raine said. "Me, too."

"Have a good afternoon, Nathan," I called after him, getting up to stand beside Susan.

We watched the boys leave, more or less together. Two Nathans could fit into one Raine, possibly with plenty of room for Karen.

Susan said, "At least they're somewhat on speaking terms."

"Yes. Nathan hasn't said anything more to me about any troubles, so let's hope it stays that way." Quickly changing subjects, I said, "Are you done with your videotaping?"

"Almost. I filmed most of the classrooms this morning and just have to get some footage of the cafeteria, then we're recorded for all posterity."

"I'm sure it'll be riveting. By the way, did you take the tape that Adam made to the police?"

She stiffened a little. "No, but I really don't see that it'd be any help in their investigation."

"Probably not, but still . . . they can judge that for themselves."

"You're right. I'll try to find it and get it to them. Just . . . don't mention anything to your friend Tommy, in case I erased the recording. Okay?"

"Erased it?"

"Taped something over it." She gestured with her camera. "We've run out of blank tapes for the camera, so we've been reusing them. That recording was made back before Christmas, so it could well be gone by now."

"Oh. Sure." Maybe I was unduly skeptical, but my instincts were warning me that all was not right.

She grabbed my arm and said conspiratorially, "I guess

it's official, now, that Adam and Karen are going to the prom together. Exciting, isn't it?"

"Yes. Adam seems like a terrific guy."

"He is, and, again, I'm just so relieved that Adam's developing a more mature sense of what type of girl he should be dating."

"Well, I have to say that Skye rubbed me the wrong way, too."

"Oh, that reminds me . . . did Emily ever find you last night?"

"Pardon?"

"She said she had to take off, but that she had a question about your latest fax for our group. None of us knew where you went."

"I was standing right against the wall, in back of the bleachers. My coat was still there, wasn't it?"

She looked at my charcoal-colored wool blazer, which I'd been wearing last night when someone stuck a threatening note in my pocket.

"Probably so," Susan said.

"Emily hasn't spoken to me, but last night someone stuck a note inside my coat that I couldn't decipher. Did you happen to see her leave me a note last night?"

"No, but she very well might have."

I saw Stephanie enter the cafeteria, which was surprising. She didn't have any children in junior high and was as likely to voluntarily attend a luncheon like this as she was to shave her head. She spotted me and gestured for me to come with her. Stifling a grimace, I said to Susan, "I'm being beckoned. See you later, Susan."

Stephanie remained in the doorway while waiting for me. Apparently she couldn't deign to actually enter the cafeteria. There was something about her expression that made her look even more self-satisfied than normal. She immediately said, "You know, Molly, you really should start going to a beauty salon."

"Bernie at the butcher's block at the Shop 'n' Go is a lot faster and cheaper. Just one chop with the old cleaver and I'm done and out of there."

"Molly, make fun of me all you want, but it's been my experience that if I don't take my own appearance seriously, nobody else will, either."

"What do mean by 'take your appearance seriously'? Do you want people to burst into tears at the sight of you?"

She gave me a wry smile. "No, just applause."

"Oh, well, that's a worthy goal. Is that the reason you wanted to speak to me? To tell me that I should change hair stylists?"

"Hardly, my dear. I thought all women knew that the beauty shop was gossip central."

"That might be, but gossip isn't—"

She held up her palms. "Molly, if you would just listen to me for a moment, you'll find out that I've all but solved the case."

"Pardon?"

"All on my own, since you've proven to be dead weight. I found the big clue we've been looking for to identify Patty's killer."

Much as I was tempted to lash out for being termed "dead weight," I was sufficiently intrigued and asked, "Which clue is that? The killer's physical description?"

"No, but the next best thing: the killer's motive."

Chapter 16

Pinpointing the Problem

I glanced into the lobby behind us. There were too many students and parents milling about to warrant the risk of being overheard. Furthermore, in the cafeteria, Susan Embrick stood in the middle of the room, her camcorder in hand, panning in a slow circle.

"Let's continue this conversation in my car," I said to Stephanie.

She grimaced at that suggestion. "My car's right out front. I'll give you a ride to yours while I fill you in on everything."

Stephanie's BMW was in the no-parking zone by the entrance. The moment we'd shut our doors behind us, I asked, "Why do you think Patty was killed?"

Playing the moment at its most casual, Stephanie put her keys in the ignition, then studied her manicured nails. "By a jealous wife or, perhaps, her lover. She was having an affair."

"How do you know that?"

She released an exaggerated sigh and studied my face. "I thought I already explained that."

"You heard the rumor at your hairdresser's?"

"Yes."

"That's hardly an oracle, Stephanie. I mean, come on. It's just a batch of women yakking while they get their hair done and speculating about a horrible murder

207

that took place two weeks ago. I can only imagine what Tommy would say if we were to try to pass off something like that to him as evidence."

She clicked her tongue and started the engine. "That's not what happened at all, Molly. Furthermore, you're going to owe me an apology for being so condescending when you hear how clever I was."

I dug my fingers into her leather upholstery and stared through her windshield. "Sorry. Go on."

She sniffed, then asked, "Where's your car?"

Still annoyed at her, I merely pointed.

She made me wait until she'd pulled into that parking lot before she spoke again. "I was waiting for my appointment, and two women were sitting next to me. They weren't talking about anything substantive, but I kept thinking—where have I heard that voice before? Then, suddenly, I remembered."

I turned to face her and asked excitedly, "One of the women was that unidentified voice on the tape?"

Not to be rushed, Stephanie said, "I recognized the voice from the tape. She was the woman who called us 'amoral' at the end of one of our meetings. Remember?"

"Of course I do. So who is she?"

"Her name's Denise Goodman, but that's not important." Stephanie stopped her car directly behind mine and shut off the engine. She rotated in her seat to face me, putting an elbow on her tan leather backrest. "I struck up a conversation with her. I said that I recognized her from a PTA meeting, which wasn't true, but she fell for it. She launched into a tirade about how she'd quit attending our meetings because she hadn't been able to stand to be in the same room as Patty Birch, when she knew for a fact that Patty had been having an affair with a married man."

"Did she say who this man was?"

"No, she claimed that he was the husband of another PTA officer, and that she wouldn't give me the name because she didn't like to spread vicious rumors."

I grumbled, "She didn't seem to mind spreading vicious rumors at the PTA meeting."

Stephanie snorted. "Maybe she draws the line at gossiping about the recently deceased."

"They'd be the ones least inclined to care," I retorted. "How did she find out about Patty and this . . . married man?"

"She saw them together a half dozen times, going into that restaurant off of Clifton Road . . . Lucinda's."

"Lucinda's? I've never heard of it."

"It opened about six months ago. I hear it's quite good. But the point is, it's next door to where this woman lives. She's been on a campaign to put the place out of business, so she keeps track of the license plates of cars and hopes to trap them on some sort of code violation . . . parking exceeding the number of allocation, noise ordinances, et cetera."

"That's all very interesting, Stephanie, but what good does the information do us? We don't even know who this man is, and Denise Goodman sounds like some sort of a crackpot. For all we know, she might be hallucinating. Or maybe Patty was with her ex-husband. She was trying to win him back, after all. Or maybe it was Chad Martinez, and this . . . Denise person only *thought* he was married, for some reason."

"You're forgetting something, Molly. She was quite clear that he was married to a PTA officer. That's exactly the way she put it. Apparently, she saw the two of them . . . the man and his PTA-officer wife . . . at Lucinda's on their anniversary."

Maybe I was just dense, but this was getting me more and more confused. "How could she have known that it was their anniversary, let alone that they were married? Did she stop them in the parking lot or something?"

"Precisely. They said as much when Denise confronted them in the parking lot." I raised my eyebrows, and Stephanie held up her palm. "As you already gathered, Denise is more than a little odd. She objects to the traffic and noise at Lucinda's, so she's being a gadfly, hanging out in their parking lot and blatantly logging customers' license plate numbers. She says she's always very polite whenever the customers ask what she's doing, but that she explains what a hardship the place is for her, and how she's hoping it will go under. That night, apparently, the two-timer's wife told Denise that they were there for a romantic evening on their anniversary and didn't have the time or patience to hear about her personal troubles."

I leaned back into the cushy bucket seat, trying to analyze this information. "Did Denise spill the beans that night? Mention right then that she'd seen the husband numerous times with another woman?"

"I . . . didn't ask."

I furrowed my brow. "Even if Denise said something about seeing the husband's car in the parking lot before, that could have tipped off his wife, who then could have found out it was Patty. Did Denise say when this took place? What month, at least?"

Her expression fell a little, and she shook her head. "I didn't think to ask. When it comes to married PTA officers, there aren't many possible candidates . . . just Jane, Emily, and Susan. And you, of course, but obviously we can rule Jim out as a philanderer since you've never eaten at Lucinda's."

Annoyed that she'd felt obliged to bring my name up, I snapped, "Since there *are* only three names, if we knew when the conversation took place, we could find out when each of their anniversaries were and identify who it was."

"Or you could simply call the three of them and say that you and Jim are trying to find a nice restaurant for your anniversary and do they have any suggestions. One of them is sure to mention Lucinda's."

"My anniversary isn't for five months."

"So?" She flicked her wrist as if to sweep me out her car with an unseen broom. "I've got to go, Molly. Now that I've done my part, you can determine which of the three Denise was talking about, then notify the police."

"No, it'd be best if you were the one to tell the police about this, since you're the one who actually spoke to Denise Goodman. Furthermore, you should do that right now, in case you're correct about this being the killer's motive."

Her jaw dropped and she started to protest, but then she threw up her hands and said, "Fine. I'll call our fine-feathered friend, Sergeant Newton, this afternoon." She started her car.

"Let's hope he takes this tip seriously, even though it's so flimsy."

"Flimsy?"

"We don't even know if this had anything whatsoever to do with the murder."

She chuckled. "Now, Molly. Bear in mind that the victim was *Perfect* Patty, somebody the whole town seems to think *I* was jealous of, and who turned out to have been the proverbial 'other woman.' Why else would anyone hate her so much as to kill her?"

The question made me cringe a little as I thought about the underlying level of resentment that some of the people I'd talked to seemed to have toward Patty. All I said, though, was "Good point."

Something must have registered on my face, for Stephanie said, "Come to think of it, you didn't bat an eye when I told you about this. Had you already learned she was fooling around with someone?"

"No, it's just . . ." I let my voice fade. "Maybe as I get older, I've learned enough about human nature that nothing shocks me."

She put her car in reverse as if ready to peel off. "I suppose that's something of a truism. Toodles."

I got out of her car and into mine, mentally trying to assess the likelihood of one of those three women having wound up in a triangle with Patty Birch. If the story was true—as opposed to a fabrication by a strange woman Stephanie had befriended in a beauty salon—the most logical choice would be Susan Embrick. Patty might never even have met Emily's or Jane's husband; I had never met Emily's spouse and had met Jane's husband only briefly that one time at Chad's dance studio. In contrast, Susan and Patty had a long and strained history, and Susan's husband and Patty's ex-husband had worked together for years.

During my short drive home, I tried in vain to come up with a better plan than Stephanie's for determining which female PTA officer Denise Goodman could have meant. I'd had enough social contact with Susan Embrick to feel comfortable with the notion of calling her to ask her opinion about restaurants. If I were to call Emily or Jane, however, and one of them was the killer, it would look so suspicious that I might as well announce, "Say, there. You wouldn't happen to have gone to an anniversary dinner at Lucinda's only to discover your hubby was cheating on you with Patty Birch, would you?"

At home, I found myself hoping that the phone would ring, and Lauren or Tommy himself would be calling to say that, thanks to Stephanie's tip, the police had at long last made an arrest. That call, however, never came. Eventually I put my frustrations into a cartoon. I drew an exhausted-looking woman with Band-Aids all over both arms and lying on a bed in a hospital room. A doctor says to her, "Okay, Mrs. Schlinklebee, it's too bad we've had to give you seventy-nine blood tests, but we've isolated the problem now of why you've been feeling light-headed and sluggish. Your test results indicate that you have a shortage of blood."

Afterward, having resigned myself, I called Susan, who had three suggestions for restaurants we might want to try and went into detail with each, but said nothing about Lucinda's. I then asked specifically about Lucinda's, and she said she'd never been there, but had heard "only positive" comments.

I thanked her and hung up, feeling slightly encouraged. She'd seemed completely at ease during our conversation, so she was either extraordinarily good at masking her reactions and modulating her voice, or she was innocent.

Skye's friend, Heather, had said it was either Emily or Jane whom she'd witnessed storming out of the room following an argument with Patty. Also, Emily had supposedly searched for me last night to ask about my cartoon, but had yet to phone me to ask. What if she'd made up the excuse about looking for me so that she could cover for slipping that threat in my coat pocket? Maybe getting writing samples from her and the other suspects would help the police identify the killer.

I decided that I would get in touch with Emily. As she was a marriage counselor, it was reasonable to think that she would know which restaurants in town were suitably romantic for an anniversary dinner. I called Emily at home, but got no answer. I then tried her work number, but her phone mail instantly picked up, so I left a message for her to call me "when she had some free time."

Within two or three minutes, the phone rang. I answered, and the caller said, "Molly, hi. It's Emily Crown.
Is everything all right?" Her voice was so full of concern
that I instantly regretted my decision to leave a message.

"Yes, everything's fine. It's just that . . . Jim and I are
having some problems, and I thought I should . . . make
a romantic evening, you know? So I was wondering if
you, as a marriage counselor, knew of any especially romantic restaurants."

"Oh, well, in that case, I'd recommend that you pull
all the stops. Have someone watch the kids this weekend. Then don't stop at making dinner reservations, but
rather make hotel reservations as well at a four-star hotel
in Albany."

Ooh. Thoughtful suggestion, but one that got me
nowhere when it came to asking about a particular
restaurant right here in Carlton. "I'm not sure if I want
to get *that* romantic. Have you ever been to Lucinda's
Restaurant?"

"No, I haven't. Seriously, Molly, even for a perfectly
healthy marriage, an occasional night away from home
is a great way to *keep* it healthy."

By all indications, Emily was also telling the truth
about never having eaten at Lucinda's. That left Jane,
but how could I make my finding out whether or not
she'd ever eaten at Lucinda's seem like idle conversation?
It would sound ridiculously suspicious if I were to call
her up out of the blue to ask. I would have to contrive
a way to bump into Jane instead. "When's your next
menopause meeting?"

"Support group. Not till next month. Why?"

A month from now to speak to Jane was far too
late. "I . . . seem so emotional these days, I could use
some . . . group support."

She hesitated. "Molly? Are you sure you don't, perhaps, need to see a therapist?"

Emily's voice had slipped into such soothing, sympathetic tones that I almost *did* become emotional. On second thought, this could be an opportunity to get a handwriting sample from her. Tommy could compare that with the note.

"Maybe so, Emily. Do you think you could write some names down for me? This is kind of embarrassing, but if you can use . . . big block-letter handwriting, that'd especially be good. I seem to have misplaced my reading glasses." I covered my eyes with my free hand. I was making a total idiot of myself! Not to mention that, if she had written that threatening note, I'd completely tipped my hand. I should never try to do sleuthing off the cuff like this!

"Let me just give you some names right now. Do you want to see a marriage counselor, or a personal therapist?"

A phone recommendation would do me no good. "Um, a marriage counselor. The thing is, though, I'm really not sure whether Jim would . . . go for this, or what type of counselor he'd feel comfortable with. But this is . . . something of an emergency. Maybe I could stop by your office today just for a minute or two. Would that work?"

Again she hesitated, but then said, "That would be fine, Molly, if that would help you. My last appointment of the day is waiting for me now. Why don't you come here afterward, at six P.M. We'll work up some suggestions for you then. All right?"

Now her voice sounded so soothing that I began to suspect she thought I was on the verge of a nervous breakdown. Who knows? Maybe I *was*. In any case, I played along and got her office address, thanking her profusely.

I stared at my phone in its cradle. Shouldn't my mention of her menopause group have reminded her of the question she'd supposedly needed to ask me about my cartoon?

Therapists were trained not to give their reactions and to modulate their voices. My question about Lucinda's might have signaled her that she was all but caught, and so her only hope was to lure me to her office and make me her second victim. Yikes! On the other hand, if she was completely innocent and simply trying to help me out of a dark period in my life, I would never forgive myself for calling the cops on her . . . telling Tommy now that I had reason to suspect her, so please send police to her office to watch over me.

Inwardly cursing at myself for getting myself into this jam in the first place, I called Jim. He answered with a cheerful, "Hi, sweetie," having Caller ID on his work phone.

"Hi. Is it still true that you'd rather join me in my investigations than try to stop me?"

He paused. "I would always rather you stopped. It's just that, short of tying you in a chair, that hasn't been possible."

"Okay, so you'd rather go with me to a quickee appointment with Emily Crown than have me go by myself, right?"

"That would depend on what type of an appointment this was. What does she do? She isn't a proctologist, is she?"

"She's a marriage counselor."

There was a long pause. "I think I'd rather see a proctologist. Are you trying to tell me something?"

"Not about our marriage, no. I'll explain it all when

you come pick me up. I have to be there at six P.M. tonight. Can you make that?"

"What else would I rather do on a Friday evening than go to a marriage counselor?"

The moment I got into Jim's car to drive us to Emily's office, Jim asked, "Okay, Molly, what are you up to?"

I flew into an explanation of Denise Goodman and the three women under extra suspicion as a result. Our discussion became heated, however, when I went on to explain about the note in my pocket and why Emily could have been the one to leave it there. As Jim pointed out, I'd neglected to tell him about that particular incident.

"You were asleep when I got home from the police station, Jim. I didn't want to wake you, and the next morning, it slipped my mind."

"You got a second death threat, and it *slipped your mind*?! Maybe we do need to see a marriage counselor!" He braked a little harder than strictly necessary at the traffic light.

"Whether or not that's the case, the idea here is for me to get a handwritten list of referrals."

He smacked the heels of both hands on the steering wheel. "This is ridiculous! The police can just *ask* Emily for a writing sample!"

"Sure, but this way she won't know what it's for and won't be disguising her handwriting."

Jim just made a "gaa" sound and looked at me as though I were the biggest idiot in the world.

"I didn't get us into this meeting with Emily with the intention of getting a writing sample. It just seemed like the opportunity was presenting itself to me, so I went for it."

Jim growled, "And what are you going to do if she

tries to print the referrals from her computer database? Fling her keyboard out the window?"

"I don't know, but I told her I'd lost my reading glasses and needed her to write it down for me in large print. Besides, I doubt she'll have information about her competitors on her database."

Jim let out a derisive laugh. "This is not going to work, Molly! If she *is* the one who wrote you that death threat, and you go to great lengths to get her handwriting, she's going to know what's going on!"

"She might already know," I mumbled, silently acknowledging Jim's point. I could probably snatch some handwriting sample from her office when she wasn't looking, though.

"Come again?" Jim asked through clenched teeth.

"She might be expecting me to come alone and want to get rid of me before I turn evidence over to the police that points at her."

"*What* evidence?"

"That's just it. I don't have any yet, but if she is the killer, she might not realize that. Due to the fact that I called her and expressly asked her if she'd eaten at Lucinda's."

"Wait. You expect me to possibly have to defend you from some armed woman intent on killing you?"

He spoke with such anger that I asked, "Do you mean you *wouldn't* defend me against a possible murderer?"

Jim said nothing, but worked the muscles in his jaw. A vein in his forehead looked primed to burst.

"She's not going to make an attempt on my life with you there, Jim. It'd be impossible to explain how we both wound up dead in her office."

"Not impossible. Off the top of my head, I can think of a couple possible scenarios."

We pulled into a space in the parking lot, shut off the engine, and sat still, glowering through the windshield.

"Well, Jim. On the bright side, we're not going to have any trouble playing the part of a squabbling couple."

Chapter 17

Roller–Skating with Buffaloes

We were both smoldering as we entered Emily's waiting room. In the self-righteous argument that was running through my head, I shouted to Jim: You tell me you want to help me with my investigations, then you get all huffy at me when it doesn't go smoothly! If I had that much control over things, we wouldn't be here at all, because Patty would never have been murdered!

Emily opened the door to her inner office.

"Hello, Molly." She shifted her vision to Jim and, before I could introduce him, held out her hand. If she was surprised to see him, she masked it. "You must be Jim Masters. I'm Emily Crown." They shook hands, and Emily ushered us into her small-but-pleasant office. I checked for a reachable writing sample on her desk or in her trash can, but found none.

"Thanks for seeing us," Jim said.

"My pleasure."

Jim and I exchanged glares as the three of us took seats in a semicircle in front of her desk. Emily had either spoken with automatic graciousness, or she was the only one of the three of us who could find any "pleasure" in this visit.

Looking smart and at ease in her gray skirt and pale yellow silk blouse, Emily crossed her legs at her ankles. "As Molly has no doubt told you, we're going to try to identify a few issues tonight and possibly look into an appropriate referral. Molly seems to feel that she would like to see a marriage counselor. Jim, how do you feel about the idea?"

He looked at me, then back at Emily. Through a tight jaw, he answered, "Whatever she thinks is fine."

Emily waited a moment, but as I could have told her, that was as much as Jim was going to say unprompted. "Do you think your marriage could benefit from seeing a counselor?"

He paused as if giving the question tremendous thought, and I had to bite my tongue to keep quiet. Inwardly I urged him to say either yes or no, but not to make us sit through this long silence. "If Molly thinks so, then yes."

"Do you often find yourself deferring to your wife's judgment in order to keep the peace?"

He gave the little half smile that always signaled he was fuming but was determined to keep a lid on his anger. "All the time."

"Good for you, Jim. That's exactly what keeps a lot of marriages going." She smiled. "I read a research report—quite extensive, actually—that showed that all these communication exercises we counselors have relied on for so long—'When you do X, I feel Y,' or, 'I heard you say X, and my reaction to that is Y'— are overrated. What really works is just the husband's willingness to listen to his wife and go along with her suggestions."

That, I thought, was because we wives were the ones who made the suggestions, as opposed to sitting around with a tight jaw, and more often than not came up with excellent suggestions—present circumstances excepted. Generously, however, I asked, "Isn't the same true in reverse? For the wife to go along with the husband's suggestions?"

"Not typically. Women tend to articulate their feelings so much more naturally than men do that we're the more natural navigators. Men are best behind the wheel, keeping things going."

"That's because we women can ask for directions."

"Right, whereas the men feel that they should always know precisely how to get where they want to go." Again, she shifted her attention to Jim. "If there were one thing about your marriage you'd want a counselor to assist you with, what would it be?"

He looked at me, and I gave him a slight nod, hoping he wouldn't miss this opportunity to "steer" the conversation in the direction I'd preselected. He said, "I'd like her to stop always making every murder case her own personal vendetta."

Emily raised an eyebrow and looked at me. "Do you do that?"

"I'm afraid so, but it isn't because I have a death wish or anything. It's just that . . . I want to help out Kelly Birch. She's a friend of my son's, and I don't see how she can even begin to heal until her mother's killer is behind bars. I mean, don't you agree that Kelly needs that to happen?"

"Absolutely, though the police are better suited to seeing to it that someone is arrested than any of us civilians are."

Jim snorted and nodded, but I said, largely for his benefit, "Not necessarily. For example, this case might have been long solved if the police saw fit to collect all of the outtakes that the girls recorded."

Emily replied, "I didn't realize that they'd lost evidence. But let's get back to the two of you, Molly."

"That's okay. We're not really seeing this as an actual session, anyway."

She blinked, but otherwise acted as though she hadn't heard me. "Same question I asked of Jim. If there was one thing that you'd like a counselor's help with, what would it be?"

"At the moment, I'd like help with knowing who killed Patty."

"Okay," Emily said slowly. "I'm sure that's true. The subject now is a marriage counselor, however."

"But this *is* affecting my marriage. Right, Jim?"

"You can say that again," Jim grumbled.

"But that would be redundant," I snapped.

In that therapeutic voice of hers, Emily said, "All of us like to feel in control. That's part of human nature. When someone we know dies, let alone at someone else's hand, that's unsettling. It can affect all aspects of our lives, our relationships."

"Right. So, for example, Patty Birch could have been killed in a fit of passion, by a jealous wife who'd found out that Patty and her husband were having an affair."

Emily looked at me. "Yes, but do you see what you're doing here, Molly? How you're diverting attention away from your marriage and your spouse?"

"I take it you think that's bad?"

Emily gave a casual gesture. "We try not to use such judgmental terms as 'bad.' "

Clearly, I was not going to get a telling reaction from Emily as to whether she was guilty or innocent. Might as well try to get a handwriting sample and get out of here. "Sweetie? Would you rather we go to see a man or a woman counselor?"

"Or, if you'd prefer," Emily interjected, "there is a married couple I can recommend who have a therapy practice that they run together."

Jim avoided my gaze and said to Emily, "I need time to think about this. Could you please give us recommendations for two male and two female counselors?"

"Certainly." Emily rose and went to her desk. "I anticipated that request and printed these out for you."

Jim shot me a nonverbal "I told you so," and I countered with a silent, "Well, Jeez! I'm not the boss of her!"

She grabbed a sheet of paper from the top of one drawer and handed it to me. Everything was neatly typed, though in big block letters. We'd wasted our time. Couldn't my stupid ideas *ever* turn out to be smart, after all? Jim and I stood up.

In a last-ditch effort, I said to Emily, "I think we'll probably go with this first guy on the list, but I've never heard of the street he's on."

"It's just three streets north from here," Emily said.

Jim, a.k.a. Mr. Won't Ask for Directions, was trying to get a look at the address in question, which would ruin my plan for getting Emily to write them down.

While practically throwing an elbow to block Jim from grabbing the sheet from me, I asked Emily, "Could you possibly draw me a map of how to get there from here?"

Emily smiled patiently. "Of course." She took the sheet back and drew me a map, complete with street names. In block letters. Ha! She returned it to me.

Jim held out his hand to Emily. "Thanks for your time, Ms. Crown. This has been helpful and very insightful."

She furrowed her brow a little, but shook his hand and said good-bye to us graciously.

We left the building in silence and headed across the parking lot to our car. "Well," I said, "I managed to get a writing sample, but the whole thing made me feel like a total moron."

Jim patted my back. "Welcome to my world. Now let's get the writing sample to Tommy Newton."

I tossed and turned most of the night, struggling to unravel what seemed to be a hopeless tangle of partial clues. The only good thing that had come of the evening was that Tommy hadn't been in his office, so I didn't have to suffer through his repeating my husband's lecture about how flawed my logic had been to think that a writing sample from Emily might be helpful. I instead left him a note with the sample, stating the three reasons that Emily was a prime suspect: the rumor about Lucinda's, Emily's having gone to look for me right when the note could have been shoved into my pocket, and that she or Jane had heatedly argued with Patty shortly before Patty's murder.

With Jim still half asleep the next morning—Saturday being his only day to sleep in—I told him that I was going to the arts and crafts fair before it opened to offer my help with setting up. My goal was to bump into Jane Daly. As an employee of the major sponsor of the fair, in years past she'd been one of the volunteers to oversee the site. If the opportunity presented itself, I could casually mention Lucinda's.

The fair itself was taking place in an abandoned one-story building a couple of miles outside of town. The building had originally been a feed store when Carlton was more rural, but had housed more than one failed business in the interim.

Already the parking lot was nearly half full and abuzz with activity as exhibitors brought in their works. To my good fortune, Jane Daly was standing sentry outside by the front door. Over her denim coat and broomstick skirt, she wore a green vest that identified her as a volunteer. Her dark blond hair was in a haphazard bun.

She gave me a big smile, at least by her standards, when I walked up to her. "Morning, Molly. We're not open to the public for another hour."

"I know, but I thought I'd see if you could use an extra pair of hands."

"Not really. But thanks. Everything seems to be going surprisingly smoothly."

"Oh, good."

"Aren't you judging again this year?" Jane asked.

"Yes, but just the youth division. Did you enter anything yourself?"

"Oh, sure. It's pretty much expected of me. The crafts store wouldn't sponsor this event in the first place if it weren't such a cash cow. Wouldn't do to not even have their own employees care to exhibit their wares."

"Don't they consider that a conflict of interest, though?"

She shrugged. "We employees aren't allowed to be judges, so I guess the owner believes that protects us from accusations of impropriety. Last year I suggested switching that around—having us employees judge and not be allowed to enter the contest—but my boss wouldn't hear of it. He was worried we'd be accused of selecting winners that had obviously used expensive materials purchased from our store."

"I guess I can see the logic. I'm supposed to come and judge tonight after you close your doors to the public, right?"

"Right. Between eight and ten P.M."

That was close enough to an opening to discuss restaurants, I decided. "Okay. We'll just have to eat earlier than usual tonight. Speaking of which, Jim and I are trying to find a new restaurant to try. We thought we'd go to that new place, Lucinda's."

She showed no reaction to the name. "Oh?"

"Provided we can find the place, that is. You wouldn't happen to know where it is, or if the food's any good, would you?"

"I haven't even heard of it. Aaron and I don't go out to dinner much, I'm afraid."

Just then a couple of girls ran up to Jane to ask for directions to the bathroom. She and I said quick good-byes, then I returned to my car and headed home. Neither Jane, nor Susan, nor Emily had shown the slightest uneasiness on the topic of Lucinda's Restaurant. Maybe the whole thing was indeed a dead end. For some reason, the concept of a "dead end" reminded me that my new parabolic skis were supposed to be ready today.

"Molly, you're picking up your new skis!" Amber said. I'd found her in the skiwear department.

"Yes, though I hope I'm not making a mistake. So far, I haven't had any serious injuries skiing. That's going to catch up with me sooner or later."

She said with a smile, "Provided you stay away from snowboarding, there's no reason to think that you're going to get injured on the slopes."

"No reason except my aging body and lack of training and athletic ability."

"Seriously, Molly, you're in fine shape for someone your age."

I narrowed my eyes. "I don't even know how to respond to that."

"All you really need to do is make sure your muscles are warmed up before you hit the slopes. Let me show you the pre-skiing stretches you need to go through."

She went effortlessly through a series of Gumby-like positions, which made me feel all the older and out-of-shape to watch. I kept up a steady patter of "Okays" and "I sees," but in fact had not listened to her instructions. Next thing I knew, she ambushed me by uttering a cheerful, "Now you try it, Molly."

"Oh, there's no point in my stretching now. I won't be going skiing till next weekend, at the earliest. No sense in getting all limber just to walk across your parking lot."

"Don't be embarrassed. There's nobody looking. Just stand with your feet a little more than shoulder-width apart and bend at the waist. I want to make certain you know how to do these exercises. Sometimes people rush things and do more harm than good by bouncing."

"I won't bounce, I promise."

She said nothing and looked at me expectantly.

Grudgingly I did as asked and bent down as far as I could.

"That's as far as you can stretch?" she asked incredulously.

"That's it."

"My God. I've seen overweight, sixty-year-old men who were more flexible than you."

"Maybe so, but I'll bet they 'bounce' more than I did."

"Do yourself a favor and, every morning, do those simple stretches I showed you."

"To be honest, Amber, I've resigned myself to the fact that I'll never be limber. But it doesn't matter all that much, because I'm not a skier like you, or even into dancing, like half of the entire Carlton PTA."

"*Half* of the members of the PTA dance?" Amber frowned slightly. "Patty probably recruited everyone. She was quite the enthusiast. She'd go out dancing once a week, in addition to her lessons."

That surprised me. To my knowledge, Carlton didn't have a wealth of places with dance floors. "Where did she go to dance?"

"Some new place in town," Amber replied with a shrug.

Naming the only "new place" I'd heard of, I asked, "Lucinda's?"

"That sounds right. Let's go get your skis." She ushered me toward the back of the store. She suddenly grabbed my arm and gushed, "Oh, good news . . . Randy talked Kelly into entering a painting in the fair after all. And even better news, as far as I'm concerned that is, she actually signed up for something the two of us can do together. Yesterday I happened to be talking about how much I used to enjoy fencing in college, and she said she'd like to try that. I signed us both up for lessons at a club in Saratoga Springs."

We'd reached the counter where the ski technicians were who'd switched my bindings from my old skis to the new ones. She went behind the counter and soon emerged carrying both pairs of skis. I tried to take one set from her, but she refused to let me. She was probably afraid that my muscles would snap if I did any manual labor.

Partway to the car, I said, "You know, Nathan's been bugging me to get him fencing lessons, too. Maybe we'll be able to carpool at some point in the future."

"Maybe so." I popped the back of my CRV open. Amber slid the skis into place. "I hope you enjoy these in good health."

"Me, too."

She smiled and took one step toward the store, then stopped and cried, "Oh, I keep forgetting. I have something for you in my car that I've been carrying around for the last couple of days. Hang on a sec."

"Sure thing." As long as that something didn't turn out to be a murder weapon with my name on it. I waited. She went to a Saab a few cars down from mine and returned with a padded manila envelope.

"I've been checking Patty's mailbox periodically, since Kelly lives with us now but still gets mail there. Anyway, this was marked 'Carlton PTA President,' so I figured it should go to you."

She handed me the envelope, which had been sent from PTA national headquarters. My heart started racing. By the size and weight of the envelope, it felt as though a videotape was inside. Could someone have sent a copy of Al's students' tape to the PTA national headquarters?

"Thanks, Amber. And thanks for the skis."

"Maybe I'll see you at the fair later today."

"Okay. Take care."

She went back inside the store. I got into my car. My heart pounded as I opened the envelope. Inside was a folded sheet of paper and a videotape labeled CARLTON PTA in block letters. The handwriting seemed to be identical to that of the death threat I'd received. The label looked as though it had been hastily stuck on top of a preexisting label.

I unfolded the sheet of paper. It was a letter, which congratulated us for the fine work we'd done this year but stated that a PTA chapter in Iowa had won. The letter went on to explain that the enclosed tape had been sent anonymously but "played no part in the decision."

The tape had to be a copy of the girls' video. There was no telling whether or not it had "played no part" in our missing out on the award, but with Patty dead, the contest was irrelevant now, anyway. Maybe it wasn't irrelevant to whoever killed Patty, however. Could the killer have sent this tape to national headquarters to make sure that Patty wasn't honored posthumously? That might have been part of the motive behind the break-in at Skye Smith's house, combined, perhaps, with the fear that the outtakes could have given away his or her identity as the killer.

Too bad Amber had given this to me on a Saturday. With my family home, I didn't want to watch the tape there. I wanted to view it and see if this was an exact duplicate of the one we'd seen at Patty's house.

I drove to Lauren's, raced up her porch steps tape in hand, and rang the doorbell. Tommy opened the door. He wore slippers, pajamas, and a blue terry-cloth bathrobe. He had a bad case of bed-head—his red hair every which way—and his nose was a deep shade of pink, his eyes puffy. He said, "Mornin', Molly," in a froglike voice.

"You're sick. I'm sorry. I didn't realize. Flu or cold?"

He sneezed into a tissue and said, "Cold," though it came out sounding like "Code." Eyeing the VCR tape, he said, "Lauren's at the drugstore. What's that you've got there?"

"It's a tape of the Carlton PTA. Somebody had sent it anonymously to PTA headquarters. It has to have been stolen from Skye Smith's house during the burglary. But I figure some half dozen people have probably handled it since then, so I'm sure any telling fingerprints were long since overlaid. I just now got it from Amber Birch, who said she got it out of Patty's mailbox a few days ago."

He held out his hand, and I relinquished it to him, saying again, "It's probably just a copy of the one you got from Patty's house."

"How was it sent?"

"One of those padded mailers. It was sealed when she gave it to me and didn't appear to have been opened."

He had a brief coughing fit into the sleeve of his bathrobe, then said, "Give that to me, too."

"Okay. It's in my car." I retrieved the envelope and handed it over. "Are you going to watch this right now and make sure the two videos are exact copies?"

"Uh-huh." He sneezed again into his tissue.

Well, obviously, he wasn't going to give me the opportunity to watch the tape with him. I felt a stab of disappointment, but reminded myself that investigating crimes was his job, not mine. "Did Stephanie call you yesterday, about Denise Goodman, the woman she met at the beauty parlor?"

"Uh-huh. We're lookin' into it."

I felt like demanding: Yes, but are you actually *seeing* anything when you do? Is "it" a tunnel? A crystal ball? Pea soup? But I knew he would blow his stack—in addition to his nose—so I merely asked, "Did you also get my note last night? With Emily Crown's writing sample?"

"Yeah. Real scintillating stuff. Hope the therapy helps you and Jim. I'll tell Lauren you came by." He shut the door.

I went home, but was not especially fun to be around. I wished I had more faith that Tommy was following up on the lead that Stephanie had given him. After giving the matter some thought, I realized I'd made an omission. I pressed the speed dial for Lauren and Tommy's home phone number. He would probably read me the riot act for interfering in his investigation, but there was no sense in my taking foolish chances just to avoid a tongue-lashing.

After four rings, their answering machine picked up. Knowing that Rachel could be the one to hear the phone message, I said, "Hi. It's Molly. This message is for Tommy. There's something I forgot to tell you, so I'll leave the message on your phone-mail at the station." Then I called his work number and, when his recorder picked up, said, "In the spirit of full disclosure, I just wanted you to know that I asked Emily, Susan, and Jane whether or not they would recommend Lucinda's. They all denied ever having been there. That means either that Stephanie's source isn't reliable, or that one of them lied about Lucinda's because she knew that incident had edged her into murdering Patty . . . which, in turn, would mean that I might have made myself a target." I paused, realizing that Tommy was going to be cursing at me when he heard this message. "Hope your cold is better. Bye."

Nathan had a friend over for lunch, then Jim took the boy home, taking Nathan with them and saying that they were going to the hardware store afterward. To perk myself up, I decided to ask Karen to go to the fair with me. I called upstairs for her and wound up having to make the suggestion while shouting through her closed door.

She came skipping down the stairs, dressed attractively in a flame red sweater and blue jeans. She announced, "Sorry, Mom. I'm going to the fair with Adam. And he's probably already on his way over here to pick me up."

"You were supposed to keep me informed of your plans. Remember?"

"I told Dad about this two nights ago!"

That was plausible. "Okay. Good for you."

She peered at me and chewed on her lower lip a little. In a meek voice, she asked, "So, like, could you stay home, Mom?"

"It's a fairly large venue, Karen. Even if we were there at exactly the same time, we might never run into one another."

"Yeah, right," she mumbled. "Please, Mom? You're

gonna see it tonight, anyway, when you're judging it. Okay?"

"Why would it bother you so much if we—"

"I just don't want Adam to get the impression that we're constantly getting spied on."

"Well, if I had it my way, you *would* be."

"Fine." She stuck her lower lip out and stomped her foot. "I'll cancel my date, and I'll stay home alone, locked in my room."

"Hey, there's an idea. Then you can grow your hair like Rapunzel for Adam to come rescue you. Since you're only on the second floor, it won't take you that long."

The doorbell rang.

Karen clasped her hands together in feigned prayer and said, "Mo-o-om!"

"Okay. Fine. I won't go."

She breathed a sigh of relief and gushed, "Thanks, Mom."

She dashed to the door. As she started to open it, I said, "Though that's not saying your father won't." If I told him he *had* to go, for instance.

Adam's face lit up as he looked at Karen. "Hi. Ready to go?"

"Just one second. I need to grab my coat." She gave me a pleading look as she went to the coat closet, apparently afraid that I'd say something to Adam that would embarrass her. *Moi?*

Adam peeled his eyes away from her long enough to give me a quick glance. "Yo, Mrs. Masters. You going to the crafts fair?"

"Not till tonight, when I judge some of the entries." There! Now was *that* embarrassing? No mention whatsoever of my surveillance operation being on the fritz or my spy team being on vacation.

Apparently unaware of the restraint I'd just shown,

Karen and Adam left, holding hands. A half hour later, Jim and Nathan returned, and the two of them went to the basement to put to use their hardware purchases. Later, Nathan showed me how they'd retooled his tongue-depressor catapult. It was now so powerful that it would be unsafe to use indoors.

Nathan went outside to catapult pine cones over state lines. Meanwhile, Jim switched on the television set and plopped down on the couch to watch a game. He made sympathetic noises during my tale of ostracism from our daughter's social life, but was apparently more interested in whether or not a batch of tall young men neither of us had ever met were capable of throwing a ball through a hoop some fifty-plus times.

I went downstairs to my office to work on cartoons, but spent most of the time sulking. I'd called Tommy hours ago; he had to have gotten my message by now. He absolutely would have called me back—and yelled at me—if he were closing in on the killer, thanks to this Lucinda's business. Damn it all! Was Patty's murderer *ever* going to be brought to justice?

My thoughts were in a constant whirl. Eventually I at least made some progress on a cartoon. An ancient-looking man on roller skates, clad in an ill-fitting sparkling suit with a cape, is trying to negotiate his way through a group of grazing buffalo. The caption reads: Bored with retirement, Evel Knievel sets out to disprove the lyrics of a song entitled "You Can't Roller-Skate in a Buffalo Herd."

Karen got home and sought me out, probably due to guilt over her shabby treatment of her loving mother, and told me that the fair was "mostly boring," but that I'd have a tough decision when it came to assigning ribbons. She then said that she and Nathan were going to watch television in Jim's and my room, because "Dad's

watching some dumb basketball game in the family
room."

I glanced at my watch. He must be into a second
game by now, or quadruple overtime. It was not quite
six P.M.—too early to judge the contest at the fair,
but getting near to dinnertime at restaurants. I called
Stephanie, who instead of "hello" said, "If this is a tele-
phone solicitor, the answer is 'no.' "

"It's me . . . Molly. I want to resolve this thing about
Lucinda's, for my own peace of mind if nothing else.
We need to stake out the place tonight. I could do it my-
self, but it'd be easier with the two of us."

"What would we be looking for? Patty's ghost?"

"For Denise Goodman. Can you help me out or not?"

"I suppose so. But it'll be at least half an hour till I
can possibly get there."

She probably had to put on her custom-designed
stakeout makeup and clothing. "Fine. Let's drive sepa-
rately, and I'll meet you in the parking lot. Okay?"

"I'm all atwitter with excitement," she replied, and
hung up.

Chapter 18

Pardon My Impertinence,
Sir Fluffy Foo-foo . . .

Not surprisingly, there was no sign of Stephanie's car when I arrived at Lucinda's parking lot. As I'd already told her, it wasn't strictly necessary for her to be here. If any woman came wandering onto the scene to copy down license plate numbers, odds were very good that she would be Denise Goodman. Stephanie's presence, however, could help me convince the woman how serious her eyewitness report might prove to be.

It was a long, boring, and cold wait. I was kicking myself for coming here when I could be home with my family. I'd told them that I was "going to a restaurant with Stephanie" and would judge the contest at the fair afterward. Maybe my punishment for my lie of omission would be to wait here for hours to no avail, and to never know whether or not Denise Goodman was simply a raving lunatic.

After half an hour, an athletic-looking man emerged from the restaurant and surveyed the parking lot. In his black suit and ruffled shirt, he appeared to be an employee. There were only a half dozen cars in the lot, including mine, and his vision stopped when he caught sight of me in my car. He gave a little wave, which I returned. I could tell from reading his lips that he was asking, "Are you all right?"

I opened my door and stood up. "I'm fine. I'm supposed to meet a friend here."

"Wouldn't you be more comfortable waiting inside?"

"Probably, but I told her we'd meet in the parking lot. I don't want to confuse her."

"Okay." He rocked on his heels a little and looked past my shoulder at the copse of trees to one side of the parking area. "The thing is . . . there's this lady who comes around a lot. She's got a wild hair up her . . . she's harmless, but she's on a one-person crusade to discourage our clientele from coming here."

"How bizarre."

"Yeah, she's something of a neighborhood kook." He smiled pleasantly. "If she tries to hassle you, just come and get me. I'm the bartender, and all you'll have to do is lean in the front door to find me."

"Thanks. I'll be fine. I don't discourage easily." Understatement of the year, I thought, as I settled back into my cold car.

I kept checking the time. At seven P.M. there was still no sign of Denise or of Stephanie. I vowed to leave for the fair no later than eight P.M. Then I tried to keep myself amused by singing all the songs I could think of with "Fair" in the title. That proved to be a poor diversion, because after Johnnie not coming home from the fair and "Scarborough Fair," I was stuck. What was the folk song with "Come 'round ye fair maidens . . ."?

A beam of white-yellow light caught my rearview mirror, which made me nearly jump out of my skin. Someone in dark clothing approached on foot, cutting through the woods, illuminating the way with a flashlight.

The person continued to come closer, stopped beside the overhead streetlamp, and turned off her flashlight. This woman did not fit the picture I'd built of her in my head. She was younger than I'd imagined—in her late twenties—and was wearing glasses, jeans, sneakers, and a bulky sweatshirt. Shaggy, strawberry-blond tresses poked out from under the hood of her sweatshirt. Somehow I'd imagined her with more of a Church Lady persona. I decided I needed to play this as coolly as possible; pushing her too hard might make her refuse to say anything to me at all.

I watched as she counted the cars in the parking lot and made notations in her notepad. If I could just get hold of those notes and give them to Tommy, perhaps they'd help him solve this thing after all.

When she neared my bumper, I got out of my car and said, "Hi. What are you doing?"

She was startled, and her hand flew to her neck, but she quickly recovered. "I'm just trying to keep a record of how many cars come here tonight." Her nasally voice was, indeed, instantly recognizable as the voice on the video. She continued, "I live next door, and I have reason to suspect that Lucinda's is breaking some business zoning ordinances."

"They are? I don't want to support an establishment that's breaking the law. Maybe I shouldn't come here, then. I was going to meet my friend here for dinner, but maybe we should reconsider."

"Absolutely. The food here's lousy and overpriced, and you can't enjoy a meal here, even if it were *worth* enjoying, because the music in the bar is so loud."

"What kind of music do they play?" I asked, just to keep her talking.

"Oh, it's . . . dreadful. Instrumental music. There's a cheesy dance floor in the bar, so it's icky, old-fashioned dance music."

"Eww. That doesn't sound like my type of place at all. That does it . . . once my friend gets here, I'll turn her right around, and we'll go someplace else. I guess I owe you a big thank you for saving our evening. My name's Molly."

I held out my hand to shake hers, but she merely stared at it. She shifted her gaze to my face. "Molly Masters. You're active in the Carlton PTA. What's going on? First Stephanie Saunders starts interrogating me at the hair salon yesterday. Now you show up here."

"Well, you're right that something's going on. Stephanie's a fr—an associate of mine, and we're trying to help the police investigate our friend Patty Birch's murder. You're Denise Goodman, right?"

She pursed her lips and glared at me, saying nothing.

"You must have children in school at Carlton, right? Well, so did Patty, and so do Stephanie and I. We just want to make Carlton a safer place, you know?"

She took a step backward and said nothing, her features still set in a frown.

"The thing is, I need to know who exactly you saw accompanying Patty Birch here."

"Why is that any of your business?"

"It *isn't*, really, but it's possible that the man's wife could have gotten so enraged at Patty after learning of the affair that she killed Patty."

She switched on her flashlight and shined the beam right in my eyes. I had to look away as she said in a haughty voice, "I'm supposed to tell *you* something like that? I don't know you from beans!"

I held up my hands, forced to squint at her, although she'd averted the beam slightly. "Fine. Don't tell me. Just tell the police."

She shook her head. "I can't! I'll get thrown in jail. Lucinda has a restraining order against me. In fact, I've got to get out of here right now."

"Fine. I'll walk you home."

She pivoted but said firmly, "Don't bother. I have nothing to say to you."

I balled my fists and followed her. "In that case, I'll just have the investigating officer speak to you."

She lifted her head in defiance and kept up her steady gait. We were now halfway through the woods. "He already did, but I've got a lousy memory. I can't even remember what we were talking about."

"You told Sergeant Newton you didn't remember anything at all?"

"It wasn't a sergeant. Just some guy my age who'd made junior policeman."

"So your memory isn't so bad after all."

"No, just selective."

"Please, Denise." I caught up to her and grabbed her arm. She jerked it from my grasp as I pleaded, "What if you could put Patty's killer behind bars?"

"Then I'd have to testify about how I met her. And I'll get jailed for violating the restraining order. And this restaurant will get all that publicity, and its business will increase tenfold. No thank you."

"Those matters are trivial compared to getting a killer behind bars!"

She spun around to face me. "Come off it! All I saw was some man stepping out on his wife. I'm not getting involved. Leave me alone."

She picked up her pace, and a pine tree bough slapped me in the face. "Damn it," I muttered, stopping to tend to my eye. Officer Bob had been correct. An eye gouge, even from a pine tree, could stop a pursuer dead in his or her tracks.

My vision already limited with darkness and now half blinded, I picked my way back through the woods to my car. By then, at least my eye had more or less cleared up. Just as I started to unlock my door, Stephanie's BMW pulled into the lot.

I stood with my arms akimbo as she shut off her engine and came toward me. "You're too late, but thanks, anyway. I already found your Denise Goodman and spoke to her, and she wouldn't tell me anything."

"She's hardly *my* Denise Goodman."

"Well, she sure isn't *mine*. The good news is, a police officer spoke to her already. The bad news is, she told me she denied everything to him."

"Why?"

"She doesn't want to get involved. Even so, the officer will surely have talked to the employees here and gotten a description of the man who came here with Patty."

"Let's hope so." She sighed. "Come on, Molly. Since we're here, let's go in and have some dinner. I'm famished."

"So am I, but I'm supposed to go to—"

"We'll make it something quick. I'm buying."

We went inside. The decor had a strong New England flavor, as though we'd walked into someone's house on the Cape. Few seaside houses came equipped with a dance floor and full bar, however. A hostess asked us if we were "Two for dinner," and I interrupted Stephanie's request for a table by the window to explain that I only had half an hour, and we would prefer to grab something quick at the bar. Stephanie held her tongue, but was clearly less than pleased.

We took seats at the bar itself, and the bartender put down the glass he was drying and came up to us. "Your friend finally showed up, I see."

"Yes, she did. But now we're pushed for time and need to eat and run, unfortunately." Though I felt silly for continuing to act like a professional investigator, I

couldn't give up this easily. "Lucinda's came highly rec-
ommended by a friend of ours who used to be a regular
here . . . before she died, that is. Patty Birch."

He narrowed his eyes, but handed us two small, lami-
nated menus. "The police were asking me about her
just last night. Far as I know, she never actually ate here.
She would just order a ginger ale or two and use our
dance floor."

Stephanie immediately said, "Her dance partner was
a tall Latino man, right?"

"No, she was always with some average-looking Joe,
about my height . . . five-eight, middle-aged."

"He was average looking?" I prompted.

"Yeah. I gave his description to the police officer. So.
What can I get you ladies?"

"Can you give us a couple of minutes to decide?"
Stephanie asked pleasantly.

"Actually, I really do have to eat and run." I glanced
at the menu and chose the first thing I saw. "I'll just
have an order of potstickers and a glass of water."

"Fine," Stephanie said. "I'll have the same thing. But
make my 'water' a glass of your finest chardonnay."

The bartender gave us our drinks, then left to put in
our order in the kitchen. I said to Stephanie, "Jane's
husband is around five-eight or so. Have you ever met
Emily Crown's husband?"

She nodded. "He is medium-height, too. And he and
Emily are good dancers. They occasionally took classes
from Chad."

"Mr. Alberti's off the hook, since I would think the
bartender would have mentioned it if Patty's partner
was bald."

"Plus his wife wasn't a PTA officer. Susan's husband,
on the other hand, is even taller than Chad."

I frowned and shook my head. "Something's bugging me about this whole . . . dancing business."

"What?"

"I don't know yet. I feel like I'm overlooking something obvious."

She swirled the pale liquid in her wineglass, then took a sip. "I'm sure you'll come up with whatever it is soon."

Our food came, and we focused our attention on that. We each had six potstickers, which Nathan had once described to me as "wontons without the soup." They were tasty, and I ate quickly, wracking my brain for whatever it was that somebody had said to me about Patty and dancing.

"That's it!" I cried, suddenly remembering. I set down my fork and pushed my plate away. "Chad wouldn't let Jane and Aaron Daly dance at that contest, remember? He felt that his dancers were supposed to represent his studio, and Aaron had gotten lessons from somebody else."

Stephanie arched an eyebrow. "So?"

"So, what if Patty was giving lessons to Aaron Daly here all that time? Remember how he came into the studio and told Jane he'd taken lessons as a surprise to her?"

She nodded and said thoughtfully, "Which could explain why Patty kept coming here with another man even though, according to your research, she was trying to win her ex-husband back."

She smiled and crooked her finger at the bartender, who came over. "Pardon me, I know you're busy, but one last question about our friend, Patty Birch."

He leaned both elbows on the bar. "Go ahead."

"This man that Patty was dancing with . . . was he as good a dancer as she was?"

"No, it looked to me like she was teaching him."

She gave me a triumphant smile. "Thank you. You've been most helpful." She handed him a twenty and said, "Keep the change."

The moment we'd pushed out the door, Stephanie said, "Well, that solves it. Jane Daly did it."

"We have no proof of that, Stephanie. All we have is a theory. And even if Denise Goodman sees fit to identify Jane and her husband to the police, that's still all we'll have—a theory."

She stopped walking, put her hands on her hips, and eyed me. "Rain on my parade, why don't you!"

"A plausible theory with corroborating evidence is better than nothing. I'm just saying that it's not the same as positive proof. Please do me a favor . . . go to Tommy's house right now and tell him what we've learned about Jane Daly. He'll probably at least be willing to bring her in for questioning, and if she's guilty, maybe she'll break down and confess."

"Aren't you coming, too?"

"No, he'll listen better if this comes from you than from me, and I promised I'd judge the contest tonight. Provided, of course, that plenty of other judges are there and Jane Daly's nowhere near."

There were only three cars in the parking lot at the fair by the time I arrived. I got out of my car slowly and reluctantly, wishing there were more people around. Just in case Jane Daly truly was the killer, I didn't want to take any chance of winding up with her in an otherwise empty building late at night.

The warm air inside the exhibition hall bore the pleasing scent of wood chips and potpourri. The woman guarding the front door was not Jane. I showed her the card identifying me as a judge and asked, "Is Jane Daly here?"

"No, she's not."

"Is she supposed to come here tonight for any reason?"

"No, she worked this morning. Can I give her a message?"

"That's okay. Thanks." I breathed a little easier and made my way over to the section where the works of eighteen-and-under artists were displayed.

I soon saw what Karen meant about my decision being difficult. The artwork was outstanding. Here I was, judging work way beyond my own ability level by artists less than half my age. What was I supposed to say to a sixteen-year-old who could somehow make a flower-covered garden come so alive, or a portrait look so haunting? Well, your work is good, yes, but I get to rule that you're not worthy of a blue ribbon because *I* can draw a pair of funny-looking rabbits in tuxedos with arched eyebrows and pink noses in the air, saying, "Pardon my impertinence, Sir Fluffy Foo-foo, but didn't you wear that very same ecru-colored cumberbunny to *last* year's banquet?"

As I made my way down the aisle feeling a sinking hopelessness at having to decide, the final entry stopped me in my tracks. It was a watercolor portrait of Patty Birch. Because of the medium, the colors had a faded, ghostlike feel, which added to the effect. It was an extraordinary painting, but so were many that I'd seen, and it was excruciating to have to decide whether or not my judgment was tainted by my added desire to see Kelly win.

I agonized over the decision. Ultimately, I decided to award her with first place. Furthermore, I vowed that I was not going to feel guilty if some partiality had crept into my judgment, because I'd tried my best to be fair . . .

at the fair. I awarded the other ribbons, including the second- and third-place ribbons.

Afterward, I felt that I'd earned the right to see the other exhibits, although I'd gotten the impression that my fellow judges had already left. As long as the door was unlocked, the lights were on, and Jane Daly wasn't around, I was in no danger of getting trapped inside for the night.

The next aisle featured paintings by the adults, and they were no better than the ones that I'd judged. One immediately caught my eye, because it was so unsettling—a naked woman shown from the waist up, screaming to the heavens. What was particularly remarkable was that the work wasn't a painting at all, but rather was a mosaic made with tiny plastic beads glued into place. It was hard to imagine somebody taking such painstaking effort and expense to build such a hideous image. The judge, apparently, must have shared some of my misgivings, for the artist had only been awarded a red ribbon. I looked at the name card that identified the artist: Jane Daly.

"Oh, crap," I muttered to myself.

"I'd like to think it's better than that," a woman's voice said from directly behind me.

I gasped and turned slowly. Jane Daly had somehow sneaked up behind me and met my gaze with dagger eyes. It was all I could do not to scream and step back.

"Hi, Jane." I gestured at the portrait. "This is a remarkable piece."

She continued to glare at me. "I would expect a fellow artist to appreciate the emotions that my work expresses, if not the subject matter."

"Oh, it does indeed express a lot of emotions. Your work depicts total despair, for one thing."

She crossed her arms and looked at her portrait. "I

wasn't sure if I should really exhibit that here or not. Obviously my judge couldn't relate to it. Can't say that I'm surprised. I started work on this last year, when Patty won with a reproduction of van Gogh's *Sunflowers* made entirely out of M&M's." She chuckled. "My mosaic doesn't exactly belong in this country-kitsch fair, along with all the knitted mouse-head golf club covers or the little-piggie oven mitts, and cranberry muffins . . . and walnut preserves."

There's such a thing as walnut preserves? Jane seemed to be in no mood to discuss such matters, and, truth be told, I wasn't, either. Whether or not she actually was Patty's killer, I was now nervous in her presence.

I glanced around me. There was nobody else in the immediate area. "The guards are probably ready to lock up now. I guess I'd better be going."

"So do you like it? My self-portrait? Would you have given it a blue ribbon?"

I looked again at the mosaic. "It's very good, plus unusual. But you're right. It's too disconcerting to be a big crowd-pleaser at a little local fair like this."

"You didn't answer my question. Would you give my painting a blue ribbon?"

"I doubt it. The piece isn't my taste."

She nodded and sighed. "I appreciate your honesty. Frustrating, really, when I think about it. You know, Molly, until Patty came along, I had won Best-in-Show honors six years running. Do you have any idea how hard that is? Out of more than a thousand entries each year, different judges each time, to win the very highest honor six times in a row? I mean, it's like . . . I was the Michael Jordan of the Carlton Fair."

"Yes, you were. Good for you, Jane. It's very impressive."

"Then, two measly years, Perfect Patty wins the honors. And I've got to tell you, Molly, that first year, I allowed her to win by deliberately not entering my very best pieces. Everybody just . . . kneels down before her and heaps praises on her and acts like I never even existed. Even though I won this thing six times, and she only won it twice."

"I can imagine how that must feel."

"So now I'm free. The weight's off my shoulders. I can enter whatever I want in the contest, but . . . it's like I lost all my creativity, all of a sudden. I look at my work over the year, and . . . I've got nothing to show for it." She gestured at her mosaic. "I mean, come on. The Carlton judges are hardly enlightened enough to bestow honors on a portrait of a naked woman screaming, now are they?"

For some reason, she started to cry.

A chill ran up my spine. "I'm really sorry, Jane. I've got to get home soon. My—"

"What am I going to do?" Jane said through her tears.

Was there anybody else here? Other judges? The guard must still be here. The place now had an eerie, deserted feel to it.

She sniffled. "Did you see the way my husband danced with me, at Chad's studio?" Jane asked, forcing a smile.

Oh, my God. Why would she mention that now? "Yes, and he obviously loves you a lot to . . . take lessons for you."

She dried her eyes and nodded. "Yes, he does." She gave her head a shake. "I've got to get home and get dinner going. Can I walk you to your car?"

I wanted to keep a safe distance from her. "Oh, no, I . . . think I might have left something over in the section I was judging. My extra ribbons."

She pursed her lips and shuffled off toward the door.

My heart was racing. I listened to Jane's heels across

the concrete floor and breathed a little easier when I heard the gymnasium-style door open and shut behind her. I pulled my keys out of the pocket of my jeans. I would give Jane a minute's head start, then get my cell phone out of my glove box and let Tommy know that, evidence or not, I was now certain that she was the murderer.

Save for my own pounding heart, the building appeared to be empty. At the top of my lungs I called out, "Is anybody here?"

My voice seemed to echo slightly among the rafters, but there was no answer.

I headed for the exit, then stopped. There was always the chance that Jane would be waiting to mug me right outside the main exit. I decided to go out through the rear exit instead.

I hurried my pace. The door was bolted. I tested the knob, but it was locked. Damn! I would have to go through the main exit after all.

I started to jog down the main row. I stopped short. Jane Daly was standing alone next to the double doors, which had been chained and padlocked from the inside.

Chapter 19

No Exit

I struggled to hide my fear. "Jane. You . . . didn't leave."

"No, and I told the guard I'd lock up tonight, so it's just you and me."

She had one hand hidden behind her back. I prayed that she wasn't holding a deadly weapon, but knew my prayers were unlikely to be answered. Trying to sound relaxed, I said, "I'm ready to go now, so you can let me out."

"Drop the routine, Molly. Neither of us is that good of an actor."

I forced a smile, still desperately hoping I could somehow bluff my way out of this. "I . . . don't know what you're talking about."

"Yes, you do. You figured out who taught my husband how to dance."

My face felt red hot and wet with perspiration. "Susan Embrick?" I bluffed.

"Patty Birch. He'd taken dance lessons from her as his anniversary gift to me." Once again, tears started to run down her cheeks. "Only that's not what I thought when that awful woman confronted Aaron and me in the parking lot of Lucinda's. And you found out about her, somehow." She winced, but then lifted her chin as if in defiance. With her free hand, she indicated

251

our surroundings. "This is my last chance. I'd been waiting for you to come back here, hoping you'd be here late. Deliberately told you judging started an hour later than it actually did."

Desperately clinging to the notion that I could talk my way out of this, I muttered, "Let's just go home and discuss this in the morning. Okay, Jane?"

As if she didn't hear a word, Jane continued: "That woman told my husband frequent customers like him were keeping the place in business. I pretended like I hadn't heard her. After dinner, Aaron asked me to dance. That's when he was going to surprise me. If only I'd said yes, none of this would have happened." She grimaced. "I was too upset to dance. I claimed I wasn't feeling well. I was so certain he was having an affair. But he'd just been sneaking out of the house for dance lessons.

"It wasn't my fault, not really. I couldn't have known. That damned Patty always had to do everything her way, to be the star. I recognized that dreadful woman's voice on the tape, calling us amoral. I put that together with some slips-of-the-tongue from Aaron and knew it was Patty Birch he'd been seeing."

She swiped at her cheeks with the sleeve of her free hand. "I didn't mean to kill her, Molly. I just . . . hated that woman so much. And when I doubled back and confronted her that night, she just kept using that oh-so-superior voice of hers . . . telling me it wasn't what I thought. That I needed to ask Aaron. So, I asked if I could call him. I went into the kitchen and grabbed the knife."

"Jane, stop. I don't want to hear this."

She ignored me, fury now marring her tear-stained features. "I came back into the living room with the knife." Jane's eyes were glassy-looking. She looked almost inhuman. "Patty was just looking at me like I was some kind of fool. Even afterward, she almost . . . she laughed at me, Molly. She was laughing at me."

Jane had me so spooked, my knees shook. "I'll help you with the police, Jane. If you'll turn yourself in now, you can—"

"No, Molly. That's not the way this ends. I can't go to jail." She took a steeling breath.

She looked straight at me. "It wasn't my fault, and I'm not going to pay for that woman's arrogance. I mean . . . what would any woman think under the circumstances?" She paused, expecting me to respond.

"Right. Any woman would have thought her husband was having an affair."

She grimaced. "You know what's funny, Molly? On our way home from Chad's studio, that time he surprised me, you know what happened? Aaron pulled out this little note card from his jacket. He said he was going to give it to me on our actual anniversary, but never got the chance . . . and now he wasn't sure he should even show this to me, considering who wrote it to me, but decided that I'd want it as a keepsake."

She let out an eerie laugh. Her eyes looked wild with fright or, perhaps, rage. "It was a note from Patty, in flawless calligraphy, of course, wishing me a happy anniversary, and thanking me for letting my husband secretly get lessons. Can you imagine how that made me feel?"

Not really. Learning that you'd killed somebody for no reason? "Jane, please think about what you're doing. It wasn't premeditated. There were all sorts of extenuating circumstances. You'll be able to get help. And I'll vouch for you with the authorities."

She shook her head determinedly. "I'm in too deep, and so are you. Everyone's always saying how you solved a couple of murders some time ago. I kept trying to warn you off . . . crashing into you on the ski run . . . the notes. You just wouldn't quit. You're just like Patty. Thinking you're so much better than I am that you don't have to listen to anything I say."

She lowered her arm to her side, but whatever weapon she hid there was still out of my sight in the fabric of her broomstick skirt.

"No, Jane, that isn't true," I said, backing away. "You're not gaining anything by hurting me. You won't get away with this. It's too late. I already told"— I paused, needing to keep Stephanie's name out of this in case Jane would go after her—"Tommy Newton earlier tonight. He knows I'm here. He'll send the police here for me any second now if I don't get home. There's no way for you to cover your tracks this time."

"It doesn't matter. I was hoping it wouldn't come to this, that you hadn't figured everything out, but one look at your face tonight and I knew this was my only chance. I'm leaving town tonight. By the time they find you, it'll be morning, and I'll be long gone. With you out of the picture and me on the lam, they'll never know for certain it was me." She lifted her right hand. She was holding a hatchet.

"Oh, my God! Jane . . . you can't possibly . . . use that on me! We're friends!"

"No. I have no friends. Just my husband and kids. She took them from me. I'll have to leave them now. I'll go back to the mountains, make a new identity for myself. I lived that way before, and I can do it again." She glanced at her hatchet. "I've used this to rough out my wood sculptures. Now it's going to help me carve out a new life."

Oh, Jesus. Help me! Why hadn't Officer Bob taught

us how to defend ourselves against an ax-wielding maniac? How could I get away from her?

He'd said to use the element of surprise—not to hesitate to be the one to strike first. I didn't have the nerve to try that now. She was too well armed.

Keep calm. I knew there was a fire alarm near this door. She was blocking it, but maybe there was a second one by the rear exit.

I backed into the table of displayed items behind me. Shit! Of all the useless categories for me to be near at a time like this—needlecraft. All I had to use in self-defense here were pot holders and quilts and knitted baby blankets.

"Jane, you're not a cold-blooded killer. You don't want to do this." Afraid to turn my back on her, I worked my way blindly down the long row of tables.

Jane was content to match me step for step. She must have figured that she would back me against the wall, then make her move. I kept backing down the aisle, dragging my hand along each of the tables. Still nothing but cloth items.

I was unable to take my eyes off the glinting sharp blade of the weapon in her hand. My God. With one blow of that monstrous thing I would, at best, be maimed for life. "Jane. Please. Think about your children."

"I *am* thinking about them. They will not be raised by their dad, their mother locked away in jail. I can't do that to them."

I felt dizzy, all but faint with fright. Mindlessly, I babbled, "But you *won't* be there for life. Not if you put a stop to this right now. You'll serve your sentence and get home to them. If you kill me and run, you'll never see them again."

Jane looked like some madwoman from a bad movie,

her nostrils flared, her teeth gritted. She gave her head a little shake. "Maybe I'll bring them. We'll manage."

I was almost at the last table in this row. This had to be the second to last. Then I might have to turn and run. Yet my instincts warned me that the only reason she hadn't struck me already was that she was waiting for just that—for the moment when I turned away.

Damn it! Still just cloth goods. Did every woman in this entire goddamned town except me have to *sew*? Where in hell was something solid! And sharp!

"You won't be able to run forever, Jane. You know that's true. Besides, I already told Tommy about the woman at Lucinda's. He got a description of your husband from the employees. By now, he already knows everything you told me. It's too late, Jane."

At last, I touched something hard. It was a small glass jar. Probably preserves.

I talked louder, hoping to distract her with my words. "You know you can't run forever."

She kept slowly coming toward me. I threw the jar at her head as hard as I could. I whirled around without waiting to assess the damage.

She let out a cry of pain and surprise. I ran for all I was worth. A jar whizzed just past my ear, and I darted around the corner.

Instinctively, I dodged behind a partition and into another aisle.

At last—sculptures!

Jane shouted, "Molly, you're the one who can't run. Face it. You're overmatched."

At least she had hard-soled shoes on to my tennis shoes. I could hear her footsteps more easily than she could mine. I took off at a dead run down this aisle. Though the partitions blocked all view to the other aisles,

I could hear her just on the other side of this row. She was shadowing my movements.

I stopped at the next display. It was metalwork. Some artist had crafted a stainless steel end table. I grabbed it by one leg and held the table like a baseball bat and waited for her to turn the corner. I tried to keep silent, but was panting for air. If she could hear my hard breathing, she would hack me with that hideous ax and it would all be over for me.

"Molly? I can hear you. I know where you are."

Her voice was directly on the other side of this partition, which looked flimsily constructed. I held my breath.

The table in my hands was heavy, and I couldn't keep my arms cocked like this for long.

I turned around and gave the second-to-last partition a thrust-kick. The partition teetered for a moment, then toppled over into Jane's aisle. Praying that she would still be looking at the fallen makeshift wall, I raced around that corner and into her aisle.

I swung at her head with my heavy little table just as she was starting to turn back toward me. The corner cracked into her temple with a sickening thud, but again I didn't stop to see what had happened to her. As she crumpled to the floor, I ran for the nearest exit.

Something hard and heavy skittered down the cement floor at me and clipped me in the ankle. I hollered in pain and fell, afraid that she'd hurled the hatchet and had struck my leg with the blade.

Despite the pain, I scrambled to my feet and caught a look at the weapon she'd thrown. It was a large, sun-shaped, metal discus. The thing was heavy, made of steel, perhaps.

Jane charged at me so fast, there was no hope of my outrunning her.

I dived back down and grabbed the sun sculpture, rolling over onto my back.

Jane let out a scream and swung the hatchet down at me. Gripping the sculpture with both hands, I held it over me.

The ax blade clanged into my shield, sending horrid aftershocks down my arms. The impact threw her off balance. I managed to get to my feet. I kneed her in the stomach before she could strike again. She doubled over, and I smacked her in the side of the face with the metal sculpture. I staggered toward the front door.

My vocal chords were making an animal-like moan as I limped across the room. It was as if I'd lost control of my own voice.

I threw the alarm. The shrill noise was the most welcome sound I'd ever heard.

A partition came crashing down. Jane stomped over the top of it like Godzilla gone mad. Blood poured from her temple and her chin. She was breathing hard, holding her hatchet in one hand, by her side.

Jesus, God! Did this woman have nine lives!?!

"You're gonna die, damn you!" Jane shrieked and rushed toward me.

My back smacked against the padlocked doors. No place to go, I charged at her. I grabbed her forearm before she could strike again with the hatchet. We barreled into a folding table. The displayed candles clattered to the floor.

The table held for a second or two. Jane dropped her hatchet. She threw her forearm into my neck. The table collapsed beneath our weight.

Jane took the brunt of our fall as I landed on top of her. I scrambled to my feet, grabbed her weapon, and raced to the window. I swung at it, shattering the glass.

There was a noise behind me. I turned.

Once again, Jane had risen.

She still looked wild with rage, ready to charge at me. I prepared to swing her hatchet, gripping it firmly with both hands. "Stop!" I cried. "I'll kill you!"

She took another step toward me. Her breaths were coming in half groans.

She put a hand to her eye as if confused why she couldn't see clearly. Then she looked at her own blood on her fingertips.

Her demeanor changed. She seemed to sag a little.

"Don't come any closer," I again warned. "I'll use this if I have to."

Outside, a police or fire engine siren wailed. Its reassuring cry grew louder.

"It's over, Jane."

She gave a glance at the shattered window. She'd heard the sirens, too.

Jane slowly dropped to her knees. She curled into the fetal position and cried like a little girl. Moving as quickly as possible without cutting myself on the glass shards, I climbed outside through the shattered window.

A firetruck turned the corner onto this road. I dropped the hatchet and waved both arms as the headlights caught me in their steady beam.

Chapter 20

Épée Log

Nathan scored a tenth touch, winning his sparring bout. He shook his opponent's hand, who, as I learned when the red hair came spilling out from underneath her mask, was Kelly Birch. Nathan yanked off his mask, reached back, and unplugged the wire that enabled his épée to be connected to a scoring device, and came toward me. "Hey, Mom, is it all right if I have dinner at Kelly's house tonight?"

"It's okay with me, but first we'll have to make sure it's okay with Kelly's . . . with Amber."

Kelly overheard and trotted up to us. "I already asked her if Nathan could come over after fencing, and she said it was fine." She leaned toward Nathan and said into his ear, "She's making lasagna tonight, and I gotta warn you, she's not exactly the world's best cook."

"That's okay. Neither's my mom."

Putting my hands on my hips, I feigned resentment at his remark. "Actually, Nathan, I *am*, in fact, the World's Best Cook. I've got an apron someplace in the pantry that says so."

Both kids chuckled.

"Hurry up and get ready, guys. Karen is waiting for us in the car."

"Why?" Nathan asked.

"She and I are going shopping after I drop you both off."

I returned to the car to wait with Karen, who immediately said, "Are they coming? We're supposed to meet Rachie and Lauren at the mall in twenty minutes!"

"Lauren and Rachel will wait for us even if we're a few minutes late."

Karen fidgeted with her nails and said nothing. She needed a clutch purse to match her dress for tomorrow night's festivities. A friend of Adam's had asked Rachel to the prom, and so the two couples were double-dating. Through some extrapolation of teenage logic, that meant that they absolutely *had* to shop for purses together.

A few minutes later, Kelly and Nathan kept up a steady patter of conversation in the backseat as I drove to Kelly's home.

Ignoring Karen's plaintive cries about the time—if she'd had things her way, we'd have pushed her brother and Kelly out the car doors without even coming to a full stop—I accompanied them inside to double-check with Amber. Not only was Nathan invited for dinner, but Amber made my day by saying that, if this recipe proved to be any good, she and Randy would like to have us all over for dinner soon.

I thanked her and returned to the car, keeping my eyes, as always, averted from the house directly across the street. The day would surely come when I would be able to look at that house without getting a lump in my throat, but with just six weeks having passed since the murder, that day had not yet arrived.

Last week, Susan had found the video of Patty spiking her drink and had shown it to me. Everything had taken place precisely as Susan had described, with Patty spiking Susan's orange juice in what was apparently a desperate attempt to coax information out of Susan that Patty hoped could help her to win back her ex-husband. Nevertheless, Susan had surprised me by saying that her biggest regret was that she hadn't forgiven Patty sooner—that she'd never told Patty how much her friendship over the years had meant to her.

I, too, missed Patty terribly, despite having learned that she'd been just as far from perfect as everyone else. Maybe we love our friends in part *because* of their flaws and their willingness to reveal them to us.

With my vision still down-turned, I opened my car door, only to find Karen in the driver's seat.

"Can I drive?" she asked.

"Sure."

I got into the passenger side. The moment I'd shut my door, Karen put the car in reverse, gunned the engine, and we shot down the driveway. Instead of negotiating the slight curve, she drove us onto the landscaping rocks.

"Karen, turn the wheel!" I cried, grabbing the dashboard for support but looking over my shoulder. She turned, but in exactly the wrong direction. "Left! Not right!" We were now practically on their side lawn. "Stop! You're going to hit the mailbox!"

Karen hit the brakes. "Well, it's not my fault!" she cried. "It makes me nervous when you yell at me!"

She'd stopped the car half on the driveway, the other half on the landscaping rocks. She unfastened her seat belt and opened her door.

"Do you want me to drive?"

"Yes. But only when I have to go backward. I can go forward just fine."

I got out, too, to check for any tire tracks or other damage to Amber and Randy's property. Everything appeared to be fine, but I intended to tell Amber about this after dinner when I picked up Nathan.

As I returned to the driver's side, I caught a full view of Patty's house. The structure and its property were as well maintained and welcoming as ever, despite the for-sale sign in the yard.

Realizing how lucky we were to have so little to yell at each other about, I gave Karen a quick hug, then got into the driver's seat, put the car in reverse, and backed the car out of the driveway for her.

I put the car in park so that we could switch seats again and said, "Well, my darling daughter, one thing I know for certain: In driving, as in life, learning how and when to go forward is at least nine-tenths of the battle."

If you enjoyed *Death of a PTA Goddess*,
don't miss these Molly Masters mysteries . . .

THE COLD HARD FAX
THE FAX OF LIFE
THE SCHOOL BOARD MURDERS
WHEN THE FAX LADY SINGS

by Leslie O'Kane

"Molly Masters is a sleuth with an
irrepressible sense of humor and
a deft artist's pen."
—Carolyn Hart

Published by Ballantine Books.
Available wherever books are sold.

For more mirth and mayhem,
look for this marvelous series by Leslie O'Kane,
featuring dog therapist Allie Babcock . . .

PLAY DEAD
The first Allie Babcock mystery

RUFF WAY TO GO
GIVE THE DOG A BONE

by Leslie O'Kane

"O'Kane delivers a satisfying whodunit."
—*San Francisco Chronicle*

Published by Ballantine Books.
Available wherever books are sold.

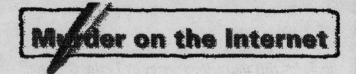